WRECKAGE

Born in Liverpool in 1966, Niall Griffiths now lives in Wales. He has published four novels: *Grits*, *Sheepshagger*, *Kelly + Victor* and *Stump*, the last two of which are being filmed.

NIALL GRIFFITHS

Wreckage

VINTAGE BOOKS
London

Published by Vintage 2006

2 4 6 8 10 9 7 5 3 1

First published in Great Britain in 2005 by
Jonathan Cape

Vintage
Random House, 20 Vauxhall Bridge Road,
London SW1V 2SA

Random House Australia (Pty) Limited
20 Alfred Street, Milsons Point, Sydney,
New South Wales 2061, Australia

Random House New Zealand Limited
18 Poland Road, Glenfield, Auckland 10, New Zealand

Random House (Pty) Limited
Isle of Houghton, Corner of Boundary Road & Carse O'Gowrie,
Houghton, 2198, South Africa

The Random House Group Limited Reg. No. 954009
www.randomhouse.co.uk/vintage

A CIP catalogue record for this book
is available from the British Library

ISBN 9780099461135 (from Jan 2007)
ISBN 0099461137

Printed and bound in Great Britain by
Bookmarque Ltd, Croydon, Surrey

But I do have an 'identity' very highly prized in our culture. Me-unreal-bad-here-inside-now-pain is not unusual.

– R. D. Laing, *The Politics of the Family*

Strife is the father and king of all. Some it makes Gods, others men; some slaves, and others free.

Heraclitus, Fragment 60

Men do not worship violence as such . . . Violence is venerated insofar as it offers men what little peace they can ever expect.

René Girard, *Violence and the Sacred*

ACKNOWLEDGEMENTS

For help of many kinds, hospitality, company, laughs, drinks, conversations, and pillows to put my head on, huge thanks to:

All at RCW, particularly David Miller and Rowan Routh; Wyatt Wilkie and Emily Charette; Mark, Jane, and Sian Jefferson (always a warm place to stay in Cardiff, but let's lay off the politics, Mark, ey?); Gruffydd, for when he can read; Jacques Peretti; Rob Williams and Oh Paxton (for many things, including a lift to Narberth when I really, really needed it, but generally just for being lovely, lovely people); the Croats – Boro Radakovic, Sandra Ukalevic, Nenad Rizvanovic, Jurica Pavicic, and all at the Konoba Hvarinin (best food in Split) and anybody else I've forgotten to mention; and all the ghosts in all the corners, watching and whispering whenever I pick up a pen.

Fine fellows all.

And i.m.
Scott Cowan
1960–2004
This one's for you
and Lou
and your family

BOOK ONE

There is no pain, or very little, only this sensation of slipping away from a place never completely solid to him anyway, never really reliable, under his feet. Slipping away from the now shattered body, the ribcage wrenched apart as if by giant hands, this red wreckage still feebly beating, a red purse to catch the strange rain descending, this fall of flaming paper. And somewhere in that soft and crackling shower is a gun and attached to that gun is a man and behind that man is a shop and behind that shop, in time if not in space, is the wreckage of a woman, an old woman, of a life so easily breakable.

What is this light in Darren's eyes. Not the giving back of the small bulbs of the dashboard nor the spread sodium of the street lights bowed and shamed nor the illuminated shopfronts that pass outside the car. Nor that which spills from pub or chipper or private home as they enter the outskirts of Wrexham on the A525 from Coedpoeth and the smaller villages beyond that and the mountains and lakes beyond them, nor even the half-moon hanging yellow over all this some pale flame there is in Darren's eyes flickering between the road and Alastair, Alastair and the road in front, outside:

—Fuckin *rich*, Ally! Fuckin brewstered, lar! See that fuckin wedge she had inside that safe? Didn't I tell yeh, Alastair? Didn't I fuckin tell yis! Pure fuckin rich we are, lad! Pure fuckin loaded, man! No cunt touches us now, man, eh, we're pure just fuckin *saved*!

Alastair has seen Darren similar before but never quite like this, never quite this high-voltage animation, never quite this heat. Always an exuberance following violence in him but that usually combined with a resignation of sorts, an acknowledgement of the necessity of an ugly job but still a job worth doing well but never this, *this*, this sparking eyefire as if flints clash in his skull or steel strikes stone.

—All this fuckin money, lar! We're *rich*, Alastair! Do

wharrever the fuck we wanner do now! Four fuckin grand nearly! He leans over to Alastair face to face jerking the steering wheel and so the car and shouts: —FOUR FUCKIN GRAND, MAN!

Warm spittle on Alastair's face. —Eeyar, Darren, straighten up. Yer takin us off the road.

—And? What fuckin odds if I did? Could go straight into that garage over there, man, an buy another motor straight off, no fuckin messin. Can do anythin we fuckin want, now, man. No fuckin lie.

They pass the garage/dealership and Alastair scans the price tags in the windows of the few vehicles on the forecourt and there is not one below six thousand. Utility vehicles of various kinds as befits the terrain roundabouts and these never come cheap.

And the way she collapsed, the old lady, all force gone in one split instant. The sound of metal on bone.

—So what now, Darren? What the fuck do we do now?

—I'll tell yeh what *you* do, lar – yeh keep yer fuckin gob shut. Unnerstand me? Not one werd of this to Tommy or no cunt else. Djer hear me? I mean it, Alastair; not one. Fuckin. *Werd*. Alright? That fuckin trap o' yours stays *shut*.

—Yeh but no, I mean . . .

Big sigh from Darren. His chest swells to touch the steering wheel and then flops back flat again. —Can't understand you, lar, honest to God I can't. Just don't fuckin get you at all. We're four fuckin grand to the better, do wharrever the fuck we wanner do an you've gorrer face liker smacked friggin arse. An I know why,

4

n all; it's cos of that ahl queen, innit? That one in the shop, like?

Alastair nods.

—Thought as much. Can read you liker fuckin *buke*, tellin yeh. Yeh were all like this after I glassed that Blackburn knob'ed n all.

—Yeh didn't avter hit her that hard, Darren.

—That hard? How else would she have opened the safe?

—Yeh but I mean yeh hit her *after* she'd given us the fuckin code, didn't yeh? No need for that, man. I mean she might be dead.

—Alright then, eeyar, tell yeh what; I'll divvy the dosh up inter two and you can get a cab and take your half back to that friggin post office and give it back, yeh? Sound alright? Check on thee ahl biddy while yer there, like, see if she's alright and if she isn't yeh can ring for an ambulance to taker to thee ozzy. Yeh? That sound alright to you, does it? That what yeh wanner do, aye?

Alastair's bottom lip protrudes, a child about to cry. The dull thunk of hammer on skull and the way she fell so crumpled. Lump hammer on bone and its awful noise felt in *his* bones too and the manner she fell so sudden so utter.

Darren makes a left turn, the brewery on their right. Lit up like a small city and the creeping smell of roasting hops and sugar into the chugging car, welcome smell masking the lingering niff of vinegary chips several hours old and cigarette smoke and engine fumes and farts and sweat the same age, unyoung.

—Where we goin?

—You'll see when we get there. Gorrer ditch the motor.

—What, get rid of the car? What's Tommy gunner say?

—*Fuck* Tommy, lar. Fuck that fat cunt. Don't need him any more, lar.

—Aye but . . .

—Tell me, Alastair, you enjoyed yerself today, did yeh? Adder fuckin boss time like, did yeh, drivin all that way inter friggin Wales to find some one-armed blert that probly doesn't even live there? Consider that a day well spent, do yeh?

—No.

—No, an neither do fuckin I. Woulda spunked the whole fuckin day if it weren't for that friggin postie and that woulda been that Tommy's fault so *fuck* that fat bastard. This four grand, like, every friggin penny of it we owe to ar *own* fuckin, what, we owe to arselves, like, an no fucker else. All ar own hard work, man, knowmean? So piss on everybody else. Fuckin initiative, man. That's wharrit is.

—Aye but the car.

Darren imitates Alastair, a high whinge: —'Aye but the car, the car' . . . He smirks. —Wharrabout the fuckin car?

—What we gunner tell Tommy happened to it? Gorrer tell him *some*thin, like, haven't we? Can't just say we ditched it, like.

Darren shrugs. —Just tell im it conked out. Tell im it fell apart on us like outside friggin Wrexham. An tell im that he shouldna sent us off on a dodgy job in such a knackered ahl piecer fuckin shite in the first friggin place. Fuckin fat no-mark arsewipe.

THUNK, that hammer went as it struck skull. THUNK. And no noise made as the old woman fell except for a dry rustle of starched apron and old skin similarly bereft of moisture because of the years spent behind that counter franking envelopes and shuffling papers until the body becomes as parchment itself. And then the world's rude reward: attack and blackness, and the body then brought to earth with one THUNK and crisp rustle as if its station has consumed it whole, the obliteration of one office never-altering.

THUNK. And then that arid keel.

—So what we gunner do? Torch it?

—*Torch* it?

—Yeh.

—The car?

—Aye.

—Nah. Don't be soft, Alastair. Fuckin fire attract every friggin bizzy from here to Chester, man.

—Like moths, aren't thee?

—Is right. *Moths* thee are, them fuckers.

—So what, then? Can't just *leave* it, like, can we? Got ar prints on it an everythin.

Darren turns left, over a bridge. Street lights thinner here in this suburb and more sheltering darkness.
—There's a river here. Gunner dump it in that. Get all yer stuff together and wind yer winda down so it sinks.

He drives into a car park and then across and out of that car park, sudden bump as they traverse the kerbstones and into a field that slopes down into a river ridged and silverscaled by the moonlight. The car labours in the field made soggy by the recent rain and Darren swings it to aim at the river then stops.

—An what then?

—What when?

—After we ditch the car, like. How we gunner get home?

Darren turns off the engine. —Not goin back to Liverpool tonight, lar. Gorra mate in Wrexham, we'll stop over at his. Get yer gear together like I've just told yeh to.

They gather up mobile phones, cigarettes and lighters and of course the rucksack heavy with plunder. They wind all windows down and exit the car, Alastair stretching his cramped and tired joints till they crack and there is a cold wind on his face and he licks his dry lips and fancies that he can hear a bird but thinks no, not here, not at this time. Birds don't sing in the hours of darkness. Maybe the shriek of a gull if you're at the seaside or the hoot of an owl if you're in the country but in the suburbs of a large town at night-time, no, no birds sing there and then.

—Got everything, Alastair?

—Yeh.

—Got the swag?

—No. *You* have.

Darren grins. Them white teeth. —Too fuckin right I av, lar. An I'm not lettin the fuckin stuff outer me sight. Handbrake off is it, yeh?

Ally nods.

—Right. Say tara to the piler fuckin junk. Come ere and give it some welly.

They move to the rear of the car and place hands on the boot and on 'three' push it forwards, gathering speed, it lurching and creaking over the uneven ground. It accelerates away from them and they let it go and stand shoulder to shoulder panting as they watch it bump over the earth down the sloping field then appear to leap off the steep bank, airborne it is for a second or two no wheel on the lumpy earth. Then the splash, surprisingly quiet, surprisingly deep in pitch. Then the vanishing roof, sinking beneath the water, and one more small surge, rise, as the tidal river buoys it and it surfaces and blows steam like a grampus or a manatee, riparian cetacean sounds only once then gone.

—Seeya, yeh piecer fuckin crap. Werst car I've ever friggin driven, you. Rust in peace, useless mudder-fucker of a motor.

Darren sniggers at his own joke. Alastair glances at him then back at the river where bubbles boil and burst and then the car is gone. No sign of its existence. All erased, submerged.

—Deep enough, djer think?

Darren shrugs. —It's sunk, innit?

—Aye but in the day, like. Might be able to see it in there when it's daylight, like.

—Long as me dabs're all washed off I'm not arsed. Pure could not give a fuck, lad. Come ed, let's goan see Dean.

Darren slings the rucksack money-bulging over his shoulder and squelches off the field and across the car park and out on to the main road spotlit by the brewery lights and Alastair follows him and here is Alastair in Wrexham, three, four paces behind Darren and like some negative image of him, the sprightly fire in Darren's eyes inverted in Alastair's which spit dark

9

sparks and beam black rays at Darren's back like anti-torches, light's antithesis. Twin shafts of shadow from Alastair's eyes aimed at the back of Darren's head, the colossal self-regard that lolls lizard-like beneath the tight black curls in the skull unslammed, unhammered. Curdle if they could those rays the bad beating blood that drives the will that bursts the undeserving, stop for ever if they could the hard dark heart that wrecks the undefended.

The blow and the noise and then the noise of the fall. The old woman's slippered feet slowly turning inwards, trauma's pigeon-toes. And the eyes and the age in them rolling back to become two red-laced eggs in a nest of creasing.

Alastair snarls at Darren's swaggering back as they pass the brewery and head towards the bus station where taxis rank. Darren turns and just catches that snarl as it vanishes.

—The fuck's wrong with *your* gob, knob'ed? Friggin kite on yeh, lar, Jesus. Still tampin over thee ahl biddy, are yeh? Got ter fuckin grow up, son. Carn handle a bit of bother then yeh should find yerself another fuckin job. Simple as.

Walking backwards, facing Alastair, Darren spreads his arms wide. —Mean ter say, like, what'd yeh fuckin expect when yeh first got into this fuckin caper? Think it'd be, it'd be, all fuckin –

—Ere's a cab.

—Wha?

—Ere's a cab, look, behind yiz. Flag it.

Darren spins, sees the taxi approaching, raises his arm. It stops at the kerb and they get into the back seat.

—Where to, lads?

—Brymbo.

Out into the traffic, around the small roundabout, back into the town.

—Friends there, aye?

—What?

—I said yew visitin friends in Wrexham? Or family?

—Yeh.

—No bloody reason to stop off at Brymbo otherwise, is there? The cabby chuckles. —I mean, that estate. Shockin. Council's got to do somethin about the mess up there. Only last week they –

Darren, rucksack held tight to his lap, leans forwards over it: —Lad, I'm payin yiz to drive, not natter. If I wanted a conversation with yiz I would've started one, knowmean? Givin yeh money to drive me to the Brymbo estate, not gab me friggin ear off, unnerstand?

—Suit yewerself then.

—I will, aye.

The cabby glances at his fares in the rear-view mirror, sees their faces, one peaked by a baseball cap, both with shaded eyes and cheekbones feral, rodential. The eyes of the one unhatted like twin candleflames back there behind him but an absence of warmth there is at his back. As if he ferries an open fridge. He just drives to Brymbo, doesn't respond when a voice directs him to street and then house number except wordlessly to drive to those places. He stops and a hand delivers money, a ten-pound note which is nearly four pounds over the fare.

—Change is yours, mate. Yeh can keep it.

And in the departing taxi fumes they regard the

house like a ravey spaceship landed in this estate, red-brick semi-detached and pebble-dashed, multicoloured lights pulsing at the windows and the swift pulse too of the techno being blasted inside. Behind the music loud voices can be heard and laughter and shouting. A dog or dogs barking. Breaking glass.

—This the place, yeh?

—Reckon so, Alastair, don't you?

Alastair says nothing. And Darren stands there a black silhouette against the sodium cone of the street light behind him. One dark shape he is and only his eyes aglow in the wet, neither rain nor drizzle just a kind of thick, damp air. The rucksack a black bulge held to his belly as if he is with child.

—Dean's an old mate, he says. —Known im years. Bit gobby at times, like, but he's alright. Used ter supply Peter the Beak with his charlie, like, which is how I met im but he don't deal any more. Still hoovers it up liker bastard tho.

—Aye.

—Aye, so we hide out here the night and get the train back tomorrer. Lerrit all blow over, like. And what's the one thing you've gorrer remember, Ally? What's the one thing yeh can't forget?

Without waiting for a reply Darren pinches his thumb and forefinger together and makes a zipping motion across his lips. —Yeh keep it fuckin shut. Quiet *as.* Unnerstand?

Alastair nods.

—I mean it, Ally; you blab off about what's in this fuckin bag an I won't wanner do it but I'll fuckin rip yeh. Believe. Don't go doin mad things like takin too

12

much coke and get mouthy or tryna impress some berd.

—I won't, man, I won't. *I* want the fuckin money too, doan I?

—Yeh, well. We'll divvy it tomorrer, back in town. Until then just keep it fuckin buttoned.

Again those black beams at Darren's back directed as he heads off down the path. Still there blackly blazing as he pounds on the door five times hard enough to rattle the jamb. Still there still there then instantly extinguished as the door is opened by a tall man very thin with spiky hair, a red Carlsberg shirt on at which Alastair smiles although it represents Wrexham Football Club and not his own Liverpool.

—Deano, my man.

—Darren! Fuck's sakes! *You* doin ere?

—Need somewhere to crash for the night, lar. Help us out, mate.

—Aye, no worries, no worries.

Dean steps aside, lets Darren and Alastair into the noise and the heat, slapping Darren on the back as he passes.

—Need a bevvy?

—*Fuck* yeh. This is Alastair.

Dean turns to Alastair, shakes his hand. —Alright, Alastair.

—Not bad.

People pass between them in the cramped hallway, boys and girls of school-leaving age carrying alcopops and spliffs. Darren watches them pass and raises his eyebrows at Dean who smiles and shrugs.

—Kid sister's party, mate. All schoolies, like. Come

ed upstairs, havin me own wee private do for the grown-ups, like. Wanner put that bag anywhere?

—Keep it with me.

—Sound.

He leads the way up the stairs, stepping over two gothy girls sitting on the third riser, white faces and black braids and one with a contact-lensed eye all red. Alastair grins at them and they grin back. Surprised they seem. A bit pleased.

Dean talks over his shoulder as he climbs: —Did I tell yiz I was in New York?

—Stega said summin about it, yeh, Darren says. —Said yiz were under the Twin Towers when thee were hit, like.

—Stega said that?

—Yeh.

—Nah, I was friggin miles away, man. Coming down in New Brighton, fuckin miles away.

—New Brighton? Wha, on the Wirral?

—Nah, in NY, man. There's a New Brighton over there, as well.

—Is thee?

—Aye, yeh. Saw all the smoke tho, an the fires, like. An me brother, y'know the one lives over there, he rolls a giant skunk spliff for us to appreciate the view more, like, an stoned as a cunt *that's* when the towers fell, like. Believe that? Thought I was trippin. Only really believed it'd happened when I switched on the telly and saw it, like.

—Yeh. Is right.

Girders twisted S-wise in Alastair's head and the black smoke and the red flame and the little distant figures kicking as if to fend off the void around them. And the collapse itself all collapsing he watched it in the pub with the sound turned down thought it was a movie only the rustle of people's unbelieving breath like the old woman that old woman it all comes down in silence as if nothing we could say. As if we finally learn the fatuity of our words even before the wreckage stuffs our dry mouths.

—Still, tho, Dean says, —friggin Septics. Think ther thee only country it's ever happened to, like. Only place that's ever been friggin bombed. Shoulda seen it, Dar, people all over the place in tears like goin 'Why, why?' Said to em, I said, 'Look at fuckin Palestine. *There's* yer friggin *why.*'

—Got *that* right, kidder.

—Yeh. An fuckin Yank bizzy overheard me in Central Park, like, didn't he? Interrogation room six fuckin hours, I was.

—Bastards.

—*Six* fuckin hours! Missed me flight home an everythin.

They are standing on the landing now, Dean telling his story disbelieving, distressed. Alastair is watching his face, the eyebrows seesawing, the pupils dilated and the wet lips rearing back over the long teeth.

—Interestin story an all that, Dean, lar, but what I need right now is a bevvy and a snorter bugle, Darren says, rucksack clutched to his chest. Alastair nods agreement.

—An that is what you shall have, my friends, that is exactly what you shall have.

There is a gurgling behind them where the landing

15

dog-legs and they turn to face it. A baby in a buggy, sucking its sleeve, kicking its legs, gurgling up at the big people.

—Me sister's kid, Dean says. —Keeps im up here like where it's safer. All them pissed-up schoolies downstairs, like.

Darren smiles. —Gorrer lot to say for imself, dozen he?

The baby grins and gurgles. Darren bends and squats, somewhat awkwardly because of the rucksack.

—What did yeh say? What did yiz just call me? Call me a cunt, did yeh? Wanner step outside then, lar? Fancy a fuckin straightener then, do yeh, gobshite?

Dean laughs. The baby grins gummy and coos and gurgles again and Darren extends a finger and the baby clutches it tight.

—You're a funny little fat feller, aren't yeh, ey? Funny little fat chookie chookie chookie . . .

Alastair swallows. Darren is making baby noises, here. Alastair is watching Darren Taylor chuck a baby under the chin and make 'coochy-coo' noises at it. This isn't right.

—He's nearly one, Dean says to Alastair. —Maddy ad im last year. She was fourteen years old. Believe that? And the dad, fuckin bad beast him, was twenty-five. Did a runner soon as he found out she was up the duff, like. Believe that shit, man? What's happenin to the kids today, man, eh?

Alastair shakes his head. Dean leads them up another flight of stairs to the attic conversion at the door of which a crustie stands, scabby guardian in camouflage kex. As they pass he gulps at his tin of Spesh and asks:

—D'yew wanner go faster? Any of yew lads wanner go faster?

Darren looks him up and down and sneers: —Faster than you already, yeh jippo twat. Get downsters with thee other binlids an fuckin be'ave yerself.

Dean laughs and opens the door. They walk into a blast of bass.

People in this room in a hovering purple light. The music is loud and a TV is on with the sound turned down, some local news programme or something showing a concerned councillor in a yellow hard hat on a building site, bulldozers and cranes around him and he besuited and whiskery. Nothing comes from his mouth. He talks but makes no noise. The real people talking in the room glance once at the newcomers then resume their conversations in the smoke-choked room within this odd and hovering lilac light, two women and a man on the bed and others on the floor and one man squatting at the stereo with his fleece ridden up to reveal the top of his arse-parting and the scribble of hair there. He smiles and nods at Alastair over his shoulder; goatee beard, Kangol hat. Alastair nods back unsmiling and takes a seat at the side of the room on the floor with his back up against the wall and Dean goes over to a small fridge at the foot of the bed and takes out cold tinnies, Heineken, and hands them out.

—Ta, lar.

Darren has taken a seat on the bed, between the two women, the rucksack on his knee. Slurps long at his can.

—The beak, Dean. Fuckin dyin for a snort I am here, mate.

—Comin up, feller.

—Been a long hard day, likes, knowmean?

Dean looks around.—Who's got the charlie?

A figure on the floor holds up a bag of white powder and Darren pounces and snatches it.

—Oi! Haven't ad *my* line yet!

—Yer've ad too *many* fuckin lines by the looks of yeh, lad. Eyes like pissholes in the snow, man. Give irrup for those in need, unnerstand?

—Fuckin . . .

Dean looks at this man and shakes his head quickly, eyes serious and big. Darren smirks and makes a loose fist and tips a small mound of powder out on to the fleshy pad between bent thumb and forefinger and inhales it nasally with an abrupt snort that can be heard even over the music.

—Aw fuckin ell . . . bliss man . . .

He does another line, murmurs, and hands the baggie over to Alastair.

—Ally. Yeh deserve this, lar.

Alastair takes it and does the same. Hears as he bends to snort one of the women ask Darren what he has in the bag but catches no reply as his head gets lost in the buzzing, the deep basso buzz. Returns the bag to the pissed-off man on the floor and nods thanks and swigs at the cold beer to swill the cocaine down his throat and leans his head back against the wall and closes his eyes languid but then the small sound of his head on the wall registers. A quiet contact only this but it resonates in his skullbowl behind his eyes and above his teeth and somewhere also in his throat, grows in his ears to clang and clatter too big, too loud.

Everything has changed.

Of course that woman. That poor old woman. Terrified she was and Darren was screaming in her face showing her the hammer and she was pleading don't hit me don't hit me and calling for her husband and Alastair too with the pleading don't hit her Darren don't hit her lar and did Darren hear? No difference if he did. Wrenching the floorboards up, the trapdoor there and roughly shoving the collapsed woman's slippered legs out of the way and opening the safe and after the THUNK with the code she'd babbled at him before the THUNK or rather between the THUNKS, the second one louder than the first the thunk followed by the THUNK and the safedoor surrendering and Darren hoisting it open and all that money inside. In bricks. Tied up in elastic bands in what amounts but large ones. Never seen so much money. And Darren roaring and ordering Alastair to take a rucksack from the wall display of such items by the postcard rack and then stuffing it to bulging with the cash bricks and in his fever to leave the shop not even stepping over the woman where she fell but actually walking *on* her, across her hips and chest and she unconscious and Alastair automatised just following all stunned, the THUNK the fall the massive money all unquestioned orders.

That fucking Darren.

Everything has changed.

That fucking money.

Everything has changed.

That woman with the grey hair and the specs and the kind face and the accent all like his grandmother, his nain in hospital and when she can talk that is what she sounds like. Don'thitmepleasedon'thitme. These women falling, sliding off this earth and not just from violence but the one commonality that turns life to a wreck – age. Just getting old. And, too, all the world's fiendish imperatives issued mainly from the society of men, the drawn-out demands of men aimed at their own impossible satiation, the virus of their terrible dissatisfaction. Anything to thaw the inside snows, whatever to warm the winters within and there is one lesson that remains unlearned; that inside as without these freezings follow a cyclical pattern and the one returning constant is ice.

THUNK the desperation. THUNK the never-learning. THUNK the constant failure and THUNK as her scalp unzipped. Very little blood from that desiccated flesh.

Alastair opens his eyes, looks across the room towards Darren. He is now nuzzling the neck of the skinny girl next to him, his chunky sov-ringed hand creeping up her shirt and she is laughing and quarter-heartedly pushing him away, her face charlie-bright, sweat-sheened and flush. Her pulse can be seen fluttering in her neck and her blouse has slipped off one shoulder revealing a black bra strap and a deep dark pit behind her collarbone and a knot in that bone where it has broken and healed badly and two hickeybruises on her neck like squashed plums. As Alastair watches, Darren's fat and ring-glinting hand creeps up from underneath the shirt like some huge white spider, the fingerlegs tickling the shoulder and the neck as if seeking a vein to puncture or bone to snap and Alastair shudders and looks away. The light has changed now, become darker. A couple in the corner are kissing with limbs entwined. In the compressed shadows between them something pale lollops and Alastair squints and realises it's a penis. On the bed Dean is cooking up while the other skinny girl in a white Stetson hat slaps her withered arm and curses as a vein fails to sound. The music still pounds on although somewhat lower and on the TV is a weather forecast showing a map of Britain covered in stylised dark clouds.

The door opens. A stranger comes in. He has a face like a once-muddy field baked into ruts and ridges by a parching sun and knees which shake beneath his tracksuit trousers and hands that tremble below his cuffs.

Dean looks up at him. —Help yeh, Pughey?

Pughey approaches the bed. —Need somethin, Deano.

—Do yeh? Thought you were dryin out?

—Aye, I yam, that's why I need somethin, mate. I'm eatin the fuckin carpets, here.

—What yiz after?

—Librium, methadone, fuckin *anythin*, man. Yew've got to help me out here, Dean.

Darren has been watching this exchange with amusement. He asks Pughey: —Dryin out, are yeh, lar, aye?

Pughey nods.

—Then why come to a fuckin party? Makes no sense to me, that, like.

—Came to see Dean. Need some calmers, don't I?

Darren laughs, rises to his knees on the wobbly bed

and waves his opened can under Pughey's nose. —Aw, smell that, man? Best smell in the fuckin world, that, innit? Go on, lar, taker good deep sniff.

Pughey does. And his head flops back on his neck and he groans and his mouth hangs open and Darren laughs again and pours beer into that opened mouth. Pughey gulps. His eyes are tightly closed and his body stands loose, simply a receptacle for the beer which Darren continues to tip laughing and the others watch beginning to laugh too.

Thunk. There will soon be an echo of that sound a reverberation several times over and it will come from the world and it will be the world this noise of yielding, of surrendering, of an enforced descent. It is all around. It is the sound of the human heart weakly knocking against its cell.

There is a notion in Alastair that goes: FUCK THIS. Not in words, no, nor any conscious verballing, it takes the form of the image of an antelope pelting across grassland towards a high and humming sun but what it means to Alastair is FUCK ALL THIS and then he's standing then he's out of the room on the landing where the crustie has curled up in a corner to sleep, his camouflage gear useless against the stained grey carpet and the stained yellow walls. Everyone can see him. His face is turned upwards, snoring, his mouth slightly ajar and dribbling into his matted beard. Alastair stares down at him for a moment then also at the baby in the buggy who is sleeping too then he descends the stairs where the noise of the party is louder, shrieks and shoutings, on to the lower landing where he goes into the bathroom and pees and swills his face at the

22

sink then stares at himself in the mirror with his hands cupped over his lower face from chin to bridge of nose so that only his eyes are visible. He regards himself like that for some time then he leaves the bathroom and enters the room opposite, a brightly lit and toy-strewn bedroom with bunks against one wall, the top level occupied by a small boy maybe seven or eight years old playing on a GameCube. Alastair can hear the Tetris tune.

—Alright, big feller?

The boy just stares.

—Don't worry, lad, I just wanner watch the news. Gorrer telly?

The boy nods.

—Where is it then, my mate?

—It's over there.

He points at a portable in the corner and Alastair turns it on, starts flicking through the channels.

—You carry on playin, feller. Tetris, is it, yeh? Crap at that, meself. Useless. What's yer highest score?

The boy answers something but Alastair doesn't hear – he's found the local news. He sits through some item about flooding somewhere and another one about a gun amnesty or something and he thinks that it may have not made the news yet but then the newsreader says something about a post-office robbery in Cilcain or somewhere. About almost four thousand pounds stolen. About how the post office acted as a bank for the villagers and how the proprietor trusted and well liked among the community was found by her husband in a pool of blood.

—You okay, mister?

In a coma in Wrexham General may not survive heavy blows to the head with blunt instrument probably brain-damaged doctors say if she should pull through.

—Mister? You okay?

Disgusting crime on a defenceless old lady. Catch the thugs who did this says the grey-muzzied copper and bring them to justice shocking wicked cowardly.

Alastair turns the TV off. The little boy asks him once more if he's okay and Alastair doesn't reply and leaves the room. Moves back up the stairs again stepping over Pughey who is spread on the risers with stinking sick across his face and clogging his hair and an empty bottle of Hugo Boss aftershave on his chest like a glass growth, a terrible tumour, and past the sleeping baby and crustie and back into Dean's room. Even darker now and the music still strong and no figure alone, paired and writhing as they are in twos. On the bed and across Darren's legs the skinny woman lies topless and supine, her ribcage almost bursting through her thin plucked-chicken skin and between yellow bruises and the breasts little more than brown nipples are three long lines of white powder. Her eyes are closed above a slack smile, her chin pointing ceiling-wards, her arms thrown back over her head and all this bare flesh astonishingly white in the curdling purple light. The stubble in her armpits like iron filings. The bruises on her torso like daubs of paint and Alastair approaches and falls to his knees and fancies he can see in those bruises a thumbprint, the whorls and swirls of some man's unique stamp.

—Just in time, Ally, Darren says. —Musta fuckin smelt it, lar, eh? Livin fuckin *large*, man.

He leans with a note rolled up in one nostril, snorts one line. The girl laughs.

—Livin fuckin *large*, lar. He hands the rolled-up note to Alastair, across the marked and emaciated and bent-back body. His face, his gleaming face, the dark eyes tunnel-like in Alastair's vision. —LIVIN FUCKIN LARGE!

Alastair takes the note, leans over the woman. What has this light been in Darren's eyes. He feels heat from skin as he snorts and maybe can taste that skin mixed with the drug as it numbs his nose and gullet and he remains like that over the bared and stretched body, bending from the knee, as the galloping antelope is brought down in the grass and there are teeth and there are talons and roaring and blood in red jets and a light within which there is no light, not at all, when he looks. Or maybe there is; he's not entirely sure. But fuck it anyway, Christ, light within light, the fuck's *that* shite all about.

OTHERS

ALASTAIR, HIS DAD

Them bucks today, yeh see em walkin around thinkin ther the big I AM givin it all this shit an thee don't know thee arf, thee avnt gorrer fuckin clue. Think theev lived, think theev got experience, like, but I tell yeh what, I piss all over em I do, ah yeh, all fuckin over em. Got kids all over ere me, all over the North-West and Wales an bleedin Ireland n all, useter purrit about like there was no tomorrer when I was werkin the dodgems, like. Ah yeh, go for a walk in the Holylands now or even the whole of bleedin Liverpool, Wirral n Chester n all an yer'll see undreds o' kids look like me, all got my eyes n nose, likes, ah yeh, my fuckin strength n all! See, that's what I was doin in them days, whatjacallit, enrichin the fuckin gene pool, likes. This fuckin upsurge in the city now, all down to me, tharriz. Times o' me friggin life, lad, eh; aller tarts'd love goin on the dodgems, like, an it was all cozzer me, standin on the back of the carts, like, an them all gigglin and actin all that shy way, SHY! Jesus, not so friggin shy in the bushes rounda back of the ghost train or in me friggin carra, were thee? Dipped me wick in evrythin, I did, undreds of em, not one werd of a lie. Thee all spread ther legs for ahl Alastair, oh aye, altho I was *young* Alastair then, of course . . . an not so much of the friggin old *now*, either, eh? Still drink em all under the friggin table, still sneak off an give ther wives the kinda seein to theev not ad fer years while ther useless fuckin husbands're sleepin off the bevvy. Oh aye yeh, that's me, avnt aged a friggin day since me twenties, well not in any of the most *important* ways like . . . Lost a birrer hair, aye, bit more white in me muzzy, like, but am still the young fuckin buck I was back then. Still got the body n all, apart from the spare tyre, likes, but Jeez, yeh can't put the bevvy away like I do an av done for fuckin years without sproutin a wee bit uvver belly, can yeh? Eh? Sign of a man this belly is, all bought n paid for. An *fuck* that ahl fuckin slapper thee other night, that ahl fuckin tan-from-a-can bitch oo said I ad bigger tits than her − not fuckin difficult that, love, I said, not with them two friggin fried eggs on yer chest. Slag. Gorrer learn some fuckin respect, these bitches, the things I've fuckin been through, women I've fucked, things av seen, things av done . . . All down to me, irriz. Not one werd of a lie.

Aye, an I can remember that one that time after thee Aintree races, which is a fuckin feat in itself considerin ow fuckin many there's been down the years . . . when was it now, late sixties? Early seventies? Roundabouts then. I'd won a fuckin ton on the gee-gees like, tidy friggin sum them days, an there she was, on the cars like, waitin with her mate. Boots up to her knees, mini on, the werks − I thought aye-aye. Early doors n all, must be fuckin gaggin for it. An that's exactly what she was, too right, shoulda fuckin heard her when I was slippin er one, all this 'oooohh yeh, oooohh yeh', derty friggin who-er this one was. Couldn't help meself, spunked off inside er, didn't I, said she was on the pill, like, so no one's fault but her own, went back to her place that night an gave it a load more in the sitting room like, her ahl mother asleep upsters. Didn't care in them days, me, fuckin wild one I was, tellin yeh ... probly woulda boned the fuckin mother n all. *Still* would. Take a few lessons from me, them young bucks can ... think thee know it all. Thee know fuckin *nowt*. Told the Judy I was gunna go get ferry tickets for us both, like, take her round Ireland with me winnins like, an the daft cow believed me; started goin on about gettin a cottage together over there, livin as man n wife like, avin bleedin babbies, usual shite that the tarts come out with. Left her packin her suitcase like, didn't I, all quiet so's not to wake her ma, jumped a cab down to the docks, overnighter to Dun Laoghaire, *straight* into the fuckin bar by the way, pissed before I passed the Isler Man. Blew all me winnins in a coupla nights, like, but I tell yeh, put me last fiver on a ranker at Lansdowne an the fuckin thing only went n won, didn't it? So there I was again, back to square one, ginch in me pocket, werld me fuckin oyster. Fuckin charmed life, me, ah yeh. The gods've always smiled on this boy, too fuckin right.

So, anyway, I'm back at Aintree for the National the followin year likes, aren't I? Gettin the cars ready, like, settin it all up, an there she fuckin is, this Judy like, holdin a baby. Like she'd been waitin for me all friggin year. Said the babby was mine an that she'd adter leave school to av it an all this kinda shite. Prove it, says I, I mean these were the days before DNA testin an all the rest of it an she says, 'I've named im after you. I've called im Alastair,' as if that's any fuckin proof, like. So I tells er she shoulda called im 'Any One of a Thousand Cocks' but I tell yiz what, am dealin with one seriously fuckin dim Judy here, like, fuckin blank look on its kite, tellin yeh, lard fer friggin brains. So I tells her okay, let's talk it through, takes it back to me carra an gives it another portion. The brat never stopped screamin once which made me think it couldna bin mine, like, cos no fuckin son o' mine whinges that much (like *my* ahl man used to say, 'Here's somethin to cry for'). And the bint's goin on, 'Oh let's go to Ireland, the three of us, take me away from all this, Alastair, let's goan live in a cottage in the hills,' an I'm all 'yeh, doll, yeh', I mean some fuckin dreamwerld this daft cow was livin in, like. Anyway, fucked it all night all fuckin ways with the brat bawlin its heart out like non-stop an I skedaddled when its ma nodded off, when I'd shagged it sense- less. An I've never seen er since. She's probly still waitin at Aintree racecourse for me, her an her son who must be about what, pushin bleedin therty now or summin . . . Tell yeh what, tho, if he friggin *is* mine, if he's *any* kinda chip off thee ahl block he'll be shaggin women all over the fuckin shop, lad, puttin it about like his ahl man did. Does. Never leaves, thee urge, like, an fuck knows what I'd do if I weren't able to still pull the berds, like, *fuck* only knows what I'd do. I'm not like them other cunts my age, avin ter pay for it with the prozzies, fuck no. Thank Christ I can still get the women.

Ah yeh, I've got undreds of fuckin nippers, me. Thousands of em round ere, in this area, like. So many that I can't remember em, not even one. None of the little fuckers, ah no.

DARREN'S VICTIMS: NUMBER 17

They did a wonderful job, those surgeons. *Wonderful* job. It took a while, a lot of time in theatre, but they really sorted it out; just a bit of scarring around the left eye, and a small curl to my top lip which Claire says sometimes makes me look like a young Elvis. She's been brilliant, Claire has, never once flagged in her support in the three years since it happened. And the counsellors, too, especially that Dr Brierly; she's been superb. Absolutely superb. If it wasn't for her then I don't think I'd be able to look in the mirror, still, even with this amazing work the surgeons have done. Honestly, she's been an angel; so understanding, so supportive. All of them, Claire and Dr Brierly and the surgeons, they don't realise what they've done for me, how they've stopped me being so afraid. Restored my faith in humanity, they have. Helped me to understand that there's *not* danger everywhere. That not everybody wishes to cause me pain.

But it's the boy, tho. Steven. My son. I fear that it'll never be the same between me and him again. I know he finds it difficult now to look at my face for any length of time, I mean sometimes when we're sharing a joke or something he'll suddenly stop laughing and look away and fall silent and I know he's remembering, he's reliving that night and that thug and that glass. And it pains me, I mean it genuinely causes a pain in my heart because I can imagine what Steven is remembering at those times, it's as if I can see it again through his eyes, I can see myself, my own face so terribly, traumatically wounded and the blood and that psychopath over me . . . Did I beg? I don't recall. Oh God, I hope I didn't beg. Maybe one day I'll be able to ask Steven about it but when that day will come God only knows. He's also had counselling, Steven has, and on the surface he seems to have adjusted well but it's the little things, the small ways in which he's changed his life; I mean he used to *love* football, he was Blackburn Rovers mad, but then he found out that Graeme Souness used to be connected to Liverpool and then he took all his posters down, stopped wearing his strip, his Sega World Cup Football game went in the bin . . . everything. He wouldn't support England in the World Cup because of the Liverpool players so he switched to the Republic of Ireland, because of Damien Duff, but then he asked me why there were so many Liverpool flags among the crowd and I told him of the big Irish Catholic population in that city and so then he switched to Brazil. Must be so confusing for the poor little tyke. Neither of us watched the final, nor even the Brazil–England game, and Dr Brierly said that I shouldn't push football completely out of my life, I shouldn't let the attack change my life in such funda- mental ways, but football, especially Rovers and Liverpool, obviously sets off the unpleasant memories, the horrors . . . Steven, tho, he can't even watch *Brookside* any more. He used to love it, it used to make him laugh, he used to do mock-Scouse accents and find it funny. But not any more. I'm the same; that accent. It makes my palms sweat, now, whenever I hear it. It makes my heart thud. Once it made me hyperventilate and Claire had to call an ambulance, she thought I was having a heart attack. And all because a *Red Dwarf* rerun came on the telly.

And yes, I know it's stupid, I know this reaction is ridiculous and irrational. It was just that one man, that one psychopath . . . just my bad luck that I happened to bump into that unhinged and unhappy individual that night. And, God knows, there are people like him in every town and city across Britain, even down the road in Blackburn, drinking cider all day on the steps of St George's Hall, but I can't help feeling partly foolish and embarrassed and naive because . . . well, Claire and I, we've had only the one argument since IT happened, and during the course of that she told me I was naive, that I never followed football as a boy, that there was no way I could understand the passions it aroused especially among more disadvantaged people and that going into a pub in the city where my team had just won, wearing their colours, was pure and simply asking for trouble. Thinking about it, I'm afraid she was correct; but it was for Steven, really, I did it for Steven so he wouldn't feel excluded at school, and besides, I thought the days of hooliganism were long gone, that fans were largely friends, now . . . evidently I was wrong. Or partly; I mean, I still remember outside Anfield that night, after the game, a Reds fan shook my hand and said well done and good luck. 'Good luck'! I had the worst luck in the world that night. If only Steven hadn't've been there. If only we hadn't've missed the train, or if only we'd gone to a different pub to await the next one. If only, Dr Brierly said, are the two saddest words in the English language. She's right.

But I'm recovering. I'm getting over it. I hope Steven is too, and that our bad dreams will stop, and that I'll be able to find another job, and that one day he'll be able to look his father in the face again. And that some day we'll both be able to accept that evil walks the world and there's really very little we can do to protect ourselves against it and that it's always been that way. In its rarity lies the hope, Dr Brierly says, and Claire has said that too, but I wonder about that, I really do. I mean surely the fact that it's there around us and we cannot defend ourselves against it . . . I wonder. It still hurts when I smile.

But they've been wonderful, tho, really, the surgeons and Claire and the good Dr Brierly. They've all done an excellent job. Really; I don't know what I would've done without them, I really don't.

DARREN'S VICTIMS: NUMBER 21

NO DON'T HIT ME PLEASE GOD PLEASE GOD GET THEM AWAY GET AWAY DON'T LET THEM HIT ME **WHAT'S THE FUCKIN CODE YER AHL CUNT GIVE ME THAT CODE OR AL SMACK YEH AGAIN** *NO DAR DON'T HIT HER MATE* **DON'T USE MY FUCKIN NAME SOFT-SHITE** *DON'T HIT HER MATE SHE'S HAD ENOUGH YEH DON'T AVTER HIT HER AGAIN*

PLEASE LISTEN TO YOUR FRIEND THE POLICE WILL **D'YEH WANT ANOTHER LUMP YER AHL FRIGGIN BITCH GIVE US THE CODE I WON'T FUCKIN ASK YEH AGAIN** *YEH MIGHT KILL HER DON'T DON'T SHE'S OLD MATE SHE'S ALREADY HURT* **FUCKIN WILL KILL HER LAR N ALL I DON'T GET THAT FUCKIN CODE LAR SEE THIS HAMMER YEH FUCKIN** NO PLEASE NO PLEASE I HAVE MONEY TAKE MONEY **THAT'S EXACTLY WHAT AM TRYIN TER DO FER FUCK'S SAKES I MEAN** *JUST GIVE IM THE CODE LUV AN WE'LL GO THAT'S ALL WE WANT I'M NOT GUNNER HERT YEH* **GIVE US THE FUCKIN** EMRYS! EMRYS! *OH JEEZ DARLIN NO PLEASE DON'T SHOUT* **ARGH YEH FUCKIN AHLD** *NO DARREN NO DON'T HIT HER* **ARGH** *PLEASE DON'T SHOUT LOVE JUST GIVE US THE CODE AN WE'LL LEAVE YOU ALONE I PROMISE* **GIVE ME THE FUCKIN TAKINGS BITCH** TAKE THEM JUST TAKE THEM **GIVE US THE FUCKIN CODE WELL** EMRYS! *OH NO PLEASE DON'T CALL YER HUSBAND LUV JUST* HELP ME SOMEONE GOD HELP ME **THE CODE TWAT THE FUCKIN COOOOOODE**

Numbers then noise. Then numbers and *a* noise. Then a lot of money.

ALASTAIR

Oh shite that fuckin no-mark bastard that was too far he went too far im I'm not avin that he's not getting away with that he's one fuckin psycho balloonhead he is that was too much that was sick no fuckin need man what do I do now oh Jesus Christ God what do I do now tell me

get that bag I'm gunner get that fuckin bag he's gunner be sorry I'm gunner fuck that bastard up BIG time

all he deserves

someone's granny someone's missis

should never have gone to Wales with him shoulda known better know what he's like he's pure fuckin sick he'll welly anyone even sweet ahl ladies he's parro about evrythin he's pure wrecked in thee ed

no need for that man no need at all he's wacko he's wacko he should be locked up

that fuckin bastard

that's it between me n im now I'm avin nowt to do with that fuckin nutter that idyit that prick he's fuckin mental loop-the-loop he is he's fuckin

gunner get *iz* man tellin yeh no lie about fuckin time that arsewipe paid too right

all he deserves

he'll gerrit

that's *it* between me n im

psycho, sicko

Tommy'll do fuck all just laugh they're as bad as each other wankers

sweet ahl granny like that like me *own* granny dyin there in thee ozzy thee age of her like so old she gets through it all through life an evrythin all them bad years an she don't deserve some sick no-mark knob'ed comin into her shop

I'm sorry my nain I'm so sorry

that cunt's gunner get *iz*

youse watch me youse just wait n see

that's it now man that's *it*

not right in thee ed that fucker not right not right
it's all gone wrong

I'll *make* it right

I *will*

what do I do now oh God what do I fuckin

DARREN

Aw man, that was so friggin easy . . . eeeaaasssyyy . . .
so *easy*, lar . . . easiest four grand I've ever made that
like no fuckin lie . . . I can do anythin in the world,
now, wharrever I fuckin want . . . snort me gack off
this slag's chest . . . no tits on it like but so fuckin
what lar I'm livin fuckin large . . . this charlie . . . the
weight of the ruckie on me knees like just fuckin
perfect lar, knowmean? . . . fuckin brewstered, man . . .
am friggin rich *as* . . . so fuckin powerful with these
big bucks I can do wharrever the fuckin hell I wanner
do an no fucker's gunna stop me no fuckin Hunter
clan no fuckin Lenny Rees no fuckin Gozzy Squires
no Tommy not even any fuckin Joey . . . all me own
werk this is so fuck *them* . . . is right . . .

. . . gunna watch that fuckin Alastair tho . . . softlad's
all fuckin tampin cos I adter give that ahl queen a bit
of a wellyin . . . knob'ed dozen unnerstand, like, that
yer've gorrer be ruthless in this fuckin game, yer not
gunner get nowt for nowt . . . lesson for life, that, tellin
yeh . . . never get anythin for nowt . . . gorrer fuckin
assert yerself like . . .

36

. . . stop movin about, will yeh, yer spillin the fuckin beak . . .

. . . just gorrer av the guts, like, thee arse, the balls . . . gorrer go out n take . . . don't owe no cunt notten . . . it's all fuckin yours, man, it's all out there, just gerroff yer arse an take it . . . grab it . . . make it just pure fuckin *yours,* knowmean? . . .

. . . keep one beam on that Alastair, tho . . . cunt's up to somethin, I just fuckin *know* ee is . . . can read that bastard liker buke . . . thinks I itter too hard, fuck's . . . she'll be alright . . . hardest bone in the body, that human skull . . . an anyway notten stands between me n what's mine, no fuckin way . . . paid me bleedin dues, me . . . no lie . . . entitled to some kinder fuckin reward arn I . . .

. . . I can do anythin, now, anythin I've ever friggin dreamed of . . . an I've dreamed of fuckin *lotser* things . . . no lie . . . believe . . .

. . . aw man, this bugle . . . she'll smoke the bone if I can gerrit up, like, cos sometimes the gack does that to me, sometimes . . . does it to fuckin everyone, man, not just me . . . but *fuck* ow it feels in thee ed . . .

. . . so good, lar, so happy . . . evrythin's gunner be alright, fuckin *evrythin* . . . it's just gunner get better n better n better . . . eeyar, Darren lad, the werld is fuckin yours . . . like that globe statue thingio in that film *Scarface* said, 'the werld is yours' . . .

. . . an it *is,* Darren, it *is* . . . oh too fuckin right yeh . . .

. . . believe.

DEAN

An Jeez that's *not* the face yeh wanner see on yer doorstep all unexpected like, now, is it? Checkin on yer little sis an her mates, like, makin sure none of em's done too many pills or too many friggin Breezers an are chokin on ther own spew, like, an bing-bong the doorbell goes an yeh answer it an who's there? Fuck me I did *not* expect this, man. Thee *eyes* on the fucker.

—Darren? The fucker *you* doin ere?

All I can do to stop meself from screamin. Ee tells me he needs a place to crash. *Tells* me, like, too much to expect that twat to do anythin as nice as friggin *ask* . . . But nah, he's alright really, Darren is; never given *me* any grief, like, personally, an I've known im years. I know how he can be, God yeh, I've seen him lose it with mushers, like, on many an occasion an there's some hard fellers, that Stega for one, who're absolutely shiters of him an that but I've gorrer say, like, gorrer admit, he's always been sound with me. Member when I first moved out here from Prenton about two years ago an Darren invited imself to me house-warmin do, like, an comes up to me all charlie'd up an says he'd like a bit of the market, like, slice of the pie, meanin the coke an billy dealership I was gunner set up in Wrexham after the Birkenhead market got too chocka an started to attract some bad, bad people, an I mean *really* fuckin bad . . . I told im no. Just that; 'No'. Fergerrit, lad, I said. An he threw his hands up, like, says fair enough, fucks off back to the party. An that Peter comes up to me, asks if I knew who that was I'd just KB'd, I says I couldn't give two fucks who he was, I didn't need any kinder partner. Coked up at that stage I was, see. Peter just laughed, told me to watch me back, fucked off back to that bird he was seein, that mad one who apparently strangled her boyfriend to death last year sometime, can't remember her name now. But yeh, never ad any trouble from Darren, that night or since; I think he kinda respected me, standin up to im, likes. Think he thought I was alright after that episode, no pushover like, knowmean?

Still n all, tho . . . he's not the kinda feller you want in yer house. Not at yer little sister's birthday bash, like, oh no. His is *not* the face yeh want turnin up on yer doorstep without warnin, like. He's clutchin that ruckie to his chest like it's, what, a baby or somethin, no, a gold-plated diamond-encrusted Stanley knife or somethin an he's got his gormless mate in tow, one ugly get with zits an a basey who says nowt, just stares round at evrythin as if he's just payin a visit from another fuckin planet. Thee've got an air about them, these two, I mean ther guilty as fuck of somethin, some bad thing thee've just done comin off em liker bad stink. An I've gorrer invite em in, like, avn't I? I mean, what else can yeh do? An call it a deathwish or wharrever but I tell em one great big fuckin lie about bein in New York when the towers came down; I don't know why I do it but I'm almost crackin up, me, I mean it's so friggin funny, I'm almost startin to believe meself, tellin em I was gettin stoned with me brother when the planes hit when the truth be told I was in a boozer in Chester. An then all that stuff about gettin arrested an taken to thee interrogation room! Jeez, it's all I can do to stop meself laughin in ther faces, ther takin all this shit in. I mean I *was* in NY, yeh, but this was months before September 2001 but I mean this is just so funny, comin out with all this crap, like, an them two just standin there gawpin, believin it all . . . dead funny. Score:

Deano	1
No-mark dead-eyed scallies	0

Got to be careful, tho . . . Darren thinks he's bein taken for a knob'ed and there's no tellin what he'll do. Out'll come his trusty ahl Stanley and I'll have a much wider gob to tell porkies out of. But it feels good, this, tellin all these lies . . . knowin there's somethin *I* know that Darren and loads of other people don't. It gives me, what, what does it give me . . . makes me feel *closer* to meself, knowmean? Makes me feel like I'm a *mate* to meself, that's thee only way I know how to describe it. Like there's somethin I share only with meself an evry other fucker thinks exactly thee opposite, that kinda thing. Sort of like that. Like I know better than *them*. Secrets, like.

I think of this later when I'm cookin up for Karen, which I know I shouldn't be doin but the poor girl's rattlin so loud she sounds liker box of Smarties, and Darren's got Gillian bent back over his knees an is snortin bugle off her chest, between her virtually non-existent tits, like. Fuckin state of him, man, tellin yeh; thinks he's some kinda rock star. Screamin at his brain-dead mate that he's livin fuckin large, I mean, gerrer

40

grip, softarse; yer not tootin grade-A Colombian off Angelina Jolie in LA, yer snortin not-very-good gack off a skanky ahl skaghead in a council house in fuckin Wrexham. I mean sort yerself out, man, get back to the fuckin real werld, eh? State of yiz. An apart from all this, yer believin a lie, you think I was someplace where I wasn't on what might tern out to be the most important day of ar lifetimes and that makes you a total fuckin idyit. Dozen it?

Pathological liar, me teachers an me dad used to call me. An maybe I am. I mean I know it's stupid, really, an not much point, burrit makes me feel good. Also dangerous, I mean if Darren finds out . . . *any* excuse for that bastard and his fuckin chaos. Burrit makes me feel good. That's just me, tho, I'm Deano, it's just the way I am; it's not *you* that's livin fuckin large, lar, it's *me*. Unnerstand?

GILLIAN

Tickles! It's ticklin me!

Ee stops me wrigglin with his big hands on me waist an I like the feeling of that so I wriggle some more when he snorts the charlie so that he'll grip me tighter. Feel his great big hard hands like if he squeezed some more I bet he could make his fingers meet around me waist . . . So fuckin horny here I yam. Got a heat in me an he'll do, this one, he's got them funny eyes, like, but there's something about him an the way he moves an I bet there's got to be something *dead* intrestin in that bag he's carrying round everywhere . . . money or drugs, I bet. *Got* t'be money or drugs the way he's holdin it dead tight to him like that, nothin else could be –

Ticklin me!

—Stop movin about, will yeh, yer spillin the fuckin bugle.

His knee presses up into me back, bendin me further backwards over his legs . . . can feel me spine bendin, feel me ribs pushin out up at the ceiling, all the bones in me body stretchin an expandin . . . reminds me of the time Nathan picked me up by me collarbones to spin me around, just messin around like, but one of em snapped. Made a sound like a stick breakin or something and didn't half fuckin hurt . . . in the hospital, like, in Wrexham General, Nayth was all sad an apologising all the time sayin he only wanted to show me how thin I was getting so that I'd eat some more, which was typical of him, that, always caring about people he was. But I was tryin to tell him I didn't mind, I *liked* it, not the bone-snapping bit obviously but when he picked me up, like, when he kinda grabbed me . . . I like it when fellers grab me . . . not *hurt* me, no, fuck that, but when they're, y'know, big an strong . . . it's like me mind empties, like kinda bein free. The three or four turns in the air I did with Nayth before me collarbone went crack, them few seconds like, seemed to last for hours an they were some of the best moments of me life. That nurse, tho, that nurse in the hospital tryin to make me press charges sayin no woman should have to put up with that, their boyfriends breaking their bones . . . called Nathan an animal she did an I nearly twatted her. Animal! That's my feller, yer frigid cow I said. That's my *feller* yer calling names.

I feel him snortin again off me chest, feel the rolled-up note run up me skin as if makin a cut with no pain. Me eyes're closed an I don't wanner open them cos I can see some great shapes altho I'm dyin for another toot but these are some ace shapes.

—LIVIN FUCKIN LARGE, LAR!

I'm laughin. That's *exactly* what we're doin. Strange thing, tho, I mean usually lyin back over a bloke's lap like this I'd be able to feel his hard-on pressin into me back but with this one there's nothing, I can't feel anythin. Maybe he just needs some more coke, like Nathan used to before he could get it up. That's probly it. Oh yeh. Livin fuckin *massive*.

CHILD

Them long sticks I don't like an them ones shaped like 's'. Ziggyzaggy ones. Can never fit them ones in . . .

Funny man in my room. With a baseball hat on his head like Michael Lewis in my class always wears cos he's got a mark on his head.

—Alright, big feller?

Must be from the party. But he's older than them ones. He's a proper mister.

—Don't worry, lad, I just wanner watch the news. Got a telly?

He's a proper mister. All misters always want to watch the news. And mums.

—What's yer highest score then?

Dunno, I tell him. He's watchin the telly. Must be somethin dead sad on cos I think he's havin a cry.

—You okay, mister?

Why's he crying? Funny man wantin to watch stuff to make him sad. Got his head in his hands now so he can't see the sad stuff any more and it can't see him.

—You okay, mister?

He can't talk. He goes back out without sayin tara. Funny man. Just wanted to come in and be sad . . . they all wanner do that. They all like bein sad and cryin loads. Haven't cried for yonks me only when I got stung on the tongue from that wasp cos he wanted my Calypso. Never gunner be like them, never gunner cry like them. They all like crying an bein sad.

Another ziggyzaggy one . . . bloop. Fuck. *Baaaaaad* word.

Tell Mum about that sad man but not that bad bad word. That funny man.

ALASTAIR

Fuckin bastard out on the landin with that skinny girl he's gunner fuckin get iz no werd of a lie he'll be hert he'll be sufferin that bastard that poor ahl lady where's the bugle give me some bugle need another bump that bastard this plan *my* plan thinks I'm soft that bastard sicko get he's gunner get iz you just fuckin *watch* me

DARREN

Oooooaaggghh yes yer fucker giz it here GIZ IT GIZ IT

GIVE IT TO ME GIVE IT TO ME SLUT GIVE
IT TO ME
ME ME ME ME ME

CAR

Against his wife Ronnie's advice, Ernie Morrison
bought the car first and only then read up on its
history. This was in 1968, two years before the saloon
models ceased production and one year before the last
model, the Traveller, rolled out of the factory for the
final time. Ernie discovered that William Richard
Morris, 1st Viscount (1877–1963) and nicknamed
'Nuffield' after his financial support to the Oxford
college of that name, opened the first Morris factory
in 1912 and that he described the making of its first
car as assembling 'a poached egg'.

—A poached egg! Ernie laughed, reading the
manual in bed, nudging his wife. —Not fried or
anything, Ronnie! Poached!

Ronnie murmured something. Probably already
asleep.

—We'll go somewhere tomorrow in our egg, Ernie
said. —Where shall we go in our egg, Veronica?

—Rhyl.

—Righty-o, then. To Rhyl we shall go. In our new
poached egg.

The Morris Minor 1000 Series V, he read, had begun
production six years ago in 1962 and the updated
model he had bought that day and which sat new and
gleaming and possible under the corrugated plastic
carport had, in competition with the Mini and the

Ford Cortina, been boosted with the following modifications; an enlarged 1098 cc engine; maximum power of 48 bhp at 5,100 rpm; a top speed of 77 mph and an acceleration rate of 0–50 in 16.1 seconds. Fair bit of power. It represented, to Ernest Stanley Morrison, the last bastion of the Great British automobile industry against European and Asian imports. Quality workmanship over shoddy and inexpensive modern mass production. Reliability as opposed to the quick fix.

They drove to Rhyl in it the very next day, and on the head of the Great Orme in a warm breeze with the flat sea so blue beneath them they drank tea and ate meat-paste sandwiches and apples and fruit cake. Ernie positioned himself so that the car remained always in his field of vision, parked at the side of the road above him, the headlights and radiator grille sparkling new in the sun. A better view than the sea, he thought, representing as it did his reward for months of long and tiring hours as a fitter in the Moreton Cadbury's. More than that, of course; it stood for mobility, success, purpose. Freedom, of a sort.

It was to be the only car he ever owned. They took it everywhere, he and Ronnie; to Pembrokeshire, where they walked the coastal path, to London to see their daughter and her family, to Cornwall, on the ferry to Skye. Once, even, to France, where they intended to drive it down to the Vendée but had to cut the holiday short and return home when Veronica fell ill, probably due to the platter of fruits-de-mer she'd eaten in Le Havre. She had an accident in the car back in England and Ernie had to bleach the stains out at a roadside rest stop; it seemed to him that the car never smelled quite right after that. And when they divorced in 1988 Ernie kept the car, insisted on keeping it in fact even although it had been the main site of Ronnie's infidelities, and this saddened her but she agreed to it and accepted without much enthusiasm her new lover's gift of a late-model Fiesta. It was too small, she thought, too poky; but then again, what was an old girl like herself doing carrying on like some hormonal lovesick teenager in the back of a car . . .

Ernie's final trip in the Egg was, of course, back to Rhyl. Again he ate a packed lunch on the head of the Orme, this time alone, and he pictured himself sitting in the car, pointing it at the sea at the head of the steep dingle and simply releasing the handbrake. But he was too old for that, he thought; suicide was a young man's prerogative. Aged felo de se seemed ignoble and hysterical and impatient. And indeed on the journey home he stopped for tea at a Little Chef and over the salad bar got chatting to a widow whom he was to live with in Prestatyn until his death in 1999 from a heart attack, two months short of the millennium's end he had always wanted to see. On his back he died, underneath the Egg, far too old to be tinkering with the failing vehicle and all the while explaining to his second wife how the Morris Minor was never allowed to develop its full potential and how that in itself was symbolic of the demise of the British automobile industry as a whole and –

Ernie? Ernie? No answer. Dead Ernie. His lifeless feet sticking out from underneath the bonnet, splayed in slippers.

Widow Twice, as her neighbours now took to calling her, put the car up for sale although it pained her to do so in the *Daily Post* and it was bought for the asking price a week later by a taciturn yet friendly Welshman who introduced himself as Leonard and reassured her that the car was going to a good home and that it would be well looked after. And for some years it continued to serve, acquiring much mileage and some dents and some stains both on the back seat and in the spacious boot, blood and oil, and on the dashboard too from a squashed cleg fly and then it came to be sitting at the bottom of the canal that skirts the town of Wrexham, murky water for passengers and weed and discarded carrier bags caught in its struts and axles, a dead and uprooted rush draped over the rear-view mirror like some odd St Christopher, journey-blesser for the firecrest newt clinging to the steering wheel or the skaters and boatmen and whirligigs that dart across the surface some feet above the already-rusting roof and that cast fast shadows upon it. Horse leeches suck at tyre rubber and ram's-horn snails decal the doors; tubifex worms reach from the black mud up towards the sump as if thirsty for that gunk and male sticklebacks will scout the wheel arches for suitable nest sites come spring when their underbellies will turn fiery red. And at the advent of that spring some children will swim through the open windows of the car and one of them will get his foot caught underneath the passenger seat and will yell for help and thus inhale water and will for some moments be clinically dead until the owner of a nearby field will rescue him and revive him and for the rest of his life until he dies in a car crash at the age of forty-four that child will yearn with an almost physical pain for a recalled fleeting peace, a vast calm and warmth that seemed to solve all confusion, annul all fear. And after the rescue the field owner will use his tractor to drag the car out of the canal into the furthest corner of his field beneath the ancient hawthorn tree and will intend to take it to the breaker's yard but never actually will and the car will remain there even after his death, almost completely overgrown and sunk in the soil, athrive with vegetative and insectile life until around the middle of this century the Wrexham expansion will creep out this way and the dissolving hulk will be bulldozed into the soil and concreted over with the footings for a new overspill estate. Rot it will until the metal will crumple like paper and become not much more than unusually acidic soil. Not much more than one deeper darkness buried in the dark earth, unsunned, just dust wet and unseen.

Veronica, of course, will have died long before this has come to pass. She will die demented in Clatterbridge hospital, rambling about a Morris Minor car. And in the lucid remnants of her mind she will wonder about that car and what became of it. Where it is now. Whether after death she might ride in it again.

STATION ATTENDANT

Knew they were up to no good, those two. Could tell it a mile off; it's easy with them types, see, the way they walk all kind of swaggery, strut around as if they own the bloody place. I'd bet a month's wages that the curly-headed one wasn't carrying around a packed bloody lunch in that bloody rucksack either. Way he was clutchin it to his chest. And his pal, as well, the one with the cap, something wrong with him, didn't have a clue where he was . . . Something wrong with them *both*. Up to no bloody good. Mischief. The one with the rucksack, he comes right up to the window, see, leans right up against the glass so that his spit sprays against it and says:

—Lime Street. Two singles.

No please or thank you, mind, and oh now *there's* a surprise – Liverpool Lime Street, could've guessed, there's no other place in Britain that them two characters were going to come from, not with their track-suits with the trousers tucked into the white sports socks and the body language of them both giving it the big I AM. Scouse scally written all over them, see. Wish they'd leave this bloody town alone, I do. This town wouldn't be half as bad if it wasn't for them; they bring the drugs here they do, trying to open up new markets I suppose they'd call it, bring the burglaries, the crime, the bloody football violence . . . Overbloody*joyed* I was a couple of seasons ago when Tranmere got relegated cos I thought we'd then seen the last of that bloody fixture, a guaranteed one-day-per-season of mayhem. Oh aye, I know the Rovers fans insist that they're not Scousers, that they're from Birkenhead, but they're not fooling me – they've got the same accent, the same clothes, the same bloody swagger. And they'd pile out of trains and the trains'd be covered in sick and urine and rubbish and graffiti, they'd terrify the women and children, like, and they'd smash up the station and people like Joe bloody Muggins here'd have to clean up the mess, and the abuse! The foul language! Only trying to earn a decent day's wage, see, put bread on the table for me family . . . shouldn't have to put up with that kind of treatment, should I? Animals, they are, nothing but bloody animals, except that's an insult to the beasts of the field . . . So yes, I was very happy indeed to see Tranmere go down. But then Wrexham followed them the very next season and the whole thing started all over again. Worse, in fact, because then I had the Cardiff contingent to contend with as well and they're just as bloody bad. Give Wales a bad name, they do. The Wrexham fans, they wouldn't be half as bad if it wasn't for the Rovers and the Bluebird fans winding them up. Bringing trouble to the area. Best thing my grandfather ever did, move from Liverpool to North Wales, best thing he ever did bar none. That city should be cordoned off, and Cardiff too; lawless places, they are. Bloody lawless. Put big barbed-wire fences around them both and let them just get on with it, shooting and stabbing each other and all the rest of it, crime and drugs and all the bloody rest of it . . .

So yes, here we go again – no 'please' or 'thank you' or anything like that, just 'Lime Street. Two singles.' And doesn't he only go and pay with a fifty-pound note? Now where on earth does a dodgy individual like that get his hands on a fifty-pound note? I didn't recognise it at first, thought it was a foreign currency or something I did. Monopoly money, see. Barely had enough change in the till.

It's just not fair. *Bound* to be ill-gotten gains, that fifty pound. Boy like that gets that kind of money legitimately and I'll tell you what, I'll eat my bloody hat. I will, I'll eat my hat. Which is part of the uniform which I wear with pride and I'm entitled to bloody do so because it's not an easy job, this, see, not with them two and their ilk. People like that. At least they bought singles; that means they're not coming back. And good bloody riddance, I say.

Crimestoppers is on telly tonight. I'll be glued to the bloody screen, I will.

PASSENGER

Oo, the *language*. Shocking, it is. Why they see the need to swear like that, I don't know. I just don't understand it. 'F' this and 'f' that, there's no *need* for that kind of talk. There are plenty of other words to use in the English language to express yourself, aren't there? Sign of a lazy mind, it is; all this 'f' and 'c' and 'b'. What are they taught at school these days? I blame the parents. No child of mine ever spoke like that, not even Robert, my eldest, and he was in the army. Fought in the Gulf he did. Lovely, polite boy. Never swore. Simply no need for that kind of language, not that *I* can see anyway.

Got their feet up on the seats as well. Typical; *such* disrespect. Others have to use those seats and all the dirt from their shoes — could be dogmuck! — will get on their clothes. Could've trodden in dogdirt or anything. No respect for others, none at all. Should think about others but this is it, this is the problem with people nowadays, they *don't* think, not about anyone other than themselves at any rate. Disgusting, it is. If I had've behaved like that when I was younger my mother would've took the skin off my behind with a belt, and rightly bloody so; it would've been no more than I deserved. Would've taught me to think on, oh yes. That's what's missing these days – discipline. Good hiding's what they need. No spine these days, no back-bone; it's all just 'f' this and 'f' that, can't be bothered, 'f' it all. What's the world coming to? What's happening to us all? I look around me and all I see is mess and rubbish. It's all gone to pot. When I was a girl during the War it was much better then, we all pulled together; there was none of these drugs or internal immigrants or bogus asylumers that you read so much about in the papers nowadays. Young people shooting each other, pensioners burglared for their life savings . . . we had none of it back then, oh no. Things were much quieter, more peaceful, during the War.

Tut tut, that language is shocking. Absolutely shocking. No one should have to hear that filth, not on a Tuesday morning, no. I should say something, really. Give them a reprimand of some sort, a piece of my mind. Let them know I'm not impressed. 'F' this, 'f' that. Awful it is, bloody awful. And that's swearing.

One of them's looking at me. The one with the curly hair and the bag, he's looking right at me like butter wouldn't melt. Oo, that face . . . it's not right. It's not *nice*. He's got a look like he wants me purse. Like he's going to have it away with me handbag any moment. Wouldn't *dare* look at me like that if my Bert was still around, if he was sitting here by my side. Give him short bloody shrift, my Bert would've, no messing about. Wipe that expression off his face quick bloody smart, Bert would, if he was able to. My Robert as well. Saddest day of my life, that, when the officers called round at the house . . . so smart, they looked. I was making a nice fish pie. It is our painful duty, they said. Died a hero, they said. Oo, they looked so smart in their uniforms. Twelve years ago now and not a day goes by without I think of them both, my Bert and Robbie. Keep expecting Robert to turn up at the door. With the flowers he always used to bring of a Sunday after church. Such a good boy he was. Such a *brave* boy he was.

He's still staring. Perhaps I'd better move to another carriage, I mean what you read in the papers about what goes on in these trains; young girls raped, old ladies mugged. Enough to keep you awake at night, it is. Enough to keep you behind locked doors, safest place to be although even there you're not completely safe, what with them bogus workmen and burglarers an all the rest of it. The *Mail*'s full of it. All the time, you've got to be on your guard. Everywhere they are, all around, these bad people. Nowhere's safe. Without your husband or your son, you're all on your own. No one to protect you. The world's a dangerous place, it says so in the *Mail*. Can't trust anyone these days.

I glance at him once as I get up and move to another carriage. Ee, these old bones. Shouldn't have to move like this, I mean I shouldn't let him intimidate me, but . . . best just to be safe. Better safe than sorry, as they say. The *face* on him, tho, the *eyes* . . . brrrr. Sent a shiver down me spine it did.

Never mind; best not to think about it. Don't let it bother you. What'd be nice for tea is a nice bit of fish from the precinct; nice bit of mackerel, with the head still on. Fry him up in butter. Nice bit of fried fish, give the head to the pussens, Winnie. Cheer anyone up, that would, and Winnie's been down in the dumps lately ever since her mother Cassie passed on. So a nice bit of fried fish for myself and Winnie and that's something to look forwards to, at least, isn't it? Got to have that, oh yes, something to look forwards to each day. Got to treat yourself, haven't you?

—See the friggin gob on that bastard, Ally?

—Who?

—Im in the ticket office. See the friggin kite on him? Fuckin 'tude on im lar, no messin. Shitehawk.

Alastair just shrugs, says nothing. They ascend the stairs to traverse the footbridge to the far platform.

—An see im when I gave im the fifty nicker note? Bet he thought it was snide, like, probly never even seen one before. That's cos yeh werk in a ticket office in fuckin Wrexham Station, lad. Get yerself a life an earn some proper fuckin dough.

They pass graffiti: TRFC ARE HERE and SCOUSERS DIE. WREXHAM SHITE and ROVERS FUCK OFF. They descend on to the platform, empty but for three dirty pigeons picking at a pizza crust; the Racecourse Ground swelling above it all, the four spotlights like the stanchions of alien craft or illumination for a titanic operating theatre. Litterfruited bushes on the trackbanks shimmy in the wind and the sky is blue and almost cloudless yet seemingly without a sun. It is cold and their breath can be seen puffing over their shoulders as if driven they are by steam.

They sit in a shelter to await their train. The shelter, of course, smells of urine as such places always do, and

on one of the paint-scabbed walls written in silver
marker-pen Alastair reads a rhyme:

JO AND SARAH
HAVE BEEN AND GONE
BUT WE LEFT ARE NAMES
TO TURN YOUSE ON

Darren wedges the rucksack tightly between his feet
and pulls his tracksuit top up over his face to shelter
him from the wind as he lights a cigarette. The smell
of the smoke entices Alastair and he lights one too
and now they are enmisted; two breaths, two exhaled
fumes. Their faces blurred behind a slender smog.

—Av a good time last night, Ally?

Alastair shrugs again. —Suppose so, yeh. Gorrer bit
borin early mornin like.

—Bit fuckin *borin?* Aye for *you* yeh dull bastard cos
you were lookin for somewhere to crash just when
things were kickin off. Shoulda got yerself a Judy, man,
tellin yeh thee were fuckin *chokin* for it. That friggin
Gillian one gobbled me dry, no lie.

They say nothing for some moments, just blowing
smoke down at the ground, each recalling in fuzzed
and thudding heads an experience of empty sleep and
sex, nullity or noise. A thin body. A slim slice of darkness under a bed where no peace was found. And
experiencing anew a sorrow and a freedom, a rue and
a potential dazzling. But some shadows across them
both alike as have been before and will again.

A faint rumbling begins in the earth. They can feel
it in the soles of their feet, through their trainies.

Darren flicks his butt out on to the trembling track.

—There's summin up with you, Alastair, isn't thee? Summin not fuckin right with you this mornin, lar, I fuckin *know* there is. You fuckin plannin summin? Summin fuckin brewin in that mad fuckin ed of yours?

Alastair's eyes slide once at Darren quickly then away again. He sucks again at the cigarette even though only the filter now smoulders.

—No, Darren, honest to God. I'm just fuckin knackered, that's all. That's all it is, lar. Truth. What the fuck would I be plannin anyway?

The rumbling gets louder.

—How the fuck should I know? Think *I* know what's goin on in them addled fuckin brains o' yours?

—There's nowt goin on, Da, honest. Ain't plannin fuck all sept how to spend my share of the swag, that's all.

Alastair smiles at Darren but it is not returned. Darren is leaning forward pebble-eyed, looking beyond Alastair at the approaching train.

—Yeh well there'd berrer fuckin *not* be is all I'm fuckin sayin. I know yer still fuckin freakin over that ahl gerl like an I can't be friggin arsed goin through it all again but you fuckin *know* what'll happen, you open that fuckin gob o' yours, don't yeh?

He focuses on Alastair now, the train slowing at the platform, the wind of its wash tossing the tight curls on his crown. His muddy eyes are ringed by dark like bruising, this doubledark stare and a muscle twitches on his cheek. Alastair just nods.

—Yeh well, Darren goes on. —I hope yeh fuckin

do cos I don't wanner atchly avter fuckin *do* it, y'unner-stand?

—Yeh.

—I just hope yeh fuckin *do,* that's all.

—I *do*, Da. An I ain't plannin fuck all.

The train stops, the doors wheeze open. They get on, sit down, put their feet up on the seats opposite. A blue-rinser across the aisle glowers openly through the glass of her gigs at them and tuts and tightens her grip on her handbag, just as Darren does with the stuffed rucksack on his lap. One lurch and jerk and the train pulls away.

—Cos I wanner know there's gunner be fuck all for me to tamp about here, Alastair. Just wanner be able to enjoy meself likes without worryin about fuck all, knowmeən?

—Yeh yeh, sound.

—Wanner hear, from *you* like, that we're all sorted an happy. Are we?

—What?

—Sorted an happy. Everythin's boss. Are you lissnin to wharram sayin or am I just dealin with a dick'ed here?

—Nah it's fine, Da. Honest to God, mate, it's all gunner be sound.

—It fuckin *berrer* be.

—It *is*, man. Stop yer worryin. It's all gunner be good. Nowt to tamp about at all, mate.

Darren sniffs and snuggles the rucksack even tighter to his torso, almost campishly aggrieved. Alastair gazes out the window at the passing estates, the wide roads easily surveyable, cul-de-sacs like islands. There is a noise beneath the chunkachunk of the train that sounds vaguely like a grinding of teeth.

—An yeh can guarantee that, can yeh?

—What?

—Fuckin ell, Alastair, ow much friggin bugle did yeh do last night? Not fuckin with it this mornin, you, no lie. No fuckin lie. Not that yeh are *anyway*, like, but . . .

A tutting from the old lady across the aisle. A fiddling with mittens.

—Guarantee what, tho?

—That everythin's gunner be sound, like you said. Cos I wanner know one thing, lad, just one fuckin thing: who's got the friggin pull here, eh?

—The pull?

—Aye, yeh. Who's got the fuckin pull?

Alastair sinks his hands in his jacket pockets, tucks his chin into his zipped-up collar. —*You* av, Darren.

—Yeh, fuckin right.

—Everyone knows that.

—Yeh. Willy fuckin Hunter and his gobshite brothers know it. Stega knows it. All the fuckin Maguire brothers know it. So why don't fuckin *you?*

Tut-tut-tut from across the aisle. Darren glares at the woman and continues to glare until she slowly stands and moves off shakily down the carriage.

—I *do.*

—Do yeh?

—Aye yeh, I fuckin well do. Yer bein parro, lar. I'm not plannin fuck all, I'm happy to av the brewsters, there's notten to friggin worry about. It's all gunner be sound, yeh don't avter tamp about fuckin anythin. Alright? Yis happy now? We'll go back to town an start spendin the money on a bender, that suit yis? That make yeh happy?

Darren nods once, his eyes locked on to the middle distance, taking in the almost empty carriage. His head lolls on the thick gimbals of his neck with the rocking of the train and like some lord brought low he seems as if this transport is for him alone. As if he is forever vigilant to the bruising of his dignity, this possessor of rare bearing and scant standing amongst the common flock of men, those who are forced to travel this way because they can't afford any better conveyance. And he this glitterer must temporarily mix but will assiduous remain unblemished and aloof.

It is a quality to Darren that Alastair has witnessed before: the chest comes out, the head tilts back, the eyes become heavy-lidded. A carriage of almost aristocratic trait that paints the world contemptible, that exposes its inconsequence. That says 'this is not important only *I* am', and it is soothing somewhat to Alastair to see this since in its all-holding only in disdain and not as usual disgust and thus not fury there is a lessening of tension, a relaxed permission. An ease in the knowing that fists will not be formed and there will be no flashing of glass or blade or even teeth.

—Gunner give Tommy a call, Da?

—Tommy? What for?

—He's gunner find out sooner or later, mate, inny? About the car, like.

Darren sighs. —Aye, suppose yer right.

He digs his mobile out of his pocket and taps in a number. Holds the phone to his ear and smiles at Alastair.

—Voicemail. Nice one. Don't avter speak to the fat blert face to . . . Tommy, it's Darren, mate. No luck in Wales, like, we just couldn't find the musher. Looked evrywhere. Think yis got snide info, to be honest. Adter ditch the motor as well, I'll tell yiz about it later, but give us a ring when yeh get this message, yeh? Alright well. Laters.

He turns the phone off and replaces it in his pocket.

—Done. Cunt can't say we didn't try to contact him, can he?

—No.

—Can't say we're tryna avoid im or anythin.

—Is right.

Chester begins behind the moving windows. Back to where they began yesterday in the car now sunken and the futile hunt and the THUNK and the falling woman and the blood and the money all this yesterday formless before them now done and behind them and this city changed now, estranged, altered now irreparable by regret for one and chance for the other. How guilt and potential in turn have coloured the huddled rooves and spires of this ancient city red and black and glowing golden in the cold remote sun.

—An there's no need to tell im just yet, is thee?

—About what?

Darren pats the rucksack on his lap in affection as if it is a child or his own belly pregnant. —*This,* lar. Don't think fat fucker Tommy needs to know about this just yet, do you?

The train begins to slow.

—I mean keep it quiet like an we can divide the

62

whole fuckin haul. Tommy don't need to get a friggin penny, knowmean? Sixty-forty split, lar.

Alastair looks.

—An don't go givin me that fuckin face Alastair cos if it weren't for fuckin me we'd have fuck all, y'unnerstand? We'd have nowt. We'd still be in fuckin Wales lookin for that one-armed bastard an wanderin around in the fuckin rain so don't start givin me them fuckin looks, alright? Sixty-forty split. Yeh can like it or fuck off.

The train stops at Chester Station. Doors hiss open. People get on, mainly shoppers returning home from this city or travelling towards the wider choice at Liverpool forty minutes or so away. They carry bags and wear fleeces against the cold and have red cheeks and take their seats talking, some small excitement about them the disposable incomes in their pockets pressing warmly. Christmas out of the way now although odd lights and decorations still linger in the larger towns.

—I mean look at all these bastards, Ally . . . could buy n sell em all, I could. Every last one of em, no lie. Werkin at ther shitey friggin jobs and takin home buttons and I'm here with four fuckin grand on me knee, I could buy n sell all these fuckers. Ther in a fuckin daze, lar. Thee avn't gorrer clue. Can't tell one from thee other cos ther all the fuckin same, same faces, same clothes, same shitty fuckin jobs. Same fuckin house n all on the same shitty estates. All adds up to the same fuckin no-mark life an we're fuckin well *not* them, kidder, are we? Eh? No fuckin way, man. Too fuckin right. Could buy n sell *all* these twats. No messin round. Can do wharrever the fuck we want to, now. You *know* it.

The train pulls out of the station. Alastair takes his baseball hat off and rasps his palm over his shaven head, the stubble growing out now.

—Me ed's bangin, Da. All that beak, like. Needin a bevvy to sort meself out, knowmean? Get me ed straight like.

—Oh no. We are fuckin *not* goin straight to the boozer off the train. No fuckin way. Need straight heads, lar, sort the bucks out like, knowmean?

—Aye but that's wharram sayin, me ed *isn't* straight. In need of a scoop or two to gerrit sorted.

Purselipped Darren shaking his head. —No fuckin way. Two scoops my arse. There's four grand here lad, d'yeh really think we'd stick to the two? Back in town, like, with all that friggin beak floatin around? He shakes his head again. —Nah, me n you, we'll gerrer few cans, go back to mine. Stuff needs divvyin up, lar, an fuckin soon *as*. Plenty of time for the boozer an it ain't today. Tonight maybe, aye, but let's get everythin sorted first before we do anythin else. Yeh?

Capenhurst Station. Alastair looks out the window and on the platform he can see himself and Darren around a table in the pub on the Lime Street Station concourse, he can see this scene, Darren beginning to slur and lurch and loosen his grip on the rucksack and his eyelids lolling lower and the rucksack money-stuffed sliding towards the sticky carpeted floor, it's there, it's present before him, it's in the future awaiting him but it's happening now too, just outside the window on the station platform, Alastair is watching it all unfold. He can *see* it.

BOOK TWO

*Very little physical pain there is but maybe a pang
in the exposed heart for the facility of life to slide,
to slip. For the fragility of it to bow and buckle
before the distant mountain and the shop between
that mountain and the old man with his gun and
the fluttering shredded curtain of flaming money
falling, landing with an extinguishing hiss in the
bloodpuddles and the chest cavity itself minced
and shattered and torn apart. For the animate
grave that trails it all even the old man with the
still-smoking gun and the drifting spots of fire
reflected in the lenses of his leaning spectacles these
imperfections of age of existence itself, all for this
the slowing heart, all for this the arteries and their
gush. For the woman in the hospital bed who
once stood upright and the thwart of all urge
redemptive and real. For the deceleration of the
pumping muscle and the sluggish thin blizzard
of burning money and the shop and the distant
mountain and the high squealing in the sky.*

It was once just a muddy pool a bit brackish from the estuary's salt. Irish monks preached and prayed on the slimy banks which caught the attention of King John who granted a city charter in 1207 to this small fishing hamlet which for more than four centuries had only seven short streets and a population that fluctuated between 500 and 800 only. What sea trade there was was conducted between the mud-dwelling fishermen and similar types from Eire, Mannan, Cymru. Exchanges of fish and boat parts and some strange faith, this channelled chandlering storm-smacked and salty.

Then it was a port in the early seventeenth century, importing New World cotton goods and exporting textiles from the burgeoning mills of Lancashire and Yorkshire. Then inevitably it became a centre of ship-building and engineering and by 1750 it was the world's first wet dock with a population of 20,000. By the mid nineteenth century it was home to more millionaires than London and home also to the worst poverty and mortality rates in Europe. By 1900 the population reached over 700,000 but then a global Depression appeared and containerisation of shipping destroyed jobs numbering in the tens of thousands. By the mid twentieth century with Britain's membership of the EU, this once-just-a-muddy-puddle place was seen to be on the wrong side of the country away from the main European markets and since 1961 has lost 43 per cent of its jobs and 34 per cent of its population.

It has turned its back to the land. Turned away from the country it barely inhabits and which it is nominally part of and looked seawards to other lands. So if this city has a soul . . .

And from oozing pool standing stagnant to world city major mercantile metropolitan capital built on triangular trading of what commodity? Transformation affected by what wet goods? Raw materials of cotton and hardware sent to West Africa for a barterable product carried to the West Indies and Virginia and exchanged for sugar, rum, tobacco and other stuffs and people were the fulcrum for this triangular transaction. People the poor and perishable commodity measured against stimulants and cloth. And the traders in them honoured now by Elder status and statuary and street name, carved and noble profiles bespeckled with the shite of pigeon and gull.

So if the city *has* a soul . . .

And after abolition in 1807 came the occurrence of more people-moving, exodi converging from England Ireland Wales and Scotland and the Scandinavian countries and the Balkans and Jews from Russia and the Pale of Settlement, a movement nearly ten million strong in less than a century less than the numbered dead of four years of war, of mechanised slaughter. Travel to Australasia and the Americas was the aim but many of these pilgrims went no further than the Goree or the Pier Head as if arrested by the stink of greasy sea and engine oil and that locomotive lotion too that exudes from human glands. And from the western shores of a close country came those escaping that which could not at that time be seen, phytophthera infestans, and that which could, the bulging greed of landlord and corralled clergy and came those too from remote colonies in Asia or the Caribbean or Africa or the subcontinent this influx boosted by bases situated during war. After which with the heavy bombing this once muddy puddle that burned for years, like a microcosm of the wider country itself saw devastation and decline into a society divided deeply by unequal distribution of whatever wealth there was and the oppositional aims of Tory rulers and militant left-wing radicalism. And capitalist employers swollen with a hunger incomprehensible to the labour organisations they sought to exploit and if that could not be realised then destroy, smash. Which venture saw some success which led to decades of entrenched unemployment which led to parts of the city aflame in 1981 like the city's buried memories of war, like a yearning to purge, the white-hot brewery of this once muddy puddle smouldering in the bitter pits of the footings that seared the feet of the leavers, the escapers, the anti-exodus of the endtimes. The trudge of the longing retracing the forefathers' footsteps away from this, this place which has never neglected its genesis in sludge and which found itself the focus for the wrath of obsessed rulers. Which made itself the paw-thorn for a system built on and devoted to the maintenance of privilege and positional power. Which found itself the target for odder bombs, softer but still endowed with massacre.

So if it could be said that the city has a soul. Built on and sunk in sumps of blood if this city *has* a soul . . .

Then maybe the spirit of here roosts in its tunnels, the Williamson tunnels branching beneath the streets and buildings, vessels for wind and darkness as if they are the blood of this place. As if they power it, as if it is sustained by wailing air and shadow. The mystery of these tracts, these hidden capillaries built to the orders of Joseph Williamson, Mole of Edge Hill, work for the veterans of Napoleon's wars and the simple philanthropy of that or something to do with an eschatological conviction, a hole to outwait Aramageddon? Or maybe the need of a man of power not just to explore but also to create some black and secret recess? To reflect his own central nervous system? To drill into the soil the trace of his own arteries or purely to provide cover when he visited mistresses? The death of his wife in 1822 drove him down into his tunnels for longer periods and down there, with the city arumble over his head, maybe he met the red genesis of his works among the talcum dead, his wealth made from the traffic of lives and darker skins. His money made from the harrowing of hearts on this earth turned tarmac which too sheathes his bones now under a car park on the outskirts of this once shallow puddle of bubbling mud.

So the city's soul rises on vast and tattered wings from the flat rust-coloured sea. It rises and soars and hovers and casts shadow over street and square and gargoyle and cupola and a million different bloods. It pays witness to despair and design, purpose and futility and the shore warehouses now peopled only by pigeon or preened for the pampered. All the living skins quick in all their common squalor and it pilots the trains into Lime Street where junkies beg and whores prop and others of their species will embark or alight and the heat of their commerce will rise and stifle the pub in the station concourse where one soul lost in this city on this earth Darren is beginning to melt into his seat and a type of excitement is beginning to flutter within another soul adrift Alastair on wings he has never until now seen or even thought could exist.

—See these fuckers, Alastair? None of em fuckin know, lar, thee ant gorrer fuckin clue . . . could buy n sell *aaaallll* these cunts, me . . .

—Is right, Da. You *know* it, my man.

—Course I fuckin do . . . all these fuckin no-mark blerts . . .

—Want another bevvy, mate? Yer runnin low.

Darren drains the dregs. Whacks the glass down on the table top where the many empties there shudder. —Same again, lar.

—Alright.

Alastair goes to the bar, orders a strong lager for Darren and a bitter shandy for himself. Their ninth drink. He orders also a double vodka and with the drinks hidden by him from Darren's liquiding eyes and with hands slightly atremor he pours the Vladivar into the lager, a mixture which Darren has been drinking unwittingly for the last four rounds. He pays the barmaid, who has bright orange skin, and takes the drinks back to the table. Darren glugs half straight off.

—Yer might be buyin the bevvies an all that, Ally, but yer still ain't gettin moren a sixty-forty split.

—That's alright, Da.

—Pure woulden av fuckin *anythin* if it weren't for me.

71

—I'm sound with it, mate.

—Just so's yeh fuckin know.

—I do, lar, I do. Av got no problems with it, man.

—Sound, well. Darren takes another long swig and stands unsteadily up. —Am goin for a slash. An I'm fuckin takin *this* with me n all.

He hoists the rucksack on to his shoulder and takes it with him to the toilet. Alastair watches him go, his swaying back on wobbly legs and then lets his eyes drift to the TV above the bar where a stern young woman announces that police are searching for two men with Liverpool accents and then an image of a post office he has seen before. A post office white-washed in a small village with a mountain rising behind it and he has seen that prospect before.

There are two young neds playing pool. Evidently under eighteen because they are drinking Cokes out of the can. Alastair gulps at his shandy and wishes it was a stronger drink and gets up and approaches the pool table.

—Yiz alright, lads?

They stare. Both of them still holding the cues beneath their chins, the blue-chalked tips reflecting greyly on skin like hypothermic buttercups. Let's see if you like slate. They stare.

—I need a favour from youse.

—Oh for fuck's sake. One of them looks to the other. —Another fuckin hom.

—Eh?

—Another fuckin queg wants to wank us off here, Robbo.

Robbo snorts. Alastair waves his hands frantic in front of his chest, palms out.

72

—Nah fuck *that*, man, am no fuckin hom. All am asking is a small friggin favour, like.

—Yeh, what? Not-Robbo tilts his head back and to the side, assessing, working out. —That's what all the puffs say. What d'yer want us to do?

—Well, owjer fancy earnin a bit of cash?

—Thought yeh said yer norra puff?

—Aw Jesus Christ, am fuckin well *not*, man, will yiz just fuckin *listen* to me. Alastair looks over his shoulder, sees a still Darrenless bar. —Yiz see the lad am with?

They look behind him, over each of his shoulders, then face him and shake their heads.

—No.

—Yer on yer own. He's on his own, Freddy, inny? Freddy nods. —Looks that way to me, like.

—Yeh, he's just gone the bog. He'll be back soon n all so av gorrer be quick.

—What does he look like?

—Who?

—This musher yer supposed to be with.

—Yer'll see im when he gets back from the bog. Big cunt with curly hair. Wearin an antwacky ahl shelly.

Robbo and Freddy smirking look Alastair up and down, from his seamsplit Le Coq Sportifs to his trackie bottoms tucked into white sports socks. They glance once down at their own feet and grin back up at his face. They're wearing Rockport and Stone Island and Firetrap and Burberry.

—Wharrabout im, well?

Alastair rubs his hands over his face. —He's a cunt.

—I bet he is, but what's that gorrer do with us, well?

Alastair sighs, glances back over his shoulders again.

Fatigue has sallowed his skin and made murky his eyes. His lips, cracked, have adopted the inverted smile of remorse and regret. —He's carryin a bag. A ruckie, like. It's fuller fuckin swag and am tellin yiz fuckin *full* of it. An youse can av some of it if yeh like.

—Ow much.

—Ton each.

—Ton fifty.

—Alright.

—Two hundred.

—Fuck off. Ton fifty.

—For doin what?

—Jackin the bastard. We're gunner be leavin in about half n hour, follow us round to Ma Egerton's, welly the twat round thee ed an al take the sack an box yiz off. Dead simple, like.

Robbo and Freddy, they look at each other. One rapid glance that shares something. —An that's it?

—Aye, yeh. But yer've gorrer make sure that yiz give im a good hard belt, like. A mean a *real* leatherin. Gorrer knock the cunt sparko.

—Sound, Robbo says. —No worries there, likes. This im now?

Alastair whirls, sees Darren back in his seat scowling at him, the rucksack clutched to his chest, the over-head lighting shadowing his eyes and bouncing in twin beams off his brow as if double subcutaneous growths there stretch the skin. He raises his eyebrows and nods sudden once: The fucker *you* up to?

Alastair moves back to the table, thanking the two lads loudly. Darren doesn't need to speak, his expression alone is a question.

—Just avin a lend of their moby, Alastair says.
—Battery's dead on mine. Tryna score us some beak.
—Yeh?

Nod. —Peter's wasn't switched on so I gave that Stega a bell instead. Says to meet im round at Ma Egerton's in thirty.

—Thirty?

Nod. —Time for another coupla bevvies first, like.

—Why didn't yer use mine?

—Your what?

—My fuckin moby. Why didn't yer use it? Why borrow them neds'?

—Just safer, like, innit. Scorin some charlie, like, just safer to do it on some other cunt's phone, innit?

Darren's thinking.

—Can't trace it back to yours, then, can thee? Never know *who's* lissenin in, do yeh?

Darren thinks. Then seems to slip momentarily into a trance for a few seconds then snaps abruptly out of it with a vigorous shake of his jowly head. Alastair smiles, but not with his face.

—Don't fuckin like that bastard, me.

—Who?

—That fuckin Stega one, Darren says. —Who d'yeh think? That fuckin Stephenson. Never liked that bastard, me.

—Aye, yer one evil cunt yerrah, Darren.

—What?

—I said he's one evil cunt that Stega. But he's the man with the beak, tho, inny? Doan avter drink with im, like, do we? Just score the coke an do one.

Darren thinks again. Even when he blinks it is

75

plodding, ponderous; alcohol and sleeplessness have turned him into cement unset.

—Aye, alright. Goan get the drinks in well, yeh tight-arsed get.

Alastair goes to the bar and will do so twice more in the following thirty minutes before they leave, surreptitiously observed by Robbo and Freddy who play several more games of pool and sip at their Cokes until they are flat and warm, the temperature and consistency of spittle. In this half-hour all four of them will talk about nothing but money, how they will spend it, what wondrous times they will have. They will talk about the horrors of being poor and about the humming power of having money. About the unique and indescribable buzz of walking around a city when your pockets bulge with cash. About how the heart thuds and the pulse races, how you relax and settle into yourself when hitherto proscribed parts of the city suddenly become accessible. About advertisements and what they offer suddenly including you in their orbit, suddenly being directed at you, suddenly welcoming you into the once arcane arena filled with creativity and profound social significance and welcomed you will be into that shining realm. They talk about the pain of unsatisfied cravings and the contempt of the moneyed for the moneyless. They talk about buying presents for their mothers and Alastair alone thinks about hospital treatment for his grandmother, going private as if that could arrest ageing although he does not voice this thought. Darren recalls a recent Sunday dinner when he made his mother cry and remarks to himself that she seems to weep quite often these days, in fact she's become a right fucking

76

whinger but he still loves her. Robbo and Freddy discuss sprees on the skank for their good clothes and how they'll soon be able to buy those Diesel anoraks they've been wanting for ages from that boss shop down Bold Street. They picture themselves wearing them, each to his own, each looking cool, each having a better chance with Madeleine O'Shea when dressed in Diesel. There is talk of the best uncut cocaine and fridges full of Baileys and holidays in Ibiza or Rhodes. There are thoughts of whores. There are thoughts of sticking the head on Tommy Maguire. There are thoughts of clearing outstanding fines, of strutting into the Clerk to the Justice's office and paying in cash and telling the stuck-up twat there where to stick his fucking penalties. There are thoughts of drinking and eating in Modo, the Blue Bar, the Living Room, 60 Hope Street. Of taking taxis, no, fuck it, *limos* to parties catered for by themselves; of lording it over tables bent with food and booze and big bowls of powder. Of impressing people. Of creating affection and admiration in them. Of the executive boxes at Anfield and, regarding Freddy, at Goodison. Of replica shirts signed by entire teams. Of buying cars, of learning to drive, even. Of how bouncers will stand aside to permit them entry and more of being ushered straight to the front of the queue. VIP lounges with footballers and musicians. Buying a kilo of pure-as cocaine and setting themselves up in business and building on it and building on it until unimaginable wealth accrues. Paying off the bizzies. Huge houses with gardens and swimming pools. Private jets. Loft apartments in London, Los Angeles. Paying some crackhead to bump Tommy Maguire or maybe merely break his bones. Never having a boss again. Answering to no one ever again. Buying property. Buying land. Investment. Speculation. Freedom and ways to live, so many different and brilliant ways to live. Then back again to merely scoring some ching and getting fucking wasted.

—Aye . . . Darren is slurring. —Could do with some gack . . . bit friggin wrecked ere likes . . .

—Come ed, well, Alastair says, standing up. —Get summin to cut through the bevvy, yeh? We're both knackered. Been a hard coupla days, lar, annit?

—'Sright.

Darren tries to stand then falls back into his chair again. Alastair helps him up and once upright he flings off Alastair's arms and snarls and clutching the rucksack leaves the pub at a reeling pace. Alastair follows, one quick look and nod at Robbo and Freddy. They nod back.

Darren staggers across the station's concourse cavernous and cold, the smooth marble floor awash with light and reflecting the long hands of the huge clock on the wall. He bursts through a line of back-packed and suitcased people at the ticket office, flailing his arms and shouting and bisecting the line, sending each half shrinking into itself. Alastair follows him, scanning nervously for police and seeing none. Darren is extremely drunk. The two neds might not even be needed here; Darren might just pass out. Ally could then give him a kicking himself and make off with all the swag and blame it on some non-existent baghead. God, what he could do with four thousand pounds. How, at least for a while, he could live. Not a life-changing amount but Jesus Christ how he could live.

Out of the station, through the automatic doors

which Darren attempts to open even as they are sliding apart so he bellows at them. Through a taxi rank and out into the drizzle, Alastair remaining several paces behind the floundering Darren, up past the side of the Empire Theatre and on to Lord Nelson Street where the thin drizzle drifts and Darren now turns to face Alastair who can see further up the street the sign for Ma Egerton's pub and its hanging baskets. And Robbo and Freddy jogging across the road on the diagonal, each holding half of a pool cue in arms bent back over their heads.

—Urry the fuck up, will yeh, Alastair . . . am needin a fuckin –

Without breaking pace Robbo or it might be Freddy one of them anyway with full swing whacks the cue-half into the back of Darren's skull. Alastair hears the THUNK bounce off brick and concrete and Darren collapses in an instant as if shot, all animation removed in less than a second. He is given a couple more whacks and then rolled over so that the ruck-sack can be accessed.

—Nice one, lads. Good effort.

Only a feeling in Alastair of embarkation. Not of any revenge or redemption but only a notion of a beginning. A step towards a place that may glow and may satisfy.

The two boys are peering into the sack. Blood matts Darren's hair and deltas the pavement feathering in the greasy rain and Alastair looks down at the crumpled figure and feels no pang, no pain.

—Fuckin ell, Robbo. Fuck me stiff, lar. The divvy was right. We're fuckin brewstered.

—Ton an a half each, lads, that's what we sorted. Eeyar, giz the sack.

Alastair's hand held out palm up expectant above the fallen Darren. Cold and oily rain spotting his open hand and the tip of his nose as it drip-drips off the peak of his cap. The tip of his nose all that extrudes beyond that peak until the fat end of a pool cue drives that nose inwards towards the face and on its way down slams the descending skull two, three times, blows cushioned by the cloth of the cap but still with impact sufficient to bring on blackout.

The two of them now on the wet pavement perpendicular: this T. They are unconscious for a few minutes and in that time, on this wet side street, only three people pass: one, rushing through the rain for a taxi, steps over them, believing them dressed as they are to be victims of each other, of a fight among themselves; another, a visitor to the city on business taking a short cut to Lime Street to catch his train home, believes them to be victims of drink and/or drugs and ignores them accordingly; and the third, a quasi-feral dipso on his way to the cheap London Road pubs doesn't care why they are unconscious in the gutter and rifles their accessible pockets but flees when the bigger of the two begins to groan and writhe. This is, of course, Darren, who awakes to rage. And then pain. Alastair awakes to pain too and a mouth that is screaming in his face, all he can see is this wet purple hole lined with worn teeth and his initial waking wish is to be unconscious again, insensible to all this, the rain, the pain, the roaring mouth, oblivious to what is here now and what must surely lie ahead. And behind.

OTHERS

VISITOR

Dear God, how I hate and detest having to come to this terrible, terrible city. I wouldn't bother, if it wasn't for the firm having an office here too, I mean I'd just stay in Manchester if I could but I can't, so . . . Seedy, that's the word for this place; seedy. And run-down? Oh yes undoubtedly but that's no excuse; I mean my work takes me to a lot of cities up and down the country, a lot of rough and run-down cities like parts of London or Newcastle or Bristol, even sections of Manchester itself, but none of them are like this place and the difference is in the people, the general popu-lace; forget what you've heard about the Scouse humour, the salt-of-the-earth people, they're extensions of their city, big and loud and vulgar and full of dark dirty little alleyways . . . That's the thing, y'see; they exult in their own seediness and shabbiness, they seem to celebrate the fact that everything here is down-at-heel. There's no shame, no sense of embarrassment; it's like Wales or Scotland – you go into those provinces and the prevailing attitude is 'we're-all-screwed-up-and-we-don't-care'. They should *do* something with themselves, try to better themselves, find some way of escaping the mess around them, instead of just . . . But oh no; I mean look at these two here, for example, here in the gutter, too drunk or drugged or both to even stand, lying across each other on the wet pavement . . . absolutely no shame. Although, knowing these people, it's probably a trap; I'll step over them and they'll reach up and grab my legs and pull me down and beat me up and take my wallet and briefcase . . . that's what this is, it's a trap . . .

No it isn't; these two idiots are too out of it to even move. Totally dead to the world, they are. And at the corner of the street I see a shaking old alcoholic eyeing them up, no doubt waiting for the coast to clear so he can go and rifle their pockets, get some change for his next bottle of Buckfast or whatever. I tell you; the problem here is the attitude. It's not loss of industry or negligible governmental investment or trickle-down Thatcherite economics or any of the other favoured and convenient scapegoats, no, the problem entirely is the *attitude* . . . the fecklessness. Spinelessness. That's why there's so much theft in this city, because its inhabitants are all so idle and unmotivated; they seem to believe that they deserve something for nothing, that they're *owed* something. It's an attitude I personally can't stand. It's pathetic. It's risible. No wonder the city's falling down. Oh yes there's investment - Urban Splash and Concert Square and all that – but it won't last. And it won't last because it won't be appreciated. Mark my words, I've seen it happen before, many times. And City of Culture! Do they *really* expect to win? Might as well nominate Gaza. Jennifer and I *did* laugh when we read the shortlist. Can you imagine it?

Sshperny oddzzsh, larr? Fordy capla khultcha, likh.

The big clock in Lime Street tells me I'm ten minutes early for the Piccadilly train although it's probably broken like everything else in this city but thank God I've not missed it; it's another hour 'til the next one and an extra unnecessary *minute* in this city would surely kill me. Soon be back in Didders with Jennifer and the girls and I'll be away from this godforsaken pit of a place for another week. Seven days. Seven blissful days at home.

I buy an Americano from Coffee Republic and am accosted by another of this place's denizens, his filthy palm held out expectantly, asking me for spare change in that grating, whining accent. I just ignore him, turn my back on him (which he flings abuse at; no surprise there), and go and find a seat on the waiting train. A window seat, so I can watch the city as it recedes, as I leave it. And good bloody riddance too. At least until next week.

Forty minutes between this place and my home and it might as well be a continent. Might as well be a world. I hate having to come here each week. I *hate* it.

ALKY

Aw fuckin junkies man . . . lowest of the low thee ar . . . scumbags, toerags . . . callin *me* bad n useless cos I liker bevvy juster fuckin jakey all that shite but fuck that man it's them friggin junkies bringin this city down . . . won't friggin catch *me* lyin inner gutter inner fuckin rain like no lie . . . no way man . . . fuckin cunts yerrah bastards could av yez fuckin all callin me

83

useless an a, anner fuckin, me, lar, *me,* what the fuck-innn . . .

Smart cunt inner suit an a briefy over deer, wait for that get to pass lar . . . knob'ed don't fuckin reelise like I was im once, *like* im . . . adder suit n house n car n missis an it can all fall apart in one week, man, one friggin week's all's it took an deer's me, fuckin nowt . . . job goes, house goes, car goes, friggin missis goes, goes off with some fuckin I.T. consultant from fuckin Knotty Ash . . . it's the terror, man, the terror . . . iss bastard in iz suit, fuckin kite on im all stuck-up fuckin gobshite like tell ee thinks he's fuckin *it* but it can fall all apart easy for im as it did for fuckin me, no lie . . . knows NOWT, that cunt, NOWT . . . g'wahn, getcher fuckin train ome yer twat an I hope yiz never avter go through what I av . . . woulden wish it on me werst enemy, man, which is now that fuckin I.T. consultant from fuckin Diddyland . . . cunt . . . wish leprosy on that get or fuckin Aids but not what I've fuckin got now lar which is sweet fuckin all . . .

Over the road, me, straight into deer fuckin pockets, no messin round. Too good an opportunity to pass, knowmean? But softarse, me; as *if* junkies as out of it as these two are gunner av any fuckin odds left . . . juster few pence like, birrer shrapnel, fuck all but lint anner big bastard, he starts movin an groanin an wakin up an I think about wellyin im one in thee ed, knock im fuckin sparko again like but nah fuck that, man, av got some bleedin self-respect still, oh aye . . . oh yeh . . . these cunts think I avn't but I know I fuckin well av . . . might be down inner friggin gutter like but some of us av still got what counts . . . birrer friggin self-respect, man . . . birrer friggin dignity like, knowmean? . . . that's all that matters won't welly this no-mark baghead cunt's suffrin imself what would be the . . . the . . .

An anyways am not all tabbed out yet inner Globe. So that's me, that's me first step. Globe. No messin round. Gerrouter this fuckin rain n all.

DRIZZLE

This is not the time of cumulus, colossal drifting cauliflowers, or of cirrus like high white slashes sharply across the bright blue, sunlight permitted through their thinness. It is the time of stratus, so much so that the sky appears one cloud only, simply a grey and murky ceiling spread from horizon to horizon over the city entire from the brown lappings of the Dee and the Mersey and out to the vast thick splat of the Celtic Sea as featureless and monochrome as the sky itself so that the city could be wedged in an envelope or between two mirrors reflecting each other's emptinesses. Tarmac-coloured ceiling very low, so low indeed that it grounds planes at Speke, covers the stranded and marooned and frustrated with no shadow and no difference just this single spread and lightless tarpaulin turning all similar, robbed of depth.

The precipitation is orographic, that decocted in air forced to rise when landform barriers lie across the paths of winds in this case the bulwarks of Eryri unseeable from this citified coastal plain yet sensed somehow as a creeping mass rising flinging shadow and felt certainly in their climactic effects as here in this forced air ascent and the resulting rainfall of drops with diameter smaller than 0.02 of an inch and descending very close together this thin drizzle defined. Slowly upwards the air moves, launched from the vast ramps of the nearby mountains carrying with it the condensed cloud droplets which have little time to grow before they become too heavy for the weak air currents to support and they fall softly, appearing rather to drift and float than fall, making a kind of moist air, a hanging sail of damp. Clean they begin but gather grease as they descend drifting through smog and thus glutinous some gather into larger drops and one of these forms in the thermals above the city's main rail terminus made sticky it is by the viscous vapours from kitchen and exhaust and the many rising methanes of the hurrying inhabitants with scalp-stuck hair and it drifts slower than the billion others, its trajectory earth-wards straightening as it gathers mass until above a side street adjacent to the station it begins to fall vertical, passing soot-fluffed chimneys and rain-run skylights and gleaming slates and gutterings choked with weed and birdshit and then it passes perching pigeons with heads wing-pitted and then windows then window boxes and the limp growths in them and then a lintel and the door beneath and then it passes below the cap-peak of a laid-low man his face turned up towards the leaking sky and this droplet lands and bursts with a tiny 'pop' in the tear duct of his left eye, the one remaining unswollen and un-discoloured by the blunt-instrument trauma recently visited on this face. It bursts clammy and humid and the eye flickers blinking open unlike its twin which cannot, damaged as it is, cannot twitch open and regard the high unbothered sky, the huge and complete shrug uncoloured, unconcerned. This one eye gazes out and up at the world then attempts to slide shut again as if too great is the exertion to take this in. As if the mere act of blinking is too much here, in this small water from far away, as hissingly insubstantial as all human plan.

A voice:

—YOU FUCKING CUNT, ALASTAIR! FUCKIN FUCKIN FUCKIN –

TOMMY: HIS CHILDHOOD

See the squat boy in the corner of the school playground. Thickset, fat some would say. See his black pumps burst at the toe joint to reveal his grubby grey socks that gather around his ankles beneath his grazed and grass-stained knees. See the much smaller boy below him cowering against the chain-link fence that separates the playground from the bomb site, the nettle-clogged heaps of rubble that were a storage depot for ack-ack guns in the not-too-distant-war. See the fence shake as the smaller boy is shoved repeatedly back against it. See the bigger boy ask yet again for money, see the smaller boy shake his weepy, snotty face, see the fence clatter and shudder yet again. Hear the sound of fist on face and then a high-pitched wailing.

It is the year of Alice Cooper and 'School's Out'. It is the year of *The Godfather*.

See Miss Wilson running across the playground as fast as her white leather zip-up stack-heeled knee boots will allow.

—Thomas Maguire! Stop that right now! You big bully!

Nimbly for a fat child Thomas skips away from the smaller boy now curled foetally and whimpering on the ground with a bleeding nose.

—Pick on someone your own size, you bully!

Thomas flicking the V with both hands, laughing, capering.

—Fuck off yeh ahl witch.

Gasp. —*What* did you just say?

—*You* heard. I said fuck off yeh ahl cow.

—Right, that's it, it's Mr Powell's office for you, my lad. Stay there.

See the chase; the wobble and teeter of the beehive hairdo. The laughing and the jeering and then the intervention of Mr Lyons the geography/PE teacher who tweaks Thomas by the ear and leads him tiptoe and full of grimaces across the playground. Many big eyes and gawps surrounding, a few hidden sneers also.

—Ow geroff me al get me dad on youse! *An* me brother!

—I don't give two shits, son. Bring them up here. How d'yeh think yer dad'll feel when he finds out his son's been abusing women? Think he'll be proud, do yeh?

—He'll stove yer stupid head in!

—You're only making it worse for yourself.

—Ow! Ow! Fuckin gerroff! Yeh big pig!

★　　★　　★

Mr Powell has long hairs coming out of his nose and a funny growth on his eyelid like a tiny brain. His breath pongs.

—Extortion! At *your* age! What in blazes possessed you, lad?

Thomas a wee bit tearful now on the seat too large for him swings his feet above the floor. There are big men around him, proper grown-ups, Lyons and Powell, and he feels very small despite his relative size. Around people of his own age he feels very, very big but here in this office he appears as puny to himself as those he daily torments.

—I mean what do you think this is? Chicago? Think you're a little Al Capone, do you, is that what this is all about? Is it?

Thomas sniffs. —Don't know.

—Don't know what?

—Don't know nothing.

—Don't know nothing, *sir*.

Sniffsniff.

Mr Lyons chips in: —And it's by far from the first time this has happened, Mr Powell. Seems to me that young Maguire here fancies himself as a bit of a gangster, don't you, lad, ey? Just like your brother did. He was *just* the same, your Joseph.

And now Tommy nods because this is exactly what he fancies himself as or rather and anathema to Lyons and Powell and their like what he for certain knows he already is. He's heard his dad and his uncles talking; he's sat with his mam and his aunties and drunk lemonade and eaten crisps as the grown-up men discussed things in the foggy kitchen. He's snuck

89

under-aged into the flicks and watched huge-eyed the films, those men in hats and suits with guns. He gets free Fabs and Screwballs from the man in the Mr Whippy van and he has always wondered why. There is never any comeuppance from the parents and elder siblings of the local boys and girls he routinely beats up and he has always wondered why and on the sole occasion when there *was* redress, a public face-slapping and forced apology in the precinct, he always wondered why this same big-brother avenger approached him the following week with one arm in plaster and offered him a long and earnest apology. So what can he do now but just nod and say:

—Yeh.

—I *beg* your pardon?

—Oh is that right? Mr Lyons says with a sneer. —Got a little Godfather here, have we? A right little Don Corleone. What do we do with gangsters, Mr Powell?

—Nowt cos yer both gunner be fuckin *dead*!

Tommy pushes a pile of papers and books over on the desk and bolts across the office for the door. A hand clamps his shoulder.

—Hold him there, Mr Lyons! I'm contacting his mother!

The clomp and scrape of Dr Scholl clogs sound down the corridor. Tommy's heart thuds. The sound gets louder then the office door bursts open and his mother comes in and glances once at him all fire-eyed then turns to the two teachers.

—Youse! Either of youse ever touches my child

again *any* of my kids and I'll take yer fuckin eyes out! Yiz hear me?

Tommy loves the looks on their stupid faces. Loves the sudden shock, the swift widening of mouths and eyes. And he loves his mother.

—Mrs Maguire, I can assure you we –

—*I'll* give yiz fuckin assure! Right across yer fuckin gobs either of youse *ever* lay a finger on my fuckin kids again! I mean it! Don't believe me an just fuckin *dare* it! *Dare* it well!

She stands and stares panting. Lyons and Powell look from her to each other and then back at her again.

—Friggin manhandlin little kids . . . should be ashamed of yerselves yer should . . . fuckin disgrace yerrah . . . call yerselves teachers?

She turns. —Come on, Thomas. Am takin you out of this bleedin place.

He follows her out and stops to point and laugh at the teachers but she grabs his arm hard enough to bruise and yanks him through the door, drags him down the corridor that claps and echoes to her wood-soled clogs and out of the school into the abrupt sunlight and out of the school grounds and across the road to a bus stop where she spins her son like a top to face her and slaps his face. Shock and ear-ringing. Instant tears.

—So yerrah friggin gangster now, are yeh? Don't you fuckin *ever* embarrass me like that again or al take the friggin skin off yer back. If I *ever* have to come up to that school *again* . . . An stop yer fuckin whinging or yer'll get somethin to cry about. Little bastard yerrah.

Blurred and swimming in his tears she lights a cigarette. Blows smoke through her nostrils like a dragon and asks an old staring man what the fuck he thinks he's looking at then points at Tommy's face with the lit end of her Regal King. The smoke makes his eyes water further, the burning coal seems further to inflame the heat in his stinging cheek.

—You an yer brother, I'm ashamed of yiz both. Honest to God, the pairer yiz, I am, I'm fuckin ashamed. Notten but trouble from the both o' yiz. God help me but sometimes I wish yer brother ad've friggin *died* of that fever.

She crosses herself. —Think I *wanner* come out to the school every week? Ey? Must think I've got nowt better to do, you. Is that what yeh think?

—Mam, I –

—I don't wanner hear it, son. Don't say another fuckin word. Yer no son of mine any more. An *you* can fuckin shurrup before yeh start n all.

The old man red-faced and tutting turns away again and the bus arrives and they get on it and the ignoring of him from his mother is worse. She says not one word to him and jerks her arm away from his when he touches her elbow and he blubbers and sobs and she simply stares straight ahead and alights at the correct stop and walks stiff-backed and merciless ahead of him homewards and he must follow and inside the house she points wordlessly upstairs and he goes to his room and there among the posters, the football posters and Bay City Rollers and Mud posters, he cries himself out and climbs under the covers and buries his face in the pillow and screams muffled swear

92

words until the word 'cunts' stops him because he can think of no worse but that is what they all are, all of them, especially *her*. A short time later he hears his dad come home and hears him talking to his mother in the front room, no specific words just mumbles, and then there are heavy footsteps on the stairs and the door opens and there is a presence in his room, big and heated. He can smell his dad. He can feel his dad standing there, outside of the pulled-up blankets, displacing air and breathing. To show his face might invite a slap so he keeps it hidden. Hot and hidden under the hairy blanket that makes him itch at night-time.

—So yeh wanner be a gangster, son?

It is a deep but gentle voice and Tommy is surprised. He expected a roar, he expected a swooping open palm. He feels a pressure on the bed and then a hand softly pulls the sheets down to reveal his face. And there's his dad; a smile, bushy sideys, a big once-broken nose. A *smile*; what's going on here? One fat hand lies just below Tommy's eyes and he can see the letters L-O-V-E big in his vision and blurred and blueing.

—I hear you've been playin at gangsters. Av yeh?

Tommy nods.

—Well, ad berrer show yiz how it's done, then, hadn't I?

Tommy nods.

—Come ed then, well. Get yerself up.

Tommy gets out of bed and follows his dad through the house and out into the car, the black Capri. No words, no directions, just out through the house and into the car.

—Know the first thing yeh need to be a gangster round here?

Tommy shakes his head and his dad reaches into the back seat and recovers a hammer which he places on Tommy's lap, between his pudgy knees. It feels very heavy. Tommy tries to lift it and can but only with difficulty and with both hands. The car starts and pulls away.

—So why'd yeh fancy yerself as a gangster, then, eh? Is it cos yeh wanner be like yer dad? Yeh?

Small nod.

—Well, howjer know that I'm a gangster? What makes yeh think that?

A shrug.

—Well, yer wrong. Cos what I am son is a businessman. That's the first thing yer've gorrer learn, Tommy; that there are no gangsters there are only businessmen. Djer understand that?

A nod. Tommy cannot take his eyes off his father, off the wedge-heeled shoes working the pedals, the chunky-ringed hands gripping the steering wheel, the wide face with the flat nose and chipped teeth and the dark eyes flicking between rear-view mirror and windscreen and the large arms beneath the yellow cheesecloth shirt and the long hair hanging down over the back of the vinyl seat. And the hairy handbacks with the blue tattoos snaking and anchoring out from beneath the flapping, unbuttoned cuffs and the gold identity bracelet. This is his dad, all bulging in the car. All sinew and confidence look at me now, Lyons, Stinkygob Powell, this is my frigging dad and I am sitting *next* to him.

—Business, that's all it is. Makin money, like. There are a thousand different ways of makin money an I just happen to use a certain way. And, y'know, when yeh grow up?

He looks at Tommy now, a sideways glance. A small but humourless smile revealing a gap where an upper incisor should be. He shakes his head and faces front again.

—Ah, yer'll find out.

—What, Dad?

—Dozen matter. Yer'll find out in a bit.

—Wharrabout, tho?

His father doesn't answer, just swings the car into the car park of a huge pub.

—Am pickin up yer uncle Dusty. Remember him, yer uncle Dusty? Baldy feller?

Tommy nods but he doesn't.

—I won't be a minute. Just sit still an behave yerself.

He leaves the car running, goes into the pub, comes back out with a stocky man in an orange boiler suit and a bald head streaked with what looks like oil or grime, coal dust maybe. This man grins at Tommy and climbs into the back of the car on the driver's side and leans and ruffles Tommy's hair.

—Y'alright, big man? I'm yer uncle Dusty, remember?

Tommy stares. This man has a Belfast accent the kind Tommy's heard on the news and some pink scars on his face. He looks at Tommy then grins again then asks the back of the driver's head: —Ye sure about this, now, Shem? Not think it's mebbe goin a wee bit too far, like?

—No. Gorrer learn, Dust, anny? *Some*time, like. Might as well be now. Been playin up at the school again, like. Gorrer learn im sometime, avn't I?

—Suppose so, aye . . . His face suddenly brightens. —Ey, did I tell yis I was on a bus there the other day there at the back, like, an who should I see but Ian Paisley, Gusty Spence an Leo Sayer. And, just me luck like, there's me with only the two bullets in me gun. Who did I shoot, well?

Shem, father, smiles and shakes his head.

—I shot that fucker Sayer twice! Make sure he's dead an can't sing any more fuckin records!

He roars with laughter. Tommy's dad does too and Tommy joins in although of course not understanding why and laughs even louder when Dusty tousles his head again and says: —Like that one Tommy, aye? Shot that fucker twice! Make sure he's dead!

Laughter again. He likes this, Tommy does, driving along and laughing with the tough and grown-up men, a hammer heavy on his lap. If Lyons and Powell could see him now. Wouldn't *dare* to tweak his ear. Wouldn't *dare* to take him into the office. They'd leave him alone all scared and do whatever he told them to do. Bastards. See Tommy now in the stylish car that George Best has advertised on TV. In the stylish Besty car with the two big tough men his father and his uncle, oh if the school could see him now.

Tommy wants to ask Dusty to tell another joke or to tell one himself, wants to feel that giant hand ruffling his hair again but Dusty suddenly serious is gazing out the window and talking, it seems, to the outside world, the city passing.

—Not sure about this, Shem, so I'm not. It's not sitting right with me, this.

—What isn't?

—The wean.

—He's gorrer *learn*, Dust, anny? Never too young to find out about these things, like. I mean say he carries on the way he is doing an in a few years' time he's at the bottom of Ally Dock in concrete wellies, how'll yeh feel then, eh? Or proppin up the fuckin motorway. How'll yeh feel then?

—Aye but still.

—An besides anythin else he's *my* lad. If this puts im off then great, sound, he's not gunner follow in is ahl man's footsteps. An if it doesn't then that's alright as well cos that means he's got wharrit takes. So either way he's gunner learn somethin, inny?

Dusty sniffs. —Aye. Suppose.

—No 'suppose' about it, lar. I *know* wharram doing.

—Wharrabout your Joseph, tho?

—Wharrabout him?

—Shouldn't he be here n all?

Shake of the head from Shem. —Gorrer bit more brains, Joey has. He'll work it out for imself, tellin yeh. He'll be able to figure it out on is own, that one will.

They skirt the city and head north, towards West Derby. Shem and Dusty talk and Tommy looks out at the passing world and the older men don't seem to notice as little Thomas does the amount of people outside who react to the car, who squint their eyes at it and then either wave or look quickly away. And the difference in the wavings, how some are meek handflaps at chest height and how some are an abrupt rising of bladed hands almost like a salute. The two big men appear not to notice these reactions but the smaller boy does, some swelling in his breast and burgeoning in his belly as merely by sitting here in this car with the two bigger men he elicits some response in all these unknown people. Just by doing nothing, just by being driven, all these pedestrians react. As if the car itself is their dream or nightmare taken form and seen passing them in city street their happiness or horror here before them on this early-evening weekday. Their nocturnal secret longings drifting by and how they do respond, rise or recoil. Tommy first grins at them all, he does not differentiate, they all get a grin, but then a thing within him tells him not to smile but to scowl instead and he obeys it, whatever ringing thing it is. See the young boy in the car, the big boy scowl jowly.

They enter an estate. New rows of pebble-dashed semi-detacheds no more than a few years old. Small front gardens and glassed-in porches. Children on Choppers or playing football whose heads swivel to trace the car as it passes now slow.

—This it, Shem, aye?

Tommy's father nods.

—Must av some money aye, livin here like. Can't be cheap these places.

—Exactly. Can't afford to pay me back but can afford to move on to a good estate like this. Makes me fuckin sick, Dust, it does. Always pay yer debts off first, isn't that right?

—It is, sure. Hear that, young Tommy?

Both big men looking at him. The car has stopped.

—*Always* pay yer debts, Tommy, his dad says. —Yeh know why?

Shake of the head.

—I'll *show* yiz why. Don't forget that hammer.

At the kerb outside one of the new, clean houses. No graffiti here, no flat planks for windows, no steel-sheeted doors. Net curtains twitch as they leave the car, Tommy carrying the hammer grunting in two hands, smiling too because this is interesting, this is a *good* game. It seems that someone owes money. He thinks that means that someone must pay.

He walks between the two men up the trail of crazy paving across the well-kept small front lawn. Some children are called then dragged bodily inside if they do not respond and doors are slammed. A dog barks four times then yelps and falls quiet.

Uncle Dusty raps on the door with his oil-stained knuckles. A soft, rhythmical tattoo; he plays a jaunty tune. Tommy smiles.

The door opens. His father says: —Iya, love, then the door is slammed shut again and seared into Tommy's eyes the woman's face and her look of terror the recognition so quick and utter and feet are raised and thrust and the door bursts inwards. Wood splinters, glass shatters. There is a woman screaming. Tommy's heart pounds hot and loud his skull throbs with each bloodbeat already he feels sick with excitement his mouth sandy dry and Dusty has hoisted him by the oxters over the threshold and into the house before he has even noticed it. He steers him by the back of the banging head down the hallway and towards the screams into the bright kitchen where his dad looks immense, King Kong-sized. There is a man seated at a round white table and a woman standing by him at his shoulder with her hands over her face and it is from behind these hands that the screaming comes. Shem is pointing at her with a ringed index finger but shouting at the seated man. The stabbing finger, the shouting mouth flinging spittle.

—Tell *er* to fuckin shurrup! Tell er to shut er fuckin trap or al fuckin break it! *Tell* er!

The man stands, puts his arms around the woman, manoeuvres her towards the back door. —It's alright, love, it's alright . . . you go in the backyard an al call yer when it's over . . . it's fine . . . don't worry, al be okay . . . go on now . . .

—I *told* yeh this would happen! *Told* yeh, didn't I, but would yeh friggin listen?!

—Shhh, now, it's alright . . . go on . . .

He opens the back door for her and ushers, shuffles her out, her hands still over her face. The man closes the door softly and turns, his arms spread in surrender. He has a kind of quiff and sideys like Alvin Stardust, Tommy notices.

Sweet, ness. I like your dress.

—Aw now, lads. It's like this.

And then he is on the floor, propped up against the fridge. His eyes roll and glaze and his head lolls and as Tommy watches his lips swell and blood leaps out on to his shirt. Tommy sees that his father's fist is clenched white and realises that he has just punched this man.

Who gurgles. Flaps his hands feebly at the height of his chest which is the height of Shem's knees. Both

Shem and Dusty pounce and Tommy behind them sees their stack-heeled shoes rise and stamp and sees their elbows working as they do when trying to start a lawnmower and between their frantic legs he sees chunks of the man, his own legs kicking in their tartan slippers, hands raised protectively to his face and those hands slapped away and how quickly that face has been changed has been altered the flesh swollen in folds purple and black lips split front teeth gone such instant mutilation. Nose smashed flat driven back above the champing jaw and there is screaming and begging in a voice gone thick what has happened to this man in so little time.

See Tommy cry. His ribs ache with the whacking of his heart. His dad grabs the man's ankles and Tommy sees his slippers fall off to expose bare feet very white and this makes him cry further. The wrecked man is dragged towards him and that smashed and purpled face is at his feet. Oh how smashed it is. It is like stew.

There is a roaring in his ear, his dad's voice: —The fucking hammer, Thomas! Wanner be top dog? Wanner be a gangster, son? *Welly* the fucker! Hit im! IT im!

There are noises coming from that pounded mouth. Faint screechings, kitteny noises.

—IT im!

Tommy raises the hammer. It takes all his strength. It is not right what has happened to this man. Tommy raises the hammer and cannot see through scrunched and stinging eyes.

—Go on, now, Thomas. His uncle Dusty's voice in a whisper. —Ye must hit him now, sunshine. Or just drop the hammer.

Little Thomas raises the hammer. He feels a scrabbling on his legs and looks down and sees the smashed man's fingers crawling up his shins, pulling at his socks, grabbing at his ankles. The thin screeching. The bubbling blood bursting on those noises high and rising. He is trying to plead Tommy thinks but his face, that face, it is not like a face any more it is burst like jam it is —

Tommy drops the hammer and vomits. Where it goes he doesn't know, he doesn't care. The spew just leaps out of him and he turns and stumbles.

—Take him to the car, Dust.

He is lifted. He is airborne in arms. There is cool air on his face then he is lying on the back seat of the Capri. Probably he sleeps because the next thing he knows he is moving and he can hear laughter.

—Djer see it, Dust? Bleeurgh, all over his kite. See it?

—I did that, aye. Straight in the mug. What the fuck has he been eatin, the wean? Looked like corn.

—Probly all them Golden fuckin Nuggets his mother keeps feedin im. Loves them things he does burrit's all the lazy cow ever feeds him. That's why he's so fuckin fat.

Tommy keeps his eyes closed. The colours there now the colours of a face, plum and black and maroon, a face so easily altered. So very easily ruined.

—What do we do with im now?

—Take im back home. Let his mother look after him, clean im up, likes. Us two can goan avver few wets, spend some of this ginch, yeh?

—Aye. Think he's learnt his lesson?

—I'd say so, aye. Poor little bleeder pissed isself n all, did yeh see? Friggin *terrified* he was, the poor little get. See im? Ee ain't gunner grow into *this* fuckin business, no way. Not one doubt about that, lar.

—Aye. In future, tell im to stick to playin cowboys n indians.

—It's all IRA v UVF at *that* school, Dust.

—Well. As long as he's a Goodie.

—Oh fuck yeh.

The car rolls on. The two men continue to talk and laugh. They *laugh*; how can they be laughing after what they've just done? What is so funny? The world to Tommy now is not what it once was. All is changed. There are things in it he didn't know existed yet the two big men can laugh still. How, though? How?

He doesn't sleep that night, little Thomas. His mother, uncharacteristically gentle, tucks him in and kisses him and tells him tenderly that he's learned a lesson and she even leaves the landing light on for him without complaining about the electricity bill but still he doesn't sleep because of the fear of the dreams that may thunder. Floods of blood and faceless howlings. But the following night he sleeps better than he ever has before and when he returns to school Mr Lyons has one arm in plaster and a bruised face and he says not one word to Thomas, will not even look at him in fact not even when Thomas whacks Toasty Fagin on the back of the burn-scarred head with a ruler. And Tommy will never return to the way he was before; something new he will become to himself as he grows, as his bones stretch and his flesh fills further out. As his hands and face spread as if rolled and pressured out by the city's winds he comes to love, at his ears, at his elbows, at his always active throat, these sea breezes strong and salted forever pushing him onwards, out into the available world.

NURSE

She's maybe not cut out for this job. She's maybe too sensitive, that's what Carl, her boyfriend, says; he says that she should find something else, or if not that then she should learn not to bring her work home, to leave it at the hospital gates. To keep the two worlds separate, homelife and worklife, not let the one affect the other. She suspects that this is simply because her work stories bore him but nevertheless he has a point, she feels; for example, look at this — she'll lose sleep over this tonight and tomorrow night and maybe the night after — this scene through the wired window of the recovery room in the Intensive Care ward:

Like an octopus the woman with all those tubes in her and her head the size of a white pumpkin wrapped in all those bandages. She hasn't moved for hours not since the emergency surgery to close her skull and remove bone splinters from her brain she hasn't moved but is still alive. A Vegetative State that may become Persistent. Robbed by two thugs is the story, they came into her post office in the little village and whacked her with some blunt instrument and stole all the takings four thousand pounds and are probably out in the pubs now living it up and laughing and boasting and waving all the money around while here she is in a coma. And her husband, Emrys the nurse heard the sister call him, he's sitting by her and holding her hand and even through the closed door his weeping can be heard. He presses his wife's unmoving hand to his cheek and lays his head on her breast and clasps her one hand in both of his and this nurse can hear his desolate sobs and knows she'll hear them in her pillow for several nights to come, more if the woman remains catatonic, more and more and more if she dies which she might, still.

Leave it at work, Carl will say tonight, hunched over his takeaway jalfrezi and not taking his eyes off *Holby City* because he fancies Lisa Faulkner and also Angela Griffin. Leave it at work. Don't bring it home with you, but what the fuck she thinks would a carpet fitter know of the sorrow that stalks the world? Of the terrible threat more terrifying in its randomness than the static stagnant sump that can be a human heart? Maybe she's not cut out for this. Maybe she should find another job, one with less potential to upset; embalmer, perhaps. Undertaker. Nothing, nowhere is safe.

And what would a man who fits carpets know, or for that matter an old woman who tends a post office. What could anybody know of this. What, truly, could anyone expect.

These are not questions, the nurse thinks; these are *not* questions. She moves away from the window before Emrys can turn round and behold her staring face.

DARREN, ALASTAIR

D: FUCKIN FUCKIN FUCKIN FUCKIN

   A: Jesus . . . me fuckin ed, man . . . me *ed* . . .

D: FUCK YER FUCKIN ED YOU FUCKIN CUNT YOU FUCKIN BRAINDEAD BASTARD SHITFERBRAINS YOU FUCKIN –

A: How? How is this my fault, Darren? Look at me, lar, cunts wellied me n all, didn't thee? How is –

D: Yeh shoulda been fuckin lookin out for me, yeh fuckin prick! Leavin *me* to look after the swag the fuckin state *I* was in . . . what's in yer fuckin ed, ey? WHAT THE FUCK'S IN ERE ALASTAIR!

(A rigid finger poking bone: THUNK, THUNK.)

A: Argh, Darren, don't, lar! It fuckin *herts,* man!

(THUNK THUNK.)

D: Don't see how it can, like, when there's nowt but fuckin *shite* in there.

(THUNK THUNK.)

A: Gerroff! It's all swollen!

(THUNK THUNK.)

D: Wannit swollen some more, do yeh? Ey? Is *this* what yeh fuckin want?!

A: Arrgghh! Gerroff! Am sorry, Da, just stop fuckin *hertin* me, will yeh!

(Patter of rain on shellsuit material. Honk and diesel rumble of a passing black cab.)

D: Utter fuckin knob'ed. No lie, man, yerrah fuckin balloon'ed, honest to fuckin God. Nowt in your skull but shite, lar, am tellin yeh. This is the *last* fuckin time we're ever gunner be seen together, me n you, believe. The *last* fuckin time. Count yerself lucky am not stampin yer friggin brains all over the fuckin road an djer wanner know why?

A: It's not my fault, Darren, honest to God, I –

D: Answer the fuckin question, dick'ed.

A: What question?

D (big sigh): Am *not* bootin yer skull up n down fuckin Lime Street cos yeh know why? Cos *you*, yeh fuckin halfwit no-mark sacker fuckin shite, are gunner go n tell Tommy what happened. Aren't yiz?

A: But, but why, tho? A mean you said yerself, T don't *know* about the postie. He don't *know* about the money, does he? An *you* said he doesn't need to, didn't yeh? Remember? We weren't gunner tell im about it, were we? That's what you said. Remember? In Wrexham?

D: Aye, yeh, I did. So in *that* case . . .

A: Darren, no! Don't fuckin hit me, lar! Look at me, I got fuckin wellied n all! Can't fuckin *see* even outer this one eye!

D: So make the most of havin at least *one* werkin one cos yer not even gunner have *that* in a coupla seconds. Yeh ready? One, two . . .

A: Darren! No, mate! I, I fuckin *saw* them! I saw who it was! Two scallies! Them two neds that was playin pool before! I know what thee look like!

D: *Do* yeh?

A: Aye, I fuckin saw them! We can find the cunts, lar! Get ar money back! It was *them* two, tellin yeh! Thee adder fuckin pool cue! Al reckernise em, honest!

(Panting. Rain patter. Traffic.)

D: Am just about managing to keep me fuckin temper ere, Ally.

A: I know, Da. An fair play to yeh. But honest, I can remember what thee look like. I *saw* them. Same two little gets that was playin pool before fuckin bush-whacked us fuckin both I *saw* them lar! Came outer the station wither pool cue, like.

D: Did thee?

A: Yeh. I *saw* them, man. No lie. Thee were *behind* yeh. Jumped yiz from the back, like.

D: Softshites.

A: Is *right*, man.

D: An yer'd reckernise em again, would yeh?

A: Oh aye yeh, too fuckin right. Know them faces anywhere.

(Rain patter. Traffic.)

D: One condition, yeh cunt.

A: What?

D: I *said*, one condition.

A: Aye, what is it?

D: That yeh leave the little cunts to me. You find em, call me an keep hold of em til I get there.

A: Sound by me.

D: We split up.

A: Yeh.

D: An yer've got til this time tomorrer, wharrever fuckin time it is. We *don't* find em in that time then am holdin *you* responsible an yer know what's gunner happen *then*, don't yeh? *Don't* yeh?

A: Al fuckin well *find* em, Darren.

D: Aye, well, yeh fuckin berrer had.

A: Where yiz goin?

D: To get me fuckin ed seen to. It's cut open, in case yeh haven't fuckin noticed.

A: Wharrabout me? Am bleedin as well, arn I?

D: Yer'll be doin a lot more than fuckin bleedin, you don't find the two little cunts that jacked us. So fuck off inter town an *find* em.

A: But me *ed*, lar . . .

D: Fuck off, Alastair. You know what to do.

A: Aye but me ed . . .

D (high-pitched, whining): 'Me ed, me ed . . .' (Voice getting fainter as he walks away.) Fuck off, Alastair.

A: But am bleedin. It herts.

D (even fainter): You herd me, Alastair. Fuck off an *find* em.

(Rain pitterpatter. Diesel engines. Rooroo of a pigeon. Somewhere in the city a siren sounds.)

EMRYS

Oh my God look at you
  Look at what they've done to you
  My own lovely woman
  My own wonderful wife
  that first moment I met you at Denbigh show you were on a horse such grace I thought never before had I seen such grace I bought you gin in the beer tent and your cheeks were flushed and your hair matted with sweat from the helmet such a colour it was all golden and your eyes happy and so blue and you were laughing and I bought you gin I remember now I cannot even see your eyes so long ago this was how long must be forty years forty years and in all that time
  How can our lives be changed like this
  So instantly
  So for the worse
  Nothing will ever
  Nothing will ever be the same again
  You beautiful woman
  What have they done to you
  and this skin of your hands so soft still I hear your heart-

109

beat the last time you lay like this in a place like this still-born the baby was and I thought you would die you cried so much I thought your lungs your heart would burst and never again you said oh never again and I never told you that the doctor said there could never be a never again because there was damage he said and tried to explain but I didn't listen I didn't want to know it was a woman's concern and none of mine but the way you cried and the amount you cried and then how the tears suddenly stopped in an instant and you said that by the end of the year you'd be running the post office in Cilcain and by God you were you

Evil they must be evil

That's the only explanation

Blame society blame their parents

All such shit

I will do something

I will DO something

I will get even

Someone will pay

and so much hardship you went through that time when the wheat failed and when they came and shot all the sheep because of the foot-and-mouth and you never shed one tear in fact since that time the stillbirth time I never saw you shed one tear as if a lifetime's worth gushed forth in that one night and was replaced by what replaced by steel in your determination you ran the post office you worked on the farm you rarely sat still life was an adversary to be over-come unique you are never met anybody else like you and the hardness in you when you shot the foxes and drowned the kittens and the softness in you when you reared the baby badger found in the barn and you were always there behind the counter guarding people's savings you were you ARE

this wonderful woman this wonderful wife never looked at
another woman in that way you were always all I ever
needed please don't die on me please don't die and leave me
alone I don't know what I'd do without you I would die
too I would follow you please recover please wake please
LIVE

God
how could You let this happen
God
she was one of Yours
how much need one person be put through
wrung dry and that's not enough for You
You want more
demand more
I'll give You more
more
blood
more
weeping
this life this life
tell me what to do
I am old, make it easier
please make it easier

please please please please take it back take it off us this
suffering this pain I cannot bear it this cannot be endured I
am not strong enough nobody is please take this off me let
her stand let me stand let both of us leave here on our feet
please this is enough I cannot take any more my heart it
will shatter it will burst I hear it cracking I feel it crumble
watch look I

please
I will get even

please
show me a sign
what do I do
someone will pay
wake, please
wake

DARREN

—Ow! For fuck's sake, man!

—It's disinfectant. Got to clean the wound.

This fuckin doctor one's takin the fuckin piss, lar. Feels like the cunt's gorriz whole friggin *hand* in there . . .

—Will you sit still?

'Will you sit still': *listen* to the fuckin blert. Not *im* who's sittin ere with his friggin ed split open, is it? 'Will you sit still'. Fuck *off*, knob'ed.

—Does it need stitches?

—No, I don't think so. It's shallow, just a surface wound, really. Bit of glue should do it.

—*Glue?*

—Yes, we can use a type of glue on superficial wounds such as this.

—Like fuckin Araldite or somethin?

—It's a special compound used first in the field in Vietnam. Binds the skin together very nicely. Not easy stitching the scalp on account of there being very little flesh up there to suture so glue and a couple of Steristrips should sort you out.

Glue? Just shows yeh, ey? Just glue yer friggin swede back together, like. Stick a birrer UHU on it, there

112

y'go lad, sorted. Birrer Bostik.

—Still fuckin herts.

—Yes, well, it's going to, isn't it?

—Yer not gunner give me any painkiller well?

Listen to im; scoffin cunt:

—I'd have thought thàt all the alcohol in your system would be doing a great job of deadening any sensation.

Oooooooohhhhh. Gobshite ere.

—I'm *not* bevvied, pal.

—Maybe not now no but you reek of alcohol. And this is a typical alcohol-related injury, I've seen it a thousand times before. Stumble, did you? Catch the back of your head on the corner of a table, mantelpiece or something?

Smug fuckin cunt. I don't answer the get, don't give the arsehole the satisfaction. Just lerrim get on with his job, bendin over me ed like the nitnurse at school an I can smell all them hospital stinks comin off his white coat, like, them kinda disinfectant mings, like. Two fuckin hours I've been smellin that shite for, waitin for *this* poncey bastard to fix me ed. Two fuckin hours, man, stuck in that friggin waitin room holdin a fuckin J-cloth to me ed that the nurse gave me an all the fuckin low-life no-marks around me, them junkies, them alkies, one ahl cunt spewin up Brasso an another ternin friggin blue. Two fuckin hours, man, believe that shit? Whole thing's fucked up, lar. Whole thing is pure fucked up. Somethin's gorrer be done. Fuckin disgrace it is. NHS my hairy fuckin hole.

An there's gunner be two more ozzy beds needed, soon, isn't thee? Oh aye yeh. Two ozzy beds or two

more fuckin grave plots, like. Pure *not* gunner get away
with this, man, them two cheeky fuckin neds. That
Ally's gunner fuckin find em an am gunner give em
a bit of thee ahl Saudi Arabias, like, take their thievin
friggin fingers off one by friggin one, slooooowwwlly.
Eye for an eye, lar, only fuckin way. Too right. Tie the
little gets to chairs, nail their hands to planks, out with
me ahl mate Stanley and . . .

Never fuckin skank anythin again. Won't fuckin be
able to. Can't fuckin *wait*, man, I pure cannot fuckin
wait.

An maybe that friggin Alastair needs a sortin, n all.
Somethin not quite right about all this, it pure ain't
sittin right with me, likes. Somethin fuckin shady about
that dozy bastard, as regards to *this* friggin caper. I
could see it in his eyes, or his *eye*, at least, thee other
one bein all swollen n closed up an everythin. A beauty,
that shiner of is; neds must've caught im a right fuckin
cracker. Maybe al just close up is other one. Or no,
cunt's been snidey so give is fuckin snipe a slice

let the punishment fit the crime

let the punishment fit the crime

an de-beak the fuckin knob'ed. Bet he was plannin
this all the way across Wales, that bastard. Don't trust
the twat. Never av. Norraz thick as he likes evryone
to think he is, he –

PAIN

—Ow Jesus Christ!

—Just one last swab, make sure it's clean.

—OW!

—There you go. All done. Don't wash or comb your
hair for a week or so and try to sleep on your front.

And don't scratch it.

—Not friggin likely to, am I?

Cunt's not gettin a friggin 'thanks', no way; fuckin *sure* he was enjoyin that, man. Didn't avter be that much pain, likes, did thee? Fuckin Brillo pad that felt like, lar, no lie.

Givin it toes out of ere, likes. Need a fuckin bevvy, a sit-down, sort through me options, like. Get me ed straight. It's chocka. I toy with thee idea of skankin some droogs, any fuckin droogs, from one of the medicine cupboards like, but only for a minute an then I think fucks to it cos I've got a fuckin thirst on me plus there's a couple of no-marks to find an teach a lesson in fuckin respect. Then of course there's money to spend, oh aye, can't friggin forget *that*, man. If there's anythin left, like, which there berrer fuckin *ad* be . . .

But vengeance, lar, there's vengeance to commit. For a start, like. An after that:

Happy, happy days.

ALASTAIR

Norraz bad's I thought it'd be really . . . swellin's gone down a bit an I can see outer me eye again . . . nose ain't bust either I mean it herts to fuckin shiters like but there's no crunch when I twist it an it ain't bruised that bad . . . gorrer headache like but av ad one of them permanent like since I got a kickin in the Copperas Hill bridewell that time . . . pig cunts . . . coppers, lar; bad, bad scallies, tellin yeh . . . can't trust em . . . just like *them* little cunts, them two neds . . . little fuckers, man, eh? Little fuckin toerags . . . can't

trust anyone these days, man . . . no fuckin way . . .
thought ad be able to trust *them*, like, a mean thee
were just kids still, but oh no, oh no . . . start young
these days thee do . . . pure cannot trust any bastard,
man . . . dead sad, like, irriz . . . dead sad . . .

Should clean the cut like, but d'yeh think there's
gunner be any soap in *these* skeezy bogs? Like *fuck*,
man . . . landlord ain't cleaned these bogs in years . . .
thee pure friggin *hum*, man . . . yeh can almost *taste*
it, like, in the backer yer throat . . . so I use a birrer
yocker insteader soap, like, just spit a birrer gob on
me finger an rub it on the cut . . . boss germkiller,
like, yocker . . . natural . . . like that ahl advert, for
Domestos or wharrever it was: Kills all known germs.
THUNK. Dead.

Thunk.

Dead.

That fuckin Darren, lar . . . he's gettin it . . . notten
fuckin surer, man, believe, I tell no lie, I shit you not
. . . he's gettin *iz* . . . an them two neds, like . . . notten,
no one's gunner fuck up me plans ere, like . . . least
not two fuckin scally kids an a complete friggin ed-
the-ball like Taylor . . . no way . . . gunner do what's
gorrer be done . . . gunner *do* it, man . . .

Jesus, why does evrythin fall to bits like this? What
goes wrong with it all? Yeh av all these plans an other
people makem all fall to shite like an it's as if there's
somethin *wrong* everywhere . . . as if under evrythin
is this great big fuck-off giant *badness,* like . . . like a
curse, aye, that's wharrit is, a *curse* . . . anythin good
yeh try an do an always somethin bad comes along
and fucks it all up . . . always . . . mean I ad it all

werked out in me ed, like, an now look, it's all in
fuckin bits, lar, bits . . . gorrer sort yerself out ere,
Alastair . . . get this shite friggin sorted, like . . .

Ferst things ferst an that's find them fuckin babyscals
. . . trawl the city like til I fuckin find em . . . get the
money . . . get that money *back* . . .

An then what?

Well, just tern up, I suppose . . . just stick it all in
a bag an get the bus back out there an just tern up
. . . say eeyar, am sorry . . . am dead, dead sorry . . .
all I can fuckin do, innit? . . . just make it berrer,
like . . .

Then get that fuckin Darren sorted. Make that
bastard pay. Wish ad never seen im with that hammer
. . . sick cunt . . . that poor ahl woman . . . God the
way she fell . . . THUNK . . . one evil twat that Darren
. . . has to fuckin *hert* people, dunny? Only way he's
ever happy, like, is when he's causin someone pain . . .
sick bastard . . .

But he'll pay. He's pure gunner fuckin pay, no lie.

Blood's washed off an I don't look too bad . . . bad
bruise on me forehead, likes, but not *too* bad . . . least,
a won't stand out in *this* friggin bar . . . evryone ere's
gorrer shiner or a bent beak or somethin . . . I spy
Kiwi's black an shiny head at the bar . . . he'll be good
for a bevvy cos he'll pay for the company, like, an I
could really fuckin go a Guinness . . .

—Y'alright, Kiwi?

—Aye, Alastair, not bad, man, aye. What happened
to the face? How'd yeh get that mark on yer ed?

—Gerruz a pint an al tell yeh.

—Brassic again?

—Yeh.

—What is it?

—Guinness. Ta.

He orders the bevvies an yeh should see the look the barman gives iz ed . . . we call im Kiwi not cos he's from New Zealand but cos he's baldy so he paints his head with black Kiwi shoe polish, all over, friggin sideys an evrythin . . . he's off iz tree . . . when he gets hot it all runs down his face an yeh can see all the scabs on is ed where the chemicals av bernt the skin . . . he's fuckin wacko, man, tellin yeh . . . an he don't friggin stand out around ere, oh no . . . just blends in like with all thee other fuckin fruitcakes and mad'eds . . . oh aye . . .

—Eeyar, mate.

—Cheers, Key.

I take the pint an neck half straight. Key's goin on in me ear burram not really lissnin cos am runnin through things in me ed:

Thievin bastard neds get found. Things are then made berrer. Darren fuckin Taylor gets *iz*.

Simple, lar, eh? Fuckin *piss* easy, man. Aye but this bleedin, this bleedin *badness* under it all . . . gorrer watch out for *that*, man . . . it'll get yeh . . . no lie . . . it just waits n waits for the best time to fuck yiz up . . . all yer plans like . . . not werth two shits inny end . . .

Jesus me *ed* . . . this pain in me fuckin ed . . . always fuckin there, lar, always fuckin there irriz . . . bangin away . . .

This pint's great, tho, sortin me brain *right* out. Kiwi asks me if I want another an I say yeh. Just one more, tho, just the one; I mean av got stuff to do, lar. Dead important stuff, like. Carn be angin round in the fuckin boozer all day, no way, man.

Oh me fuckin *ed*.

ROBBO & FREDDY:
SOME WORDS AND PHRASES

1. YES! YEEEEEEEEEEEEEEEESSS!
2. Fuckin rich! (x 8)
3. Lar. (x 17)
4. They went down liker sacker shite, didn't thee?
5. Man. (x 8)
6. No fuckin lie. (x 4)
7. We can do fuckin *anythin*. Fuckin *anythin*.
8. We're free! Fuckin *free*!
9. Set arselves up in biz.
10. What yeh fuckin talkin about?
11. Loader fuckin beak.
12. Great big mounder bugle.
13. Step on it. (x 2)
14. Sell it on. (x 2)
15. Then buy *two* big moundser bugle.
16. Fuckin brewstered we'll be.
17. Tommy Maguire.
18. Willy fuckin Hunter.
19. Peter the Beak.
20. They'll sell us some.
21. We're gunner be fuckin *rollin* in wedge.
22. Spain.
23. YEH! (x 8)
24. A fuckin shooter. (x 4)

25. Laughin.
26. Gunner be fuckin *well* sorted.
27. Is right. (x 11)
28. You *know* it. (x 11)
29. YES! YEEEEEEEESSS! (Again, and repeat to fade.)

EMRYS

Ah, Frank, my old friend. I knew you'd turn up. Knew as soon as you heard . . .

—I came as quick as I could, Emrys. I was right in-a middle of-a calving but I got Maureen to take over and came straightaway. Soon as I heard.

I take his hand. It feels so strange. This I think is the first time I've ever touched another man sober and by design in my life and it feels so alien, so utterly odd; I didn't expect it to be so *rough*. It's like sand-paper, or a cow's tongue – hard and raspy and so, so dry. Is this what we're like, to women? Do we feel like this to them, rough and unwelcoming? Like, like *stones* or something? Leathery like animals?

—I've, I've had a word with the doctor. He's told me what there is to know. It's not looking good, is it?

The tears just burst out. Just gush out. Frank takes his hand away from mine and I think he's embarrassed and uncomfortable but then he has his arms around me and my face is at his shoulder. I can feel the prickles of his shirt against my skin and I can smell sweat and silage and cigarette smoke and earth and the deep stink of large animals and this is exactly what I need. These smells, the warmth of my oldest-known friend against me, this is exactly what I need. Is this what men are like to women? Do we smell good to them, do they need our arms around them? Are our shoulders strong enough for them?

Frank lets me rest there till the tears dry and I can't cry any more, by which time his shoulder is soaked. He pats my back and moves away from me, over towards the drinks machine. I've been sitting here in this waiting area for the past hour; the surgeon wanted another look at my beautiful wife, another check-up he said, so he banished me here. But she's *my* wife. I should be back by her side.

—Coffee, Emrys.

Frank hands me a steaming styrofoam cup of hot, black coffee. I look into it and its blackness.

—When was the last time you ate?

I shrug. Honestly can't remember.

—Shall I get you something? Sandwich or something?

I shake my head.

—You should eat, Emrys. You staying here tonight?

I nod. —Yes. They said they'll make me up a cot in the room.

Frank nods. —If you should need anything.

—Yes.

—I mean *anything*, Emrys.

—Yes.

Ah Frank, my old, good friend. So good to have you here.

—And you're accepting it this time, my friend.

I look up at him, at his face; see the grey beard with the chaffs caught in it, the yellowing of nicotine at the corners of the mouth. Such a *worked* face, that;

a face made by forty years in the fields and on the hills. Is mine like that? Do I too have lines deep enough to wedge a coin in on my face?

—You *have* to, Emrys, don't you? You *need* a gun in the house, now. Don't you agree?

I nod.

—Please tell me that this time you'll take it. I'm not saying that you wouldn't be here if you had've accepted the shotgun in the first place, but . . .

But that's *exactly* what he's saying. And I fear that he may be right; I mean, you don't even have to pull the trigger, all you have to do is *show* it . . . Just before last Christmas or was it the Christmas before, there was an attempted break-in at the shop and Frank tried to persuade me to get a gun, even went so far as to offer me one of his own, an old but reliable double-barrelled. I was toying with the idea of taking it but then the Tony Martin thing happened and I imagined myself in that position, not only in jail but also with the death of a sixteen-year-old boy on my conscience and that was it for me, no thanks I said, I'll take my chances. But *now*, though . . . well, Christ, things are different, now. Things have changed.

How they change. My beautiful woman, the way she looked astride that horse. All that promise and youngness in her. And the way she looks, *is*, now, here in this hospital.

Those bastards. Those two evil bastards. It was old Mr James who saw them; out walking his dog and he saw the two of them running away from the shop with a bulging rucksack. A baseball hat, he said, one of them was wearing a baseball hat, and they were both yelling at each other in Liverpool accents. Didn't see what car they drove away in because it was too dark but I reckon he was hiding from them, that's my suspicion. He didn't want to get involved. Like everybody, that's what they always say, isn't it? 'I didn't want to get involved.'

Cowards. I am surrounded by bloody cowards. This world is made up of craven bloody cowards. There are one or two exceptions. But *only* one or two.

—I'll take it, Frank. Gladly.

He smiles and pats me on the shoulder. —Good man. You'll feel safer with it in the house. *I'll* feel better, too. Will you be home tomorrow evening? Shall I bring it round?

I nod. —I'll nip home between six and seven, barring any changes in . . . you know . . .

—Yes. I can show you how to use it.

—No need. I was born on a farm, Frank, I've lived and worked on one all my life. I know how to use a shotgun.

He smiles. —Of course.

There is a burning sensation on my hand and I realise I have involuntarily squeezed the styrofoam coffee cup and some of the liquid has spilled over on to my skin. It will blister there, later. I should run it under some cold water but I am too tired to move. I am exhausted. Remembering how she looked, on that magnificent horse . . . it has sapped my energy. Every last shred.

I will accept the gun.

DARREN, HIS GRANDFATHER: SAPPER LEON TAYLOR OF THE LANCASHIRE FUSILIERS

As soon as the three-inch mortars struck the ground he dropped his rifle and ran. No; the moaning minnies were still airborne, crackling in over the treetops and his Lee Enfield and attached bayonet were lying in the mulch before the shells landed and he hears shouting and bellowing and sees faces in his vision splintered as he passes them and the earth heaves and then there is the unmistakable thump and concussion of a six-pounder anti-tank shell and the ground shrugs and tosses him, he is for a moment aware of being upside down and then the wind yelps out of him as he lands on his back in something soft, mud. Thick mud. His face is in it. He is inhaling mud. He flops and writhes like a landed fish on to his back and blinks mud from his eyes. Hears his own breathing stentorian as loud in his head as the bursting shells and the screaming and are they projectiles and body parts pouncing across the skyslice above the irrigation ditch or are they merely impurities, blots of dirt, in his demented vision?

Whatever they are he must flee from them. He must get away. He twists his arms backwards around himself to remove his pack and retrieve his entrenching tool but it is split and scorched by shrapnel and things spill; an enamelled dark brown mug, a cutlery bundle, a water bottle useless with rotten cork and torn felt covering and the Housewife holdall it too ripped and spilling in its turn as if in imitation of the bigger pack, balls of grey darning wool and fawn thread and black thimble and brass buttons and needles wrapped in tissue, these things artefacting the mud and sunk in that by Sapper Taylor's knees as he rips his mess tin from his burst pack and begins whimpering to dig with that. The sky whines and shrieks above him. Chaos on the earth. His panting and pleading louder in his ears than the screeching flame and hurled metal deathbent and hysterical spitting heat and pinpricks on his head knocked helmetless.

Dig, dig. He has been airborne. The shellburst threw him as a man would fling a stone, carelessly and without effort. He can smell shit. Something also metallic like blood and thick, syrupy in his nostrils. Just muck in his eyes that he scoops and removes and scrabbles at just hide me hide me hide me.

—Oh please God fuckin get me out of this I will be good I will be good I will never again I promise to do Your bidding promise I will never –

Two immense swords clashing in the darkening sky above his back, above the ditch that shelters him. Strike and spurt sparks zipping in streams across that dusk and the rending of their metal is like a horde of screaming men.

Shouldn't be here. Shouldn't fucking be here. Here men will be instantly stripped of courage and aggression and will become as children sitting in their own shite pleading for mother for God for sanctuary for –
        cowardice
—No fuck off no fuck off it's too much this is I didn't *know* I didn't –
        cowardice

And not even time to kill a man. Not even time to destroy a Nazi shoot the bastard see him crumple bayonet-charge them feel their bastard bodies give, plunge and twist like the corporal showed after grinning he stroked his bayonet lovingly held at his crotch like a dick back at the training camp back in Sussex back where he was

safe

A scream and the earth heaves. Another scream.

—Oh Jesus Christ oh Jesus Christ help me hide me I –

He vomits.

—Don't let me die I want to live don't let me die don't let me pleasepleasepleaseplease –

This groove he's made in the soft dark earth exposing two cones of rust, bullets from some earlier war, he curls himself into, hands cupped to his chin. His thin whimperings. Only a few feet above him he sees tracer bullets slash the sky in complete contravention of all he'd been told that such armaments were against the rules of warfare and will not be used but what he hadn't been told and what gushes over him now as he lies in the ditch cowering and crying awash in his own fluids fevery hot and fear-drawn is the utter helplessness in the face of these demons who have put so much thought and practice have *applied* so very very much of their concrete collective will into the destruction of other peoples. These demons *love* war. They *are* war. Two decades ago they were crushed and in that short time they have built themselves back up again into this; this planet-wide wall of flame. What in God's name can you do against this? What the fuck am I doing here?

Where is this even the sign said OUISTREHAM. Three fucking hours in France or is this Belgium just not home THREE hours only and now this, this cringing cowering mud pain terror.

PAIN. A burning spot on his lower leg he is aware of this now with the adrenalin running out and he reaches down to feel and his fingers sink into his calf. Sucked into warm mush and sharp jagged chips of something what can they be but bone.

—Oh God . . . Oh God . . . helpmehelpmehelpme please please . . . oh God save me . . .

His inner child wailing this high-pitched pleading. He pulls what's left of his pack on top of him but bits of it still burn and he shoves it off. The explosions and screaming have ceased and he can hear voices now talking in a tongue that is not his.

He sits up. There is another figure close to him, in the ditch. There is enough light still for him to recognise this figure as Ernie Riley who he went to school with and to see also that there is a wound in his throat like a second mouth a toothless mouth on the side of his neck that drools blood black in the fading light. Wrecked muscle hangs in fronds over a jagged lightless hole.

Gunshots. Those non-English voices getting closer, louder, punctuated by single scattered shots. Ernie is trying to speak and more blood flicks with each attempted and aborted word. He clutches at Leon's legs and his stiff fingers jab into the calf wound. Leon bites a scream back and jerks his leg away. Ernie's eyes beg.

Shouldn't even fuckin be here. Should be fighting

with them demons and not against them those lords of war they will win, surely win, will walk the world. Straddle seas. Such ravening slaughterers what am I doing here pitched against them.

Someone will pay for this. Someone is going to pay for bringing him here to this muddy ditch in France beslimed as he is reduced to this caked and cringing state. They can light up the sky with the inferno of their will. Someone *must* pay.

Louder, the voices. Very close now. Ernie is scrabbling at his chest at the soaked serge of his shirt. His hands clench in the debris from the pack now utterly without use and something hard presses against his right palm. A familiar shape.

His jackknife. Made by C. Johnson & Co. of Sheffield. Marlin spike, tin opener, bottle opener, screwdriver. A useful little tool.

And stainless-steel blade. A very useful little tool.

He thumbs the blade out. Ernie is on top of him now, his gaping neck-wound up against his face and he pushes him away and looks elsewhere as he plunges the blade into that wound and rips to the left. Instantly his hand is hot and wet and Ernie bucks and twists and falls back against him facing upwards at the wounded sky. His face pressed against Ernie's skull in his oily matted hair, hot fluid pumping into his eyes, into his silent-roaring mouth.

cowardice

They scrumped apples together, once. Sagged school and went fishing in the canal and caught nothing. Stole soda siphons from the backyards of pubs and cashed them in in grocers' shops and with the pennies bought gobstoppers that turned their mouths purple. Met each other in the recruitment office on Lime Street. Drank beer together.

So cowardice

No, someone. Someone will pay.

A light sweeps across the ditch. Ernie has now stopped twitching and gurgling on top of him and he holds his heavy body tight to his chest. A nearby voice in the darkness grunts and speaks:

—*Er ist tot. Ja, sie sind alle tot.*

And this is how it sounds, the end of the world. Armageddon speaks in an excited voice, the voice of a child delirious with damage, his horrible and hectic excitement in those mere words.

This is it.

I will make someone pay. I promise the world that someone will pay for this.

Unconscious under a corpse, sinking slowly in filth. Torn, tattered, bone exposed to the rent air still spongy with cordite and burnt meat. These two tangled inside the crust of the upheavaling earth and which is dead and which still lives can be discerned only by the ongoing trickling and not clotting of snatched blood.

This is it.

THE SS MALARKAND

It was a barrage balloon, broken and rogue, that ignited the fire. An insane floating whale it drifted across the dark water of Huskisson Docks on 1 May 1941 and collided with the moored SS *Malarkand* which had in its hold 1,000 tons of high explosive bound for the

Middle East. These flames unquenchable, insatiable, then guided the *Luftwaffe* in towards their target and the burning ship with its apocalyptic cargo was hit with high-explosive bombs which explosions produced more explosions and so on until the entire hold itself exploded. The following day, as dawn rose, a dockside crane four miles away eighty feet up in its girders sported an odd, new growth: the *Malarkand*'s five-ton anchor. Huge and hanging there above the staring crowd, transfixed, men and women and children. The ship itself still burned and around it the oily sea still lapped but a flame had been struck that no water could douse and awe at the might that could toss steel tonnage as a child might flick a fly. Minds, hearts stilled before the force that stalked the world and attenuated by terror down into a reactive arsenal of two: revenge or collaboration. Resistance or conversion. And nothing within that of any understanding of the terrible power of destruction to simplify or maybe there was as whatever reaction stripped further and unadorned terminally eroded revealed at its barest bones just the one awesome imperative: to live and live and live. Not just live, but live for ever.

ALASTAIR, HIS GRANDMOTHER: HER LEAVING

It being an evening on which the sun still beamed although sunk low enough to diadem the peak of Moel Eilio they had made a table outside under the yew tree out of two rain barrels and a door and on it stacked bowls and plates of food and drink; a huge boiled ham, deeply pink and leaking, jugs of butter-milk and beer and water from the spring so fresh it writhed, mounds of potatoes boiled in their skins like speckled eggs and also speckled eggs themselves hard-boiled, fried carrots and loaves of bread which when tapped echoed and green bursts of lettuce and cabbage and a crusted wheel of cheese the rind of which reminded Kate of the skin of her own hands and heels, farm-calloused as they were. There was butter like a melting yellow boulder oozing whey and onions slow-baked in their skins and a long flat barky slice of fried liver. This last had been prepared especially for Kate being as it was her very favourite but the nervous acids in her stomach would allow her to do no more than nibble. Added to this the word itself and its two syllables and the hint in them of where she was going and it was like imbibing her impending loss. Like taking into her her creeping fear and it curdling inside her, thrashing, like a pregnancy to a viper.

Usually at such times as these their words would flutter like fritillaries, jostle like midges in the clean air between them; *yr hen iaith* would burgeon here among the hills and skim off the lakes as for centuries it had done but this day, it had been decided, would be exclusively given over to Saesneg so that Kate's tongue and palate could grow accustomed. As a kind of rehearsal, a foretaste of what was to come. Occasionally their lips flapped and tongues shuddered and throats juggled as if gulping under the alien strain of this strange language although all were fluent in it and had been for a generation or two, yet the eldest present had memories of the Knot and the weight of it around her neck and shoulders and on that she not unfairly blamed her stoop, her hunched back which had come premature, in her mid-teens. And the butter churned on the farm had a gentle, murmuring quality to it, it was soft, pliant, malleable, creamy on the tongue with a spark of salt at the lips and a tender coating on the gum and tooth all plap and mimble and so it was *not* 'butter'; it was and always would be *ymenyn*.

Kate's father leaned with a jug.

—Cwrw, Katie?

A tut from her mother.

—*Beer*, Katie?

And another tut. —She's had *three*, Aled. She do not wish to be drunk arriving at the Johnsons', do you, cariad? Fine show that would be.

—Ach, nonsense.

Her father filled her cup. The beer, golden and headless, tinkled as it fell and hissed as it settled. She smiled at her dad and tipped the cup to her lips and drank, just sipped. This beer was something she had always loved. She would spend the next six decades in the big city trying to recapture the taste of this home-brewed beer in party and pub and off-licence and would always, always fail.

—Yew drink, bach. Settle yewer nerves.

—Do not be scaring her now, her younger brother said. —It's not *London* or anywhere she's going to. It isn't far.

—No, but, her *much* younger sister said, —it's very big, but. Ellie Siop went last year with her taid and it's bigger than Bangor, she told me. Bigger even than Chester, she said.

—Stop yewer stories now, blant, her mother said and then in response to her husband's raised eyebrows: —*Children.* It *isn't* very far. Wmffra Evans goes there every month and back and he's an old man, he's sixty-three. And my mam used to as well, didn't yew, Mam?

The grandmother mumbled, asleep. Striped by shadow of branch her old shrunken body slumbered around beer and gin.

—Will it be safe from the war, tho, Dad?

—Of *course* it will be, bach, the mother said.

—Safer than here, even, Aled said. —Plenty of essential industries in the big city, see. The Johnsons, they work in armaments. Rich? DuwDuw. More money than everyone in Caernarfon all added up.

—Everyone?

Aled nodded. —So eyr needed, see, for the war effort. Needed to make more guns. But round yur, see, all-a people round yur, all *we* can be is soldiers. Us men. We're not needed yur, see, so to the Brass we're just . . . we're . . .

Unable to find the word he looked to his wife for help but her lips only tightened.

—Expendable, Kate said. —Yewer all expendable. That's the word.

His eyes lit up. —That's the word, Katie, aye. He looked to his other offspring. —See why yewer sister's got herself such a good job? See why she's off to the big city to make her living? *Clever.*

He raised his cup to Kate and drank. His eyes sparkled at her over the rim.

—Will *I* be needed for the war, Dad? Will *yew*?

—DuwDuw son, no. It'll all be over before yewer old enough to go.

—How do yew know?

—I just do. Too young to understand yet, yew are.

—What about yew? Will yew be going?

—Ach. The mother leaned and cuffed lightly her son on the back of his head. —Shut up that talking now. Kate's last day yur it is. War stories, DuwDuw. It's yewer sister's last day.

—Not for long, tho, Mam, is it? Yew said it wasn't far. Be back soon yew will, won't yew? The youngest daughter looked at Katie with wet eyes.

—Course I will, Kate said and smiled and sipped at her beer and nibbled at the liver congealing in grease on the plate and true it *wasn't* far, could in fact be travelled in a day from here, Capel Garmon (neolithic burial chamber, multi-chambered, central chamber topped by enormous capstone; the White Horse Inn, views of Eryri from chamber or village cemetery), to there, Liverpool (docks and enormous buildings and hurrying hordes of all hues), yet between the two places was the sharp sky-puncturing spike of Moel Eilio and beyond that Yr Wyddfa itself and the Glyderau and the Carneddau, such colossal ramparts, impassable, their bulwark bulk seeming to jeer at the very notion of human traffic across them. And scattered among them in their valleys split as if by nothing but wrath or on their cold plateaus and wailing moors the lakes, Llydaw and Ogwen and Cowlyd, blood-freezing and black as tea stewed milkless or as old blood in the byres. And beyond them the Gwydyr forest and beyond that the River Conwy and then the Vale of the same name with its crags and streams and then the smaller mountains, Moel Seisiog and Moel Llyn and the Mynydd Hiraethog itself that empty wilderness cut only by drover's trail and sheeptrack and lost in its bogs the bones of the waylaid or the wandering and discernible in its winds ever-wailing the souls of those dead as many over the aeons as those then disintegrating under gas and shrapnel in a distant country all testament to the million varieties of human extinction. And still beyond that the sea at Prestatyn and the River Dee which must be traversed by ferry above the mud at low tide black and reeking or indeed skirted at Chester this route in fact taken by the train to the Birkenhead docks where warships appeared in the water beneath the tall and claw-fingered cranes facing the other docks across the murky Mersey where also other vessels would appear, those outgoing filled with singing and a cele-bration of sorts and those returning drifting silently into dock themselves like phantoms, these huge ships cargoed with pain and loss, and floating across the gang-planks those who have left their limbs and more commonly their minds elsewhere. Then across the conurbation the bricks and cobbles and human mass, that huddled hysteria that characterises port cities and what might Katie find there in that storm of mingled life? Only something *not* found in the pool-eyes of lambs or in the gentle tumbling of milk to curd. Only something *not* found in songbird or bee or flower or the sweetening of grass to hay and the sugary burst of that from a cow's mouth on a morning before the swelling sun has melted the frost and the grass still spears pallid from the meadow and maybe not found even on the shrieking peaks where the rain falls enraged enough to bounce thigh-high from the old stone underfoot and where sky-high lofty lightning illuminates abrupt and sudden thunders. But shared perhaps in field and grotto in rock agleam with schist and brickwall fluffed with soot, the slice of knife or grunt of gun in trough or gutter, pit or drain down which fluids flow to one set end, and mirrored and indeed culminated in the mass movement of men to a killing field enormous, continent-wide bloodfeast and frenzy just these teeth that snap and blades that gleam and shear the transmogrification of mammal to meat and such red necessity. And that the sum of any plunge into the beating breast wherever it may be found on high crag or pavement slab, peak or dockside will uproot only the proof if it were ever called for that the throb that drives the shovel can only simply be purely because the engine red and fleshy that propels these green needs will buckle and break time and time over only because things die, things die.

—Of *course* I will, Katie said again, to her whole family but primarily to her sister because she was still regarding her with big and seeping eyes. —As often as I can. Every second weekend I'll try to come back, I will. Don't none of yew worry about me. I'll be fine, see. I'm not going to be going very far at all.

And then suddenly she had an appetite and she ate the now cold slice of liver and some potatoes and a baked onion with butter mashed into it and salt. The sun sank further behind the mountain and as it did more people appeared, friends and neighbours from villages more seawards than Betws Garmon, Groeslan and Creunant and Caeathro. Tales were told of more names annihilated in Flanders and healths were drunk and memories toasted and food was eaten and songs played on fiddle and harp were danced or wept to accordingly and loss rolled down into the valley from both the mountain and the coastal plain and its smell was unidentifiable yet had something in it of the clear and sharp and unsullied. Kate's grandmother awoke to sing toothlessly 'O Jesu Mawr' and then fell asleep again. Much later than intended Wil Roberts of Fferm Llandwrog appeared in his charabanc which contained only enough room in it for himself and Kate and her luggage so after wet and exhausting farewells under the blackening mountain he drove her to the train station at Caernarfon where with mere minutes to spare she caught the train to Bangor where she caught the train to Llandudno where she caught the train to Chester where she caught the train to Liverpool where she arrived at the Johnsons' house by horse-drawn cab through the city that drew from her gasps and tears and on two occasions smiles. As it was morning she was fed and allowed to rest in a huge bedroom where she only wept. She spent a decade in that house, in service, during which time in 1917, when she'd been there two years, her father died at Cambrai, part of a tank crew which caught a direct hit from an Austrian howitzer and of he himself there was nothing left to bury so they interred an empty coffin in the sloping cemetery outside Capel Garmon which in the last three years had crept closer and closer still to the village. The Johnson patriarch died after a long illness when hostilities ceased and his wife took their children to a different town and Kate then found work as a convalescent nurse, helping soldiers to recover from or perhaps simply cope with is a more apt phrase their various injuries, their missing limbs or faces or smithereened minds. In the late 1930s she intended to quit this job but of course there soon came another influx of these broken beings the convalescence of which occupied another decade during which her brother was killed in Burma and her sister took their now ancient mother with her and her new husband to America, north New York State, where shortly after arriving their mother died too. Kate lost her Cymraeg, slowly but never entirely; there was a Welsh-speaking chapel in Toxteth that she attended and she met in that city many others who shared her first tongue, but since diurnal exigencies were conducted in English then her first language dribbled away like a thaw of something, some kind of melt. In the fifties she left nursing for good and turned to hotel portering, in one of which jobs she met a Greek man, a chef who, after getting her pregnant, suddenly vanished and left her at rather too late an age for mothering to give birth to a girl, alone, although afterwards she was visited frequently by the many friends she had made, men with false limbs and glass eyes and the women who cared for them. This daughter at a very young age fell pregnant to what Kate called a roustabout and indeed she was not surprised when this man refused to recognise the child, unsurprised but not unsaddened; the desolation of her daughter and the helplessness of her grandson scoured her raw heart. Her daughter then turned increasingly to alcohol for comfort as in fact

Kate herself had been doing secretly for some years and it fell to her to look after this first child, named Alastair after his father, through primary and secondary schools into his drifting and desultory years when he began to run with the wrong crowd and, Kate was sure, turn to drugs and crime. The second-born grand-child was of necessity adopted by Kate too; a straw-haired girl who began to suffer eczema in her infancy and was called Scabby at school, although she now suffers rarely from that affliction and has developed a certain attractiveness. She has lived in London for some years. By the time of Alastair's first custodial sentence for persistent shoplifting Kate hadn't worked for some time and was claiming a state pension and had been subject to a constant heaviness in her chest and bad pain in her joints and, most worryingly, unpredictable blackouts; the last straw came when she awoke in a butcher's, blood in her eyes from where she'd hit the counter edge as she toppled, surrounded by concerned faces. Terrified only that she'd have to go to hospital and wouldn't be able to have any brawn for her tea and indeed shouting very loudly about this problem, an ambulance was called and she was taken to the Royal and there she lies now. She has been there quite some time and her mind has rapidly disintegrated and her lungs are filling slowly with fluid as are her joints and her heart is weakening and will soon become too feeble to pump any blood through her furred arteries. She will die soon. She is very old; nearly a century of years on this planet she has lived. In her own way she has not forgotten whom and what she loves. Life is a confused cloud. Her grandson will soon appear to her through that cloud but she will probably not recognise him. Across an ocean her younger sister still lives, now in Canada, not America; she has three children and seven grandchildren and one great-grandchild. At times she wonders about her elder sister Katie and if she is still alive. The last time this sister wrote, about ten years ago when one of her grandchildren went off to fight in Iraq, the letter was never answered and nor was it ever returned. Nor was her grandchild, at least not alive; the transcription on his tombstone in Alberta which the sister hopes Kate will see one day although the possibility of that is extremely remote simply reads:

HERDD
PERFFAITH
HERDD

WHORE

God, that Tommy. Changes his 'tude like David fuckin Beckham changes his 'do. Mean, me an Vix come in ere to give im is wedge, like, an ee grins all nice as pie and gives us back a score each, tells us to get ar nails done or summin an then his man Lenny brings in that no-mark Darren an all of a sudden Tommy's all 'right, youse two, fuck off, werk to do'. Mean, ere he is the BIG MAN all of a fuckin sudden showin off like, in front of his boys. But ee coulda been nice about it, couldn he, I mean he coulda just said 'see yiz later' or summin but no, oh no, he's gorrer come on all friggin dead aggressive tough guy like, so he tells us to fuck off and get back to werk. Back to bleedin werk, he sez! Fuck *that*, man. It's been a busy friggin day what with the Eurocash conference, like, an ten sweaty Continentals in one afternoon is enough for me so I give Vicky a look like come ed, it's Breezer o'clock an we gerrout of there quick-quick, that scally Darren checkin ar arses out as we do. Oh aye, never mind that he's got his face all swollen like an a shaved patch on the back of his head where he's been cut an what looks like fried friggin *onions* all over his kite that he fuckin reeks of, never mind all that, ee can still manage to check out ar arses, like. Yeh, so I give the divvy a wiggle of summin he'll never get cos he can't afford *this* werkin girl, oh no, no way. Lenny, God bless im, just gives us a little smile an looks away, gettin all shy like he normally does when we're around. Sound feller, Lenny. I *like* Lenny. Got this lovely accent, like . . . dead soothing it is . . .

But God that fuckin Tommy.

Outside on the street in the drizzle I turn to Vicky.
—Where now, Vix? Few bevvies in Concert Square is it?

She looks at me, her eyes all funny in that black eyeliner inch-thick.

—Jeez no. Avn't we gorrer get back to werk? Isn't that what ee just told us?

—Who, Tommy?

—Yeh.

I put me hand on her shoulder and steer her in the direction of the city centre and all the bright bars down there.

—Fuck what T just said, Vix. He'll av his hands full

tonight, did yeh not see the marks on that Darren's head?

—Saw that gash on his scalp, like . . .

—Aye, an his kite all puffed up. That Lenny one must've given him a few digs, I reckon. Tommy's got some business to attend to if yeh ask me an he's gunner be occupied all night so *fucks* back to werk. Let's goan get bevvied. Don't worry about that Tommy. We'll goan av a laugh, alright?

She still looks unsure. A Beemer pulls up at the kerb, winda comes down, cigar smoke an a red an worried face peers out.

—I, ah . . . I look for ladeez business to–*night*, mm?

Another foreigner. Honest to God, is that all thee do at these conference thingios, buy sex?

—Not now, love, I tell him. —Try Faulkner Square.

—Where *iz* zis Fuckenah Square?

—That way. I point in the vague direction of Tocky.

—You show me?

—*That* way, I say again an walk off with Victoria. Whether he drives up there or not I don't know cos I don't look back at him. Don't hear his engine, tho.

—See, Vix, what yer've gorrer know about Tommy is he *needs* yeh. *Needs* the dough yer bringin in. Ee knows full well that if ee starts gettin too snotty with yis then yeh just gunner tell him to do one and goan werk for someone else. Yeh? Tellin yeh, he'll shit imself, you do that. Dozen av many girls werkin for im, see, an he's scared yer'll just go off an start werkin for the Hunter brothers or someone. Yeh don't need to worry about Tommy, darlin.

Ah, Victoria; she *needs* this reassurance. Feel dead

sorry for her, I do. Mean she's only been werkin for Tommy a matter of months like, she's still findin out how things werk. She used to werk on her own, housecalls an that, all upmarket kinda stuff likes but she went into a, what, a *depression* I suppose yer'd call it after her best friend killed her own boyfriend, strangled him to death during sex like. It made the papers an the news an evrythin. She was let off, this girl, Vicky's mate like, verdict of accidental death or misadventure or summin an then she vanished, just took off like, an no one knows where she is now but the thing is, see, is that Vicky blames herself; she told me once that she took this girl out on a job, over to Heswall I think it was to whip shite out of some masochist an she reckons that this gave this mate of hers a taste for it, like, y'know, unleashed her inner violence kinda thing an that's why she was able to choke her boyfriend to death. All her own fault, Vicky says it was. So after it happened, like, she stopped werkin an started drinkin an lost a lot of money in earnings like, so she came to me for advice when things started *really* fuckin up an I guided her towards Tommy. She needs swag quick, T will help her out, an fair play to him he did; gave her a big wedge like to get herself sorted, pay off her debts n stuff, an she could pay it back in instalments like, by werkin for him, bein one of his girls, which is what she's doin now an, considerin the interest the stingy get charges, will be doin for years to come. So yeh, I feel dead sorry for her; mean, she's tied to Tommy now. All that stuff about the Hunter clan was shite, I just said it to make her feel better;

Tommy'll fuckin *mark* her if she leaves him, or doesn't pay him back. Or, rather, *he* won't, but he'll get someone else to do it for him; Gozzy Squires or one of them creepy fuckin blade-merchants. Nasty pieces of werk, them, tellin yeh. Probly cut her up for free. Got them friggin *eyes* on em, like . . . like that friggin Darren one. Looks at yiz an his eyes just go straight fuckin through yeh, no messin. Wonder what he's been up to, to gerrer whack like that . . . wonder what's happenin back there now . . . what Tommy's doin to him . . .

—So forget about im, Vicky. Time we got hammered, innit?

She gives me a small, very red smile. —Aye, alright, well. Where to?

—Dunno. Somewhere classy. Modo?

She laughs. —*Look* at us, Kathy. We'll never gerrin.

She's right; mean, ere we are in arse-freezin skirts an platform leopardskin thigh boots, push-up bras an evrythin . . . guy on the door'll take one look at us an berst out friggin laughin. But I av an idea:

—Eeyar, well. Mine's just around the corner, we'll goan get changed, yeh?

So we do; go back to mine, wee Damien's asleep thank God an I slip the childminder another flim to stay over. She's alright; stuck into a vid an a Chinky, like. I lend Vicky some kex an a jacket an we head off into town. Hit Modo first, cocktail or five, y'know . . . Soon gorrer smile on her face, Vicky has. Round about midnight in the Baa Bar she's wellied enough to start dancing on her own, slinkin all sexy like, an just for a moment I gets a glimpse of the *old*

144

Victoria, the one I first met just out of school; cocky an confident an smart, dead sexy. I expect that moment to last only for an instant an then vanish but it doesn't, it hangs around. An that makes me glad.

TOMMY MAGUIRE

Thee get moren more fuckin cheeky evry fuckin day, tellin yeh, bolder, like, start dead early thee do. Mean at *theer* age I was on the dip down fuckin Bold Street like, but *dese* lil cunts, I *ask* yeh; tryna set emselves up in fuckin bugle, at *theer* fuckin age? When I was *theer* age I though a bugle was summin yeh blew into, Roy fuckin Castle likes, knowmean? Thought it was a fuckin trumpet, lar. Thought it was.

Just a coupla fuckin kids tho. Need a friggin lesson like I got by me ahl fuckin man, lesson in fuckin *fear*, man, lesson in fuckin *life*. Knew wharry was doin my dad no fuckin lie pure *knew* wharry was up to that cunt. Pure did it fuckin *right* he did he *knew* wharry was doin.

Oh aye yeh.

Them fuckin little neds tho, lar, them two, that fuckin Robbo and Freddy thee call themselves. Gorrer fuckin *admire* the little cunts inner way I mean the *cheek* of it, like. Got some arse like comin ere sayin thee wanner set emselves up, askin fuckin *me* for advice! Gorrer laugh like really, double fuckin brave. Remind me of meself, likes, when I was theer age, fuller fuckin 'tude but dem other two cunts, that fuckin Alastair, that fuckin Taylor one, I tell yiz summin's goin on with dem two knob'eds, I fuckin shite you not. Fuckin well *up* to summin, thee are, I can fuckin tell. Don't find the thievin one-armed musher in Wales an then thee av ter ditch the fuckin motor? Not fuckin right, that. An now I hear all this about this big fuckin wedge floatin round the city with theer fuckin names attached . . . summin not right. Pure not fuckin right. Summin's goin on, I fuckin *know* it.

Tommy, man, Tommy. Yer bein taken for a *cunt*, lar. Theer callin yiz a no-mark. Theer pure fuckin *laughin* at yeh be'ind yer back. Thee all think yerrah fuckin dick'ed. Yer bein pure *laughed* at, man. Theer all *laughin* at yeh. Fatfuck Tommy theer callin yeh, thick as fuckin shite. Do somethin about it, man. *DO SOMETHIN ABOUT IT.*

I will I will. I'm *goin* to. Just you fuckin *watch* me, lar, just you fuckin *watch* me. Shut up dem voices in *no* time, lar. No fuckin time at all.

Need a fuckin lesson, thee do. An *I'm* the fuckin teacher. *Mi*ster friggin Maguire. *Sir.* Sounds boss, dozen it?

THE POET

God, there's always *one*, isn't there? Always *one* ignorant fool who just doesn't grasp the etiquette. I mean, look at him – the cheap shellsuit tucked into the cheap white sports socks, the shaven head, the baseball cap, that troglodyte pallor and those dead, dead eyes . . . Here he comes; he's going to walk to the toilets between me and my audience and horribly interrupt my flow. But I'm not going to let him; I'll ignore him; I'll embarrass him when he comes back out. He's probably gone in there to take drugs anyway, some sleazy cheap concoction.

> and then I saw you
> staring
> as one would at a saviour
> and in my whisky
> I
> wanted you more than

The toilet door closes. I hear someone in the audience snigger at his shellsuited back. What's a scally like him doing here in the Egg anyway? During a Poetry Event? This is an artist's place for God's sake. I doubt he's come in for the bulgar-wheat salads, he's probably trying to find a safe place to indulge his addictions because he's been barred from everywhere else, all those vile places his type usually go. Doesn't he realise how difficult it is, to stand up here and read out work that you've sweated and bled over? Doesn't he have any respect? I mean, I'm *alone* up here, truly alone.

> the swan wants flight
> more than the stars need us to augment them
> and in my whisky
> my four cans of beer
> now I know fear

Maybe he's one of those Scum Novelists researching his next Vomit Novel. Every year one comes out, some anti-intellectual spewing, some proudly plebeian vitriol or bile that everyone seems to need to make a fuss over and they're all the same, exulting in filth and inverted snobbery. I *bet* that's what he's doing in the toilets, making notes for his next Vomit Novel. That's all they are, just pages of exploitative nastiness; lacking in any kind of sensitivity or compassion and all written in the same grubby little voice. Oh, authentic depiction, they say! The voice of the common man! It all lacks vision, it lacks commitment, it lacks . . . *artistry*. And still they go on as if it's still the year of *Trainspotting* and not the twenty-first century, as if they don't realise that people are tired of them by now, all this sordid concern with the one voice and the one time. Society doesn't need the Vomit Novel. It never did.

> *And I came to you on my wings*
> *of Art*
> *through the terror*
> *like –*

Only it just doesn't realise it yet. The New Sensitivity, that's what I'm creating here; an outward-looking return to the pure Romantic sentiment. A reinvention and thus re-invigoration of a lyrical poetics into social life, into the world. I'll enrich it. I'll reinvest it with value. And by this time next year it won't be *their* names displayed in Waterstone's window it'll be mine, Andrew Boswell, fulfilling my duties to the world, my service. And as soon as my name is known I'll turn rapidly to criticism because someone needs to stem the flow of filth, someone needs to protect and guide the populace, steer them towards what's right; *someone* needs to ask the question, 'Is it desire for fame and money, or a simple failure of talent?' Society needs someone to ask such questions. The people need someone with the guts to come right out and ask such questions. And that someone is me: Andrew Boswell. Remember that name.

> the bee navigates the thorns
> the petrel the storms
> because I, I –

The toilet door creaks open.

$$I, I, I \dots$$

I stop here, caught on the 'I' at this rude interruption. My audience watches me, expectant, and I glare at the scumbag over the top of my page, my poem. He suddenly realises I'm looking at him, feels my glare as he passes and looks up at me with those lifeless eyes from the shadow of the peak of his cap. The whole café is watching, agog.

—The fucker *you* fuckin lookin at, yeh knob'ed? Wanner fuckin photie, do yeh?

Oh God that voice. They all sound the same. Aggression, lack of education, makes their voices thick and heavy and I can see the deeds this one's committed in his face, his eyes; half-witted, mindlessly violent deeds. Which is all he'll ever do. But I'm safe because all eyes are on us and he won't do anything if I retort: —What am I looking at? Evidently someone without the manners or bladder control to wait for me to finish.

He laughs like a drain and shrugs and leaves the café. We all hear him thumping down the stairs. He displayed his lack of intelligence there in full public view, swearing like that. Sign of a stunted mind, that quick recourse to swearing. The language has been degraded, debased by people like that and their Vomit Novel chroniclers and I will be the man to make it beautiful and valuable once more.

—Sorry about that, I tell my audience, and shuffle through my pages. After *that* little episode they need something to relax them, make them feel at ease again. I find just the thing: —This one's called 'Skimming Stones Against the Tide'.

Written on West Kirby beach last year – the playful bounce of the intellect over the dark depths of the psyche, *that's* what this is about. And about being the only New Sensitivist writing at the moment. And it's what we need and I don't mean simply here, now, in the Egg, I mean here, now, in the world. We need this exploration of the human heart and mind, don't we? It will, *I* will, help us to understand ourselves; me, Andrew Boswell, will help us to understand ourselves, and keep the world safe from the Vomit Novel. Remember my name.

DARREN, HIS MOTHER

He'll be the friggin death of me, that boy. Honest to God, he's gonner drive me into an early grave. Nowt but trouble since the day he was born and Jesus Mother and Joseph *what* friggin trouble; forceps delivery, he was. Didn't want to come out; twenty-four hours' labour like, and he *still* had to be dragged out into the world kickin and screamin. And he's been nothing but bloody trouble since. God knows what he's been getting up to recently; my dad, ar Leon, he said he saw him in the Cracke yesterday with injuries on his face and stitches in his scalp, like, and he was all het up as well, a man on a mission, me dad said. Always so angry, that boy is. Maybe the lack of a father is to blame, I don't know, but I can't imagine that if *he* was still on the scene anything'd be any better. Bad piece of work, that man was. I still remember that day, years ago now like, I remember him sitting at the kitchen table with the footy *Echo* and ar Natalie sitting there n all, she must've been about fourteen, an I remember bending down to take the chops out of thee oven an I heard a sound, like a hissing and a tutting sound, an I turned with the hot pan of sizzlin meat like, an Mary an Joseph the *disgust* on that man's face. Still remember it now as if it was only yesterday, that *disgust*; an I *knew* what he was thinking, of how ar Natalie or one of her friends would look bendin down like that an he just didn't want me any more and hadn't done for ages, me, this ahl fat-arsed cow. Lettin herself go. Letting herself go! Who friggin *wouldn't* after five children an the bloody torment thee eldest put me through . . . But that expression on that man's face, I'll never, ever forget it; that sheer disgust for me and my age an decay an how completely unlike ar Natalie I was. Beginning of thee end, that day was. Couldn't bring meself to put up with him any longer an he moved out soon after, God knows where he is now. Still married like, can't get divorced like, but God am glad he's gone, out of me life. Got rid of him without the mortal sin, I did. And I'm *well* shut of im. So yeh, if that get was still around I can't imagine how it'd be any better for ar Darren like but then again I can't imagine how it'd be any *worse*. How could it possibly be any *worse*?

He's unhappy, Father Donaghy said. You must understand, your son is a deeply unhappy young man, that's what Father Donaghy said. And I'm sure he's right but that makes it all the worse for *me*, cos I mean I brought him here, didn't I? It was me brought him into this world, like, I gave him his unhappiness. But I just don't understand his anger . . . Where does it come from? Tell me, where does his anger come from? His dad wasn't an angry man especially, he was just friggin pathetic, so why's my Darren so full of this rage? Father Donaghy couldn't answer that. He just said that we can never understand the ways of God and why He afflicts His children so, only that His love is a, what, an antidote for all the pain and suffering in the world and that the world is, at the moment, in a time of crisis, and Father Donaghy's certainly right about *that*; I mean we had this conversation not long after them planes had gone into them towers an I couldn't get them images of the falling bodies out of me head . . . I saw them in me sleep. Dreamt that I *was* one of em, falling like that. An then there was Afghanistan, with the pictures of all them poor people being bombed, an the *wrongness* of all that – the poorest country in the world being bombed by two of the richest . . . An Thatcher killed more people in this city in ten years, only not with bombs but she's still responsible for it

152

like, the despair, an pretty soon it's gonner be Iraq again an the pictures of children, so many of the innocent children hurt and killed and they've got nothing to do with all this, nothing to do with it at all but they're the ones who'll suffer, aren't thee? They're the ones who always suffer.

But Bush and Blair and that friggin Thatcher, they'll all have to answer to God. *All* of them. That friggin bin Laden in his cave n all, they'll all have to stand there in front of Him an justify their lives and their actions and what're they gonner say *then*, ey? How're they gonner defend themselves *then*? Me too, oh aye, I'm not gunner escape . . . an what am *I* gonner say? How can I excuse meself, what reasons can I give for bringin a baby into this world who hates the world? It could've been *him*, hijacking one of them planes . . . he's got the anger . . . Jesus, this world is full of holes that we can all any one of us fall through. It's like in the Holiday Inn, the Holiday Inn in town where I clean, there's three great big photographs in the foyer that I polish every mornin of the skylines of the three cities Liverpool's twinned with; Shanghai, Dublin an New York. And what're thee gonner do with the New York one now? Them two towers are still there, in the picture like, but they're not there in real life any more. So what're thee gunner do? Take a new picture or leave thee old one up, thee old one that lies? Cos everyone knows that them towers don't exist any more, that there's a great big hole where thee once stood. *Everyone* knows that. So what're thee gonner do? *Somethin* has to be done, dunnit? Aye but what, tho?

He's become a gangster. *That's* what he is. He's been

mentioned in the *Echo* an everythin, 'underworld activi-
ties' thee said, an I caught him once burning clothes
in a bin in the back alley, washing himself down with
petrol as well in the yard, an he's knockin round with
them Maguires, nasty pieces of work, like. Thinks he's
friggin Al Capone now. I asked him over Sunday dinner
last, just came right out with it an accused him of
bein a gangster an all he could say was 'Mum, am *norra*
gangster'. Just that – 'I'm *norra* gangster, Mum.' He had
me in tears. Ar Natalie was there with her feller and
their baby and their *little* baby, juster few weeks old
like, an he looked . . . he looked so bloody beautiful,
like. Untouched. An I remember how Darren would
look then an how he looks now, what he *is* now an
it breaks my heart, it really does. Just like Bush an
Blair an Thatcher an that bin Laden one he's also
gonner have to answer to God an what's he gonner
say? How will he defend himself? He can hardly string
two sensible words together as it is, not without using
the 'f' word between them, like . . . so how's he gonner
avoid it? How's he gonner avoid being damned? An
why aren't thee others like him, his brothers an sisters?
Why is it only him who behaves like he does?

I fear for him, I do, I fear for his life on this earth
and his soul in the next. So many holes for us to fall
into and most of us can never get back out again. He's
broken my heart, that child of mine. Honest to God
he has.

One moment I'll always remember till me dying
day; he came back from the school one day when he
was about ten and I asked him how it went and d'you
know what he said? 'How was your day, son?' I asked

and d'you want to know what he answered? 'Boring an pointless, Mum,' *that's* what he said. About ten years old he was. And the thing is, he probably really *had* gone into school that day cos, if only for three words, he was articulate and he could express his feelings without shouting or breakin things. An I got a glimpse of the boy he could be, just for that one moment . . . of an energy inside him that, with help, might've been steered towards something positive. But then the next day the Truant Officer brought him home an that was thee end of that. I've never seen that potential a second time from him. Not even a glimpse.

But he's my lad an he's unhappy an he's breaking my heart, he really is. I don't know what to do. Big black holes are waitin for him an I don't know how to keep him away from them, he's gonner fall in. Maybe he fell in ages ago. Them Maguires are bastards, just smaller versions of Bush and Blair an bin Laden and that Thatcher one. There's no difference – all of them, thee all target innocence. Why does He let this happen?

Father Donaghy. I'm goin round to see Father Donaghy an I'm gonner ask him why he thinks God lets innocence be destroyed. An I'm not gonner leave til he's given me a satisfactory answer an then I'm gonner ask him how I can defend meself before Him an then I'm gonner ask him what's gonner happen to that big picture of New York in the Holiday Inn foyer, the one I have to polish every day, the one with them big buildings that don't exist any more, the one with the hidden hole. Cos all these things need answers, an I can't do it by meself, can I? No. No one can. Daft to even think otherwise.

ALASTAIR

Where where where where where
  WHERE
  Ow to find two neds in a city fuller fuckin neds when every second ned looks like the neds I'm after . . .
  where the friggin hell
  needle in a fuckin haystack, lar, no lie, no mess . . . how'm I supposed to find em . . . little twats could be friggin anywhere . . .
  But:
  Find em. Then money. Then return. Then laugh at Darren freakin fuckin out cos he's back to square fuckin one. *Then:*
  Then
  ?
  Worry about it *then* . . . just now do what yer know yer've gorrer fuckin do . . . deal with this, man . . . sort it fuckin out . . .
  First time in yer life man this this this this *thing* . . . what is it . . . just avin this fuckin *thing* to do . . . nowt else just this *thing* to do . . .
  . . . ow me ed . . . pure *bangin* man . . .
  but this *thing* this *thing* I've got this *thing*
  d'yeh know wharrit is I'm . . . I'm what . . .
  what if she's dead? Thee ahl queen that cunt hit with thee ammer, what if she's carked it? What then?
  I
  don't fuckin know
  just know that this *thing*
  I've

got this *thing*

got this *thing* to do.

DARREN

I'm norra bad guy. No way. Know some people think I am, like, but I'm norra bad guy *rerly*. I've just adter do bad things sometimes, to defend meself an get what's mine by rights, like, an live the way I wanner live I've sometimes adter do some bad things.

But I've never wasted anyone as far as I know but if what I'm suspectin terns out to be true then that Alastair one is dead. Pure fuckin *dead*, lar. No lie. Cunt's a corpse.

Only one werd for this shit: **BETRAYAL.** Sums it up, that one werd. No two ways about it, lar, that Ally is one betrayin twat an that's that.

Gorra keep calm, tho. Just calm it down, like, think it through. Lose it an yer'll get nowt done, end up locked up an that Judas cunt'll be walkin around laughin. That *cunt*. Laughin. Fuckin laughin at me walkin round with his swag an I was gunner buy me ma a prezzie with that swag cos thee ahl queen's been on a lowey lately about summin, just dead sad aller time like, an I was gunner buy her a prezzie to cheer her up a bit like, but that twat Alastair has fucked all this he's

all me fuckin plans, man − fucked over − battered − smashed in bits this ain't fuckin right it ain't fuckin *right*

betrayal

Thee. Werst. *Thing* yeh could ever do to anyone is stab em inner back like this, graft with em an then

157

nick all the swag. Like that gobshite Colm who did the runner with Joey's droogs, meant to be livin some-where in Wales now. Or that Belfast musher Gillespie who T managed to track down an is now fertilisin a field on the Wirral somewhere an that's gunner happen to that Alastair that thievin bastard that Judas that fuckin

calm down yerself

don't lose it lad keep it togeth

BETRAYALBETRAYALBETRAYALBE-TRAYALBETRAYALBETRAYAL

shame and

some fuckin shame

he's fuckin well *dead*, man. I kid you not that twat is *dead*.

JAPANESE TOURIST

Ai!

OLD LADY

Gah! Me ankle! Jesus Mary Mother an Joseph God an all the saints me ankle!

LENNY REECE

Surprised at Tommy I yam, see. Never seen him this upset I haven't an I'm surprised cos *he's* surprised; I mean, could he not have seen this coming? Didn't he *know* that at some point a feller like Darren would rip him off? It's happened before, many times, so why's he gettin so hot an bothered *this* time? It's not because

Darren's a slimy stoat scally who yew carn trust as far as yew can throw him but simply because yew carn trust *anybody*, an I'm shocked that T doesn't seem to know that. I mean, that's why I entered this game in the first place, see, cos I knew from an early age that the world was all dog eat dog, all betrayal, all survival of the fittest like, an looking arfter number one so what was-a point then of joining it? That's what I asked myself; why join-a workforce, like, the rat race, when with the right kind-a backing an-a gun I could make a life for meself in whatever way I wanted to? Which is why I'm *yur*, now, having me ear barked off by Tommy on-a mobile:

—I mean it's the fuckin lack of trust that herts, Len, know wharram sayin? I mean I gave them blerts a cushy number to keep em sweet, like, a jaunt inter Wales, piecer piss, fuckin day out rerly, likes, an I find out thee've binned the fuckin motor I gave em an screwed a fuckin postie without tellin me. Without even friggin *askin* me, likes. Just went n did it off theer own backs an thee weren't even gunna give yours truly a cut, weren't even gunna fuckin *tell* me about it. Believe this shit, Len? Can't fuckin *believe* it, me, no lie. Notten down for cunts like that, is thee? Notten fuckin *down* for them, lar.

I make a tutting noise. —Shockin, Tommy. What's wrong with these people, eh?

—You *know* it, man. Summin's gone dead wrong somewhere along the line, like, too fuckin right. I mean, didn't I always treat em proper? Avn't I always fuckin done *well* by em? An *this* is how thee pay me back. Bein taken for a cunt, I am, Lenny. Tellin yeh, these little gets don't half need a lesson in fuckin manners, like. No –

Lie. —T, I'm entering the underground now, see, so me mobile's about to go dead. What do you want me to do, here?

—Well I want yeh to fuckin well. You in a *bar*, lad?

—No, no, I told yew, I'm at James Street underground. Tell me what yew need me to do, mun, an I can get straight on it.

He tells me to find Darren. Find Darren! In a city that contains a hundred bloody thousand Darrens!

—Will do that, Tommy. Carn promise anything, like, but I'll do me very best.

—Aye an when yeh do yeh bring the cunt here an am gunner fuckin –

—Signal's gone, Tommy. Yewer breaking up. Later.

I close my phone and put it back in me pocket an gesture at-a barmaid for another pint-a dark. As she's pourin it she asks me where I'm from an I tell her an she tells me that her mother's from-a same area.

—Oh aye? So yur's some Welsh in yew, then?

She nods. I smile. Wonder if she wants any more.

Chat to her for a bit then she goes off to serve somebody else, a Taylor clone; tracksuit tucked into-a socks, all-a sovereign rings. Never goin-a find him around yur, am I? Might as well look for a specific pigeon; thousands-a them too an they all look exactly-a bleedin same as well. Altho Tommy did say that Darren's been given a dig by them two other scallies who came round to see him, trying-a set up some sort-a coke deal, so Darren'll probably have a few bruises or somethin, providin ey were tellin-a trewth which of course is doubtful in itself. Yur's no honesty in people any more, if yur ever was; lying, deception, it's a condition of exis-tence now, see. It was a shock at first like, cos, bein brought up in-a countryside like, yur is no lying; every-thin an everyone is just out-an-out brutal. No sneakin around or games-playin like, it's just eat or be eaten, all out in-a open, see, not hidden. But yew get used to people bein sneaky an it doesn't take long before yew realise to look *under* an *behind* what people're tellin yew, cos on-a surface, it's never-a trewth. An why Tommy's all upset by that revelation baffles me, mun. I mean has he always trusted Darren? Has he never entertained-a notion that Darren or someone else just like him would rip him off, first chance he got? This might mean, shockin as it may seem like, this might mean that Tommy, even, has somethin inside him that's offended by human snakey-ness. Or no, forget that, mun; all it means is that Tommy needs a sense of what, indignation, he *needs* to feel righteously insulted so that when he gets out-a pliers or-a Stanley knife he can feel justified. Morally vindicated, see. *That's* what it's called.

Jeez, these papal pagans and eyr twisted, twisted morality. An yur's me among em with my own Methodist jihad. Next time yur's a home game at Anfield or Goodison I'll hijack the sky-camera blimp an float it into Paddy's wigwam. Just float it on to-a spikes, all gentle. No one'd be hurt an even I, suicide hijacker, would probably get out safe n sound if I climbed careful down-a fireman's ladder. *That's*-a way to do it. See, Osama? No need to cause all that pandemonium, is there, now? Just make a bit of a fool-a yewerself, that's all it takes. The futile gesture, mun – us boyos are used to that, see. An that's all everything is, in-a end, innit?

I finish me pint an leave-a pub, turn left up towards-a city proper. Now where is a nasty piece-a dark-hearted work like Darren Taylor likely to be? Pub, crackhouse, brothel, church . . . that's narrowed it down to several bleedin thousand, that's all. But I'll find him, I *know* I will; the sun's beamin down on me today, I can *feel* it, mun, even through-a drizzle. Luck's name is Leonard. But first: *food*. I can smell onions. Yur's one-a them burger kiosks round-a corner, if I remember right. That'll do for me, mun.

ALASTAIR, HIS GRANDMOTHER KATE

Someone   is someone there?
Who is there?   Pwy sy' yna?

A shadow . . . a voice
Cysgod

One of those men those men with the wounds those blasted children arms gone legs gone minds gone no hope for them no hope
   dim gobaith dim gobaith
   I cleaned them
   I washed them
   Helped them cope those poor ruined men

Back to

Nain

162

Nain?

Who's there?

eira

eira

mynyddoedd

My leaving I   left

I ate   liver
they gave me   liver
to eat they   gave me   iau

Pool   pwll

Alastair my grandson is that you?
My lost child is that you?
Are you

here I

angen   ANGEN

Alastair?
I cannot hear you my boy
I cannot hear you

through this

163

hiraeth

in me it kills me it hurts me it is destroying me

hiraeth

Alastair are you here to wash my wounds to rub
cream into my inflamed stumps to help me help me
sing again remember like I helped you no you were

in *this* war

dros y mor

My children *all* my children floating drifting *cut*
from me
You leave
you have gone
You

mynyddoedd

they burst in my head

eira ar Eryri

it's falling in my breast

ANGEN

No pain at last

Alastair my grandchild
have you gone

have you eaten   iau

Like me
don't go you   should never have gone

            because

back again
you can't
can never   go
                 I will
                 go

                 Gadael

                 Rwyf wedi blinon lan
                 aaaaahhhhhhh
                 nawr
                 aaaaahhhhhhh

                 and none
                 there is no shame
                 no shame
                 in leaving

165

Some small augmentation now to this city's sense of rage and shame and although it cannot be witnessed swimming in the oily harbour pools or prowling the roof like one of the feral felids that are a further secret populace of this conurbation it is nonetheless here. Not in any acceleration or deceleration of the general pace of living nor in any inflective altering of the collective voice if such a hubbub polyglot and motley, pidgin and patois could ever be encapsulated in such a term but nonetheless here it is. Devoid of tangibility or immediacy maybe it can be located in some incipience that hangs like a stormcloud or smog in a coming perturbance, in the individual lives that are yet to be startled in some specific way and which move at the moment unknowing and thus in a bliss of some sort, universal if acknowledged but since it never is then scarce-seen, lurking rarefied in these individual lives. Maybe something of it in the chance splat of the raindrop on the pecking pigeon's head and in the sudden flight of that dirty bird from the gutter and the startling of the Japanese tourist and in his flinching and his accidental striking of the mother with the pram and in the toppling of that pram and the spillage of shopping but not child and the overlooked tangerine and, later, the old lady's foot which will squash that fruit on the slippery sidewalk and which will buckle and maybe in the weakened decalcified ankle bone that will snap. And maybe then in the citizen who will stop and administer and the ambulance driver and the concerned family members who will gather at hospital bedside and so on and so on and so on and maybe in such a causal chain unheeded and unstated, maybe only in its waiting-to-happen, maybe only in the falling raindrop and the as-yet-undisturbed city bird pecking in the gutter at a discarded kebab are such tiny additions detectable; these new sparks of rage and shame located as yet only in the what-is-to-come, the what-will-be.

And, too, there is something else. Something that can be seen in propulsion, in matters of striding, in a notion of happiness even bound as that term is to ideas of determination and purpose and goal and aim. In a sense of something to do. In the eternal perversity that drives the heart through and between the diurnal traffic and that which appears desultory and often is on some level beneath the need for bread or attire because how can the way be possibly lit by a purpose that remains unknown? How can the route through a plan be followed if its architecture was drawn up in a language arcane? Or if the training of a light upon it casts only a deeper, blacker shadow?

Darren moves from pub to pub, and does not drink in any. In each, there are surreptitious glances at the discolorations and scabs on his face and the stitches in his scalp but his eyes are seldom met and in every bar he stands among the seated drinkers with his big bruised head pivoting on his big neck like a predator seeking prey. Twice he is asked by bar staff who he is looking for but on each occasion he merely shakes his head and leaves the pub and moves on to the next one to be ticked off on his mental itinerary, a list of the places where Alastair might be. One of these is Ye Cracke.

The barman recognises his face, even under the blueness and blackened blood. He's seen it many times before. Heeds the mental alarm bells that clatter in his head but does not ask anything of Darren, only keeps one eye on him as one of the old men who daily gather in the corner by the beer-garden door, the old feller with the limp and the cane, shouts him over:

—Hi, Darren! C'meer, son!

Darren goes to him.

—Alright, Grandad.

—Jeez, lad, what happened to the face? Battlin again, av yeh?

This old man pushes a stool away from the table with his cane and Darren sits down on it and shrugs.

—Ah, y'know, Grandad. Just some gobshites in town, like, that's all. Too many of em.

—Oh aye?

—Aye, yeh. Two against one, like. Did me best like but . . . adder friggin pool cue, one of em.

Darren shrugs again. The old man's faded blue eyes drift over the beaten face of his grandson and the pupils are as black as the Guinness that rises to touch the thin bloodless lips that slowly sip. He replaces the pint on the table top and shakes his head sadly and in disgust.

—Two against one, ye say? Tooled up n all? Ach,

friggin cowards. Nowt down for them types. If there's one thing I can't stand it's –

—Shite-arse spineless bastards, Grandad, yeh, I know. Yer've said before.

—Aye, well, you watch out for them toerags, son. Only look after themselves, like, an don't give two fucks who else might suffer as a consequence. Cowards. Human race's fuller them, lad. See, in the war, we –

—Ah, Grandad, I'm rushed off me friggin feet. Don't av the time right now.

—Oh aye, well? What is it yer've got to do that's so important that yeh haven't got the time for yer ahl grandad? Not gunner be around much longer an yer'll regret it then, won't yeh?

—I'm lookin for someone. And indeed Darren's eyes do now scan the bar. —Got somethin to sort out, likes.

Who?

—Alastair.

—That dopey sod, always wearing the cap?

—That's him, yeh. Seen im?

—Not for a few weeks, no. Last time I saw *him* he was with you in the Caledonian.

A plangent chord rings out. A band is setting up on the long bench beneath the big mirror; fiddle, bodhrán, squeeze box, acoustic guitar, penny whistle and gob-iron. Warm-up notes ring and wheeze and tootle in the smoke-strata'd air.

—Yeh, well, knob'ed's gone AWOL. Need to find him soon as.

—Ach, you've got time for a pint, sure. Yer mother's been askin about yeh, worried sick she is. Cheer her

169

up a wee bit if I can tell her I shared a glass with yeh, won't it? Surely yeh not so busy that ye can't share a pint with yer grandad, by fuck.

Darren sighs and rubs a hand across his face then winces and sucks air as he irritates a tender spot beneath his eye. The old man opposite him, he is of his blood. The old man opposite him still limps from a wound suffered when fighting overwhelming odds, a fight which he seems to recall sharply and clearly because he has recounted it to Darren in tremendous detail and often enough so that Darren could tell the tale too. The old man opposite him and who is of his blood, he fought his way hand-to-hand out of an irrigation ditch in France into which a shellburst had blown him and armed only with a pistol and a knife and an entrenching tool and trying to protect his old school-mate Ernie Riley who sadly died of his wounds. The old man opposite, he has seen and done things at the furthest extremes of human experience. He is of the rarest breed of men and also of his blood. The closest thing to a hero Darren has ever encountered and something of what drives him and has driven him through the shocks and horrors of the world successfully for nearly eighty years in some wise must drive Darren too.

—Aye, go on then, Grandad. I could merda a Guinness.

—Good boy.

The old man shouts to the barman and holds up two fingers, lumped and warty and arthritically crooked of knuckle and with deep orange nicotine discolorations at the tips. The barman nods and pours the pints.

—Have ye eaten, son?

—Nah.

—Could yiz go a ham roll?

—Nah, yer alright, Grandad. Guinness'll do.

—Pint of the black soup, eh?

—Yeh.

Without counting in and thus seemingly of telepathic timing precise and coordinated completely the band launch into a reel, a frantic swirling tune which instantly into this quiet mid-afternoon fuggy pub injects a note of hysteria or rather concretises the hysteria that constantly hovers in such places, in the grey layers of smoke that hang and drift and the sets of boots and trainers on the dusty floor or bar rail and certainly the contours of the faces that confront alcohol with aggression, isolated as they are and must always be from the sun and traffic both human and mechanical that blares beyond the windows of frosted glass. The lifting loops and movements of this music expanding then contracting and repeating themselves more frenzied with each fevered recalled phrase jabbers of the ditch and drink and desperation it was born in like a secret tongue concocted subterranean or in some other place where the sanctioned thief could never reach between sweating stone or sap-bubbling branch, any place where steam might gather both surrounding and enervated by the heart heated by all defiance and insistent in its relentless hypnosis of the reaching blood. Behind sockets and sterna such common force could stamp itself on the indifferent world only in this one unique expression and its high-tensile resistance, each instrument fluent and conversant with the next in this language alien to the human tongue yet familiar to and in fact borne over in many breasts, able to reflect the landscape it leaps from even if that be smoke-yellow ceilings and booze-stained wood and torn cushion, providing these brush against the tingling skin and the gulping eye. Only that these bellies have sifted a hundred hungers and found one they can accommodate, that the hearts are aware that the staying of their pain will be brief and fleeting, only until each instrument and the fleshy hands and throats that draw such huge sounds from them will dwindle and fall mute.

—D'yeh like the reel, Darren?

—Aye, Grandad, yeh. It's sound.

—In '45 I was demobbed with a bunch of Irish fellers over in Galway. Stayed there months, I did, *months*. Loved it, me. Learnt to play the banjo. Bet yeh didn't know I could play thee ahl banjo, did yeh?

—News to me.

—Aye, well, there's a packet of things yeh don't know about me, lad.

—Bet there is, Grandad.

Darren drinks his Guinness quickly and orders two more and hears the old man's voice like glass against glass in his ear, behind the music. And further behind it there is Alastair and those two fucking neds and vengeance like a hooded shade with spread vulture wings and behind that further still is a thing burning hot and blood red but as long as the music leaps and frantics and the old warrior who is of his blood continues to growl words Darren can drown it, let it momentarily fade like the throb of pain in his bruised face and scalp split and stuck. Can, while his head is otherwise engaged, convince himself that there is no shame here, in this mid-city pub on a weekday early afternoon, among these people of courage and defiance, no shame whatsoever. Little fucking scallies just caught him unawares, that's all. Bushwhacked him from behind, like. Little fucking cowards. They'll get it. Like all cowards the world over, as the old man says, they'll get fucking *theirs*.

The music must stop, eventually. It always does. But Darren'll be up and moving long before then.

Alastair needs a piss. There's a growing pressure in his bladder as if in there a fist is slowly clenching. He's not bursting yet but he's getting there and as he walks down Rice Lane and past Ye Cracke he hears an Irish jig start up suddenly inside and considers availing himself of the toilets in there but reasons that it will probably be dead busy and the two fucking neds, that Robbo and Freddy they call themselves, won't be in there because Ye Cracke doesn't have a pool table and they seemed big big fans of the game when he first met them in Lime Street Station bar. That and betrayal, oh fuck yeh, big frigging fans of *that* as well. Little pair of shites. Probably down Bold Street now spunking the entire wedge on trainees and fucking anoraks but not for bleeding long, oh fuck *no*.

He exits Rice Lane, traverses the cobbles on to Hardman Street where outside the ten-til-ten offy he gets begged on four times and God he thinks these *must* be frigging desperate if they're asking *me* for odds. Do I *look* like I've got any spare change, lar? He passes

St Luke's, destroyed sixty years ago by *Luftwaffe* bombs and left as a charred shell to commemorate that war and in the grounds of its blackened wreckage just beyond the padlocked gates some stela has been erected, a tall upright monolith attached to which is an empty bowl, monument to those who died in the Great Hunger and too to those who fled from that wasting many of whom washed up on these shores here and built the railways and the waterfront and also places of worship like this one now devastated, a scorched hulk central to this city of many edifices flame-gutted alike although not all at Nazi hands. 'An babhla folamh' are the words carved into this standing stone above the empty bowl which to Alastair has always looked horribly, howlingly empty, a terrible void that never fails to make his stomach groan whenever he passes it. Sometimes the sky will fill it with slimy rain and it then becomes a birdbath for sparrows and starlings and pigeons and other city birds but for the most part it remains empty adjacent to the charred church hollowed by flame and sprouted around by large flowering shrubs through which once drifted the attenuated shapes of junkies jacking up until for a reason recondite and known only to their peculiar migratory instincts they moved to the gardens of the Anglican cathedral, the spire of which can be seen skyscraping over the burnt twin of St Luke's like an overlord, a terrible perpetual reminder of this world's wrecking whims.

Alastair remembers the unveiling of the empty-bowl monument. Remembers Mary Robinson getting out of the limo, and all the cheering crowds. And remembers too her phalanx of bodyguards, big fridge-like men in overcoats with cropped hair and reflector shades and gun bulges. They were dead cool, he thought. Dead friggin don't-mess-with-me-cunt. He'd like to be one of them.

He crosses the road on to Renshaw Street and sticks his head around the door of the Dispensary but sees only old men and a pool table unattended and slanting beams of diluted light and he intends to cut across on to Bold Street to check the greater number of pubs and caffs there but the need to urinate is now urgent so he veers into the Egg, climbs the narrow stairwell plastered with flyers for bands and plays and readings and squeezes through the thin doors into the caff proper where ah good fuckin Jesus there's a *poet*. He's between Alastair and the toilets, standing there before a small audience single figures and going on in a poncey non-local voice about 'savers' or something, some such shite. About 'wanting whisky' or something. Ally shifts from foot to foot, not wanting to disturb this reader embarrassing as he is or indeed expose himself to the audience small as it is but it's no good, he's gunner pee his kex, so he darts across between the poet and his audience and hears a sudden silence broken only by a tut and a snigger and can feel eyes on him but fucks to that he's in the bogs and his knob is out of his trackies he's letting it all out steaming, relief.

Aaaaahhh.

Shakes off, washes his hands. Thinks about waiting in here for the poet to finish but that might take ages and he's got important stuff to do so he leaves the toilets and re-enters the caff. The poet's now saying something about a frigging *bee* or something for God's sakes and as Alastair reappears he gets caught on one word stuttering:

—I, I, I, I . . .

Eyes again on Alastair. Oo such disapproving eyes in a soft groomed face scar-free and creaseless a face in which the fiercest thing that has ever resided is a perverse desire for more worse hurt. Alastair addresses it:

—The fucker *you* lookin at, knob'ed? Fancy a photograph, do yeh?

The poet sniffs. —What am I looking at? Evidently someone without the manners and bladder control to wait for me to finish.

This amuses Alastair. He laughs loudly and leaves the caff shaking his hatted head in humoured bemusement at the people of this world and their forever estranging ways and turns left on to busy Bold Street and checks out several emporia thereon, pubs and bars and caffs and also the shops selling designer clothes and shoes because truly where else if not such places would a pair of teenage scallies suddenly monied possibly be.

At the bottom of Bold Street by the side entrance to Central Station a swaying beggar is being addressed by two policemen. One of these officers looks a lot to Ally like one of those who gave him a wellying in the Copperas Hill bridewell some time ago although he does not recall much about that night nor indeed since it of his life before, not in any great detail any more, no, not really. As he draws level Alastair stares hard into this officer's face and is met by pebble eyes and a muzzied smirk which might mean that he *is* one of Alastair's assailants or might just as easily mean that he *isn't*, Ally isn't sure. He doesn't with any certainty know. Only that there is a knotty fibrous lump on his skull beneath the skin and he has headaches with a greater frequency and of greater pain than before, just that.

Fuckers. Fuckin bizzies. Bad, bad scallies, no lie.

He moves on through the city. Sock-tucked shelly and basey and shaven skull beneath that and stubble and blue eyes and ears like satellite dishes on each side of his head, no different from a thousand others yet unique in his stride and purpose although many others round-about seek money too and also revenge. In many faces he sees Darren's unyielding glare and that spurs his steps down on to Matthew Street and into all the bars there and through the tourists milling around the Beatles Experience and up then into the business district and down past Ma Boyle's and on to the Dock Road and along that thoroughfare until he re-enters the city via Chinatown and there is no Robbo, no Freddy, although there are very many of their sort. Drizzle has yet again begun to hang and drift and at the sides of hissing roads people gather in doorways and bus stops and under brollies and St Luke's reappears again rain-darkened, fallen timbers akimbo through the glassless webs of the windows and giant-leaved plants deeply green and visible through those holes and the entire thing hulked and harmed and scorched and steaming and apocalyptic, this ever-present ruin bellowing of wreckage among the unheeding human commerce about.

Drifting Alastair, yet how he drifts with one purpose, that purpose becoming need. Need becoming desperation. Fucking Darren. That hammer. That old lady falling. Fucking two little scallies Robbo and Freddy they call themselves can't trust anyone these days man no lie. Whole world's falling apart.

Mid-afternoonish, he finds himself at the hospital. He is tired and pissed off and gritting his teeth against futility and the attendant frustration. He is thinking about extinction and has been doing so for some time so he stands in a bus shelter away from the rain and smokes a cigarette and then enters the hospital into a too-high disinfectant heat and retraces the route he has taken many times before, along corridors and up several flights of stairs as if seeking a destination made deliberately difficult to reach, this hot scoured warren seemingly designed by a race of mortals agog to deny or at least hide that which makes them so. As he nears his destination he starts to smell it again, coppery rot, a ferric morbidity and if this is mere fancy or otherwise he cares not either way because he can smell it, *smell* it, he always can.

A nurse stops him. A big woman with a kindly face despite the hairy wart on her upper lip like a beauty spot in negative. Her name tag says: WENDY MURRAY RGN.

—Can I help you? You look a bit lost.

—No, I'm sound. I know the way. Just looking for me granny.

—D'you mind telling me her name? Sorry to have to ask but y'know. Can never be too careful these days.

Alastair gives a name and the nurse gives a small smile.

—Oh yes, Katie? She's down on the left in Ward H.

—I know, yeh.

—She's asleep at the moment, I think. Try not to wake her. She's over a hundred years old, you know. You should be proud. Did she get a telegram off the Queen?

—Erm . . .

—Well, be gentle with her. She, erm, she hasn't been quite with us for the last few weeks . . .

Alastair nods. Comprehends fully the world in which his granny lives now and has done for some time and can almost grasp how torn and scrambled it must be in her head. Spatial, temporal, shredded and dispersed. Can almost imagine how blasted everything must get after passing through the sharkskin desiccation of such old ears, such old eyes.

He thanks the nurse and squeaks down the corridor to Ward H. Skeletons in beds with candyfloss hair. Eyes implore through rheum and some colourless sunken lips attempt to smile, one or two to speak. One withered hand like a fistful of driftwood twigs reaches towards him out of a nightie sleeve hanging loose.

The end bed. Kate. His grandmother.

THUNK.

Christ she looks old. Not surprising; she was born in nineteen friggin hundred or something like that. Aye but she's always seemed ancient anyway cos she was dead late having Ally's mum but fuckin hell she was always there for him and she fed him he would've starved if it wasn't for her cos the mother was never out of the bleedin pub. Aye and Katie'd drink too often to excess but when bevvied she wouldn't hit Alastair she'd hold him she was always there when he was sad and the stories she'd tell about being in service for the rich people in Toxteth when that place was wealthy and the hospitals she worked in looking after war victims *both* world wars no arms legs eyes ears faces minds some of them. God the life

God the fucking *life*

—Nan? Nan? Can yeh hear me, Nan?

The shut eyelids do not twitch or flicker much less open. Alastair takes her hand very gently, feels it just tepid with what wanes within it and the skin like the fibre of his tracksuit, somewhat satiny, unmoist. Feels the faint pulse in it as if a separate life more animate is ensnared there, a smaller yet mightier animal kicking to be free with the final scrap of its strength.

—Nan? It's me, Alastair. Can yeh hear me?

THUNK.

That bastard. That evil bastard.

God her *face*. All her hard history written in this face, life with its razors and the harrowing of years. And, at her birth, say we were presented with an itinerary of her life to come, a blueprint for the years ahead and told that this is how it will be for her, this is the pattern her life will take; would it not appear utterly unbearable? We'd think no, surely, one person cannot take that much anguish. Any one person does not deserve that much pain. And seem it must as a pre-planned scheme to wreck a life with suffering and reel we would at the cruelty and the record that nor is this unique. That this begins to hover an inch below the ceiling at the moment of the click of the first formed zygote. And any response alternative to mere endurance would be favoured completely but that is all this carapace mudbent and moribund immediately has.

Alastair bites his lip.

—Nain?

Soft but instant response. Eyelids flutter and the pulse seems to quicken and does the handskin warm or is that merely the fancied wish of the scally who clasps that hand.

—*Nain?*

The lips part with a delicate rip, almost undetectable. A word escapes:

—Eira.

And then another:

—Mynyddoedd.

Words which Alastair does not clearly hear but he feels them on his face as the gentlest breeze or as the soul departing a minute life, a songbird, say, or a skink. A cold and bare whispered drifting like the breath of ryegrass or animus of ice.

He holds her hand a touch tighter then releases it and stands to leave. He sees the tiny rise and fall of her sunken chest beneath the bedclothes and sees her eyelids ripple as she dreams and would stay longer, perhaps to fathom those dreams or at least attempt to, but there are things of huge importance that he is compelled to do.

THUNK.

That bastard.

Leave here, Alastair, and rejoin the city, move among those with life enough able still to betray. Pure got to *find* that fucking money, lad.

*   *   *

—Onions on that, love?

—Yeh, loads.

—Eeyar. One sixty please, love.

—Ta.

—Mustard there if yeh wannit. Or red sauce.

Squeeze. Ketchup leaves the nozzle with a wet red fart.

Bite, chew, swallow. Stay under the awning out of the drizzle keep yourself and your hunger dry. Bite. Oh and fuckin look at that; tomato sauce all over the shelly. Bastard.

—What can I get yeh, love?

—Cheeseburger please. With onions. And a cup of oh hello there Darren. Fancy meeting *yew* here.

FUCK. —Lenny.

—Been lookin for yew, I yav.

—Oh aye? Why's that, well?

God he looks big this Lenny. Bigger than he usually does. That leather coat buttoned up across his chest and them buttons about to ping off.

Drum of rain on the awning.

—Cracking shiner that is, mun. Nose looks chipped an all if yew don't mind me saying and how many stitches did they put in yewer noggin?

Bite, chew, swallow. Don't answer this Welsh bastard. Enough left of the burger and it still hot enough to stuff into this fucker's smiling face and –

—Tommy wants a word, Darren. Quick as yew can finish yewer dinner ey an let's go see him, aye?

—Don't think so, Lenny, no.

—What?

—Pure *is* not gunner happen, lar, me goin to see T

with youse. *Is* not gunner fuckin happen. I'm just gunner eat me berga likes an then I'm gunner –

—Two pounds please, love.

—Thankyew.

—Ta.

— . . . go lookin for that fuckin Alastair an then am gunner –

Lenny takes his cheeseburger in one hand, removes the top half of the bread roll with the other and rams the steaming meat and melted cheese and fried onions into Darren's bruised face. Darren roars and the woman in the serving hatch yells about taking it elsewhere and Lenny spins Darren so that he can clutch him backwards to his chest and apologises to the woman and bundles the bellowing Darren away towards the cab rank opposite the Hanover Arms just a matter of yards away.

—Me eyes! It's in me friggin *eyes* yeh cunt!

Lenny locks Darren's wrists together behind his back in one big hand. Darren's wounded scalp fills his vision, the glued slit like a slash of bared bone across the blue patch shaved bald. Shoppers stare then look away quickly and rain falls. Darren bellows about cutting Lenny up. Lenny smells onions and melted processed cheese coming off his captive's head and reflects on how hungry he is. Waste of a good bastard burger, that. Two quid n all.

Rain falls.

—Al fuckin *merda* yeh yeh fuckin cunt al fuckin –

—Okay now, shut the gob. People're looking. Just accept it, Darren mun. Tommy only wants a quick word, that's all, see.

—Al rip yer fuckin face off cunt al fuckin –

—Aye, yeh, am sure yew will, mun. Yur we go now, nice an quiet, ey?

He scans the street for prowling police and sees none then scans the taxi rank for a tame cabbie and sees one, big silver head, and marches shackled Darren over the road through honking fuming traffic and bundles him into the taxi without releasing his wrists.

The cabbie regards them in the rear-view mirror with some alarm. —Aw, Lenny, wharrer yeh tryna do to me, lad? Get me inter fuckin trouble, you.

With one hand Lenny grabs Darren's nape and forces his head down between his knees. Muffled roars, arms flailing. With the other Lenny digs some notes out of his jacket pocket and passes them through the hatch.

—Stop yewer skriking, Shirl. Buy yewer missus something nice on-a way home.

—Yeh but for fuck's sakes, Lenny. Mean ter say, like. Droppin me in the shite here you are. The taxi edges out into the traffic. —Out of order this, lar. Where am I takin yiz, anyway? Tommy's gaff?

—The office, aye. Quick as yew can, like.

—In *this* fuckin traffic? Jokin, aren't yeh?

Lenny looks out at the city behind the windows running with greasy rain. Bent-double Darren has ceased thrashing but continues still to roar, a muffled voice rising up from somewhere near the vehicle's floor. The rage rising off his hunched back and cut skull smells to Lenny somewhat appetising.

The mug of tea Alastair ordered is growing cold but he's not going back to his table in *this* state, no way, not with this water running down his battered face. Crying like a fucking babby, man. Disgrace this is. Got his face in his hands and his shoulders are shaking and he's gritting his teeth to dampen the sobs so that the other visitors to this toilet won't be able to hear him. Fucking sad. Fuckin blubbin away here what kinda man Jesus Christ how the fuck are yeh ever gunner —

Mountains and lakes and he was a child once and so was she more of a mother than his own frigging mother who is now where? So old so old like that and the words she whispered that voice like a ghost itself that body almost broken who she is and the THUNK of that hammer and the fall and crack of the pool cue on skull and the screaming in his head and the blackness and nowt goes right nothing ever goes right he's tryna only fucking tryna gorrer get that fuckin money back gorrer fuckin gerra grip stop this stop this it's all fucked up the *mess* we're in how the fuck do we how do we ah Jesus friggin Christ what is wrong here it's all gone wrong when will it ever

get a fuckin *grip*

get a fuckin *grip* man

Sobbing Alastair who weeps as a child weeps, in the delusion that their tears can ever alter anything. In the hope forlorn and fatuous that all external assault may cease in the flood of shed and stinging brine as if their waters are uncommon, scarce enough to startle, as if rare enough to arrest. As if as if as if as if

He delves in his pocket and pulls out a bunch of keys. With the tip of one of them he starts scratching in the paint of the cubicle door, more words among the many already scored in or scrawled on, those legends scraped and scribbled he now adds to:

DARREN TAYLOR SUCK'S BIG COCKZ

DARREN TAYLOR LIKES IT MMM UP THE SHITTA

FUCK ALL YOUSE ARSE-BANDITS

DARREN TAYLOR IS FUCKEN DEAD

And maybe writing that last will make it happen. Draw it down from the leaking sky a spell a promise a a a a

Alastair again, back out in the city, searcher in a shell suit, quester in a cap. The water now on his afflicted face only from above and not any more from within, yet shared of salts it is and of a similar mineral consistency, the drizzle without, this drizzle within. With face upturned he tastes it and whether from that one-cloud sky or dreg from reddened eye he cannot tell, cannot discern any difference. Just this wet and heavy lees that sheens all features alike.

Two figures in the dark back street between warehouse hulks all up until recently deserted and dilapidated yet some now renovated in the last few years. Once they stored cotton and sugar and tobacco and flour and oil and other such staples, stored them in amounts vast and attended by a workforce of similar size, then to lie unused and empty for several decades although some now converted into offices or even living quarters and others still as they have been for many years, shot through with slanting sunlight and inhabited only by pigeon or rat and a few vagabonds who in corners too build nests of rag and shredded paper like their counterparts rodential or avian and like them again survive on the city's leavings and lean on the generosity of the odd few of its denizens. Call these spaces crumbling, cavernous, shot through with slanting sunlight some unusual kind of a home and the ghosts of gone commerce carried by the wind that wails through broken window and subsidence crack, not only the clank of cog and pulley or gabble of a hundred different tongues but also the wailing of those who were broken to build this city's parts, those enslaved, their pulverised bones in the mortar of these storehouses now and their blood in the buried sumps long unused now drying to red scale and the many voices which lift the wind, form the wind that moans and shrieks and draws up from the vast flat empty floors little dancing devils of dust and detritus, fiend-friend and familiar to those souls lost and desolate which roost in the shadows of these high halls.

The drizzle so thin and fine doesn't exactly fall as instead saturate the air. Lenny and Darren stand by a door of reinforced steel and face each other, a few feet of wet air between them.

—You're fuckin *slashed*, Lenny, Darren says. He might as well be remarking on a new jacket that Lenny wears for all the flatness in his tone. —No lie, lar, you are pure fuckin ribboned. Sometime in the future, like. You're fuckin *sliced*, lar.

—Am I?

—Oh aye, yeh. Don't you worry about that, lad.

That fuckin kite o' yours is Stanley'd an that's that. Consider yerself marked.

—Consider meself quakin in me shoes, Darren. Tremblin with fear I yam, see.

—Yeh, you fuckin well *will* be, knob'ed. *No* cunt treats me like this, knowmean?

—How else was I gunner get yew to come? Send out a fuckin invitation is it?

Darren shakes his head. —Don't wanna hear it, lar. You're gunner need a friggin *calculator* to count the stitches *I'm* gunner give yeh.

Lenny laughs. —Ee, yew an that Stanley knife. Like a kiddie with a toy yew are, see. Favourite teddy bear, like. Just can't leave it alone, can yew?

Darren says nothing, just extracts a curl of fried onion from his ear and examines it and flicks it away. Lenny leans and rings for a second time the bell next to the reinforced door and this time hears heavy steps clump along the hallway behind that door and the galumphing tread and woof of a big dog.

The door opens a crack. A Rottweiler's massive head black and beige and jowly snarling sniffs the air. A blue rope around this dog's neck and wrapped around the wrist of Jamie 'Gozzy' Squires, his lop-eyed leer above the tightly buttoned neck of his anorak and his shaved head haloed by the fur-spikes of its collar.

—Oh would yeh fuckin look who it is. He grins at Darren, fixes him with his one good eye while the other one regards the sky. —Got some fuckin explainin to do, you av. Wanner start now, well?

—Fuckin geg out, Gozzy. Al speak to Tommy and

only Tommy. Ain't got werd fuckin *one* to say to youse so just fuckin geg out, will yeh.

—Gerrin. Gozzy pulls the dog to one side to allow Darren and Lenny entrance. Lenny ruffles the dog's huge head as he passes it and leans to whisper endearments in its ear enamoured as he is of large powerful animals and Gozzy leans too to secure the rope lead's D-clip to the collar and for a moment their heads are clustered like that to form one beast three-headed. Three-faced hybrid of human and dog leering all three with bared teeth and tongues aloll at this strengthened threshold.

A swagger on Darren as he walks down the corridor lined each side with boxes of DVD players and Megadrives stacked eight, ten high. Dark corridor this towards a lit portal at the end and through and into this light. Some kind of office with a loud central point of two young women, their big hair and leopard-spotted thigh boots and displayed tan midriffs and made-up faces blaring in Darren's eyes that still sting from hot grease.

Tommy sits between them on a swivel chair. The cheeks of his arse spill out over each side of the seat and in this position he looks like an immense 8 topped with a perm, Rockport boots planted flat and splayed on the floor and chino trousers tucked in. He glances once at Darren with eyes like slate chips pressed into lard and tucks a thick wad of paper money into the breast pocket of his red Kappa jacket and then looks back at the women, his eyes upwards, standing as the women are.

—Right, youse two. Fuck off, well. Get back to work. Money to be made out there.

They leave. One of them glares at Darren as she passes and Darren stares and checks out her arse which she wiggles all exaggerated in more of a fuck *you* than a fuck *me* way. Lenny stands aside to let them pass and smiles at them then looks sort of shyly away. Gozzy just leers one-eyed. Their stack heels clomp down the corridor and the front door opens then slams shut and drabness descends into the room. It is as if a macaw has just exited a bank.

Pugnose Tommy sniffs the air doglike.

—What's that friggin stink? Slike onions.

—It's him, innit, Lenny says, nodding at Darren. —Had to put me burger in his face to get him to come, didn't I?

Glance at Darren. Back at Lenny.

—So yer've ad no dinner, Len?

—Not a bean. Starvin, I yam.

—Get yerself in the kitchen well an knock up a butty or summin. Take Shay Neary with yiz.

Lenny takes the dog by the collar into the adjoining kitchen and closes the door. Tommy spins and stabs something on a computer keyboard and the screen goes blank then he spins back and points a banana finger at Darren.

—You. Fuckin knob'ed there. Sit down.

Darren looks for a chair. There are three but in one is Tommy and in another is Gozzy and in the third in the far corner leaning back against the wall is Jez Sully, hands locked across his belly, steroid-swelled muscles stretching his skintight white polo neck.

—Wharrav I just said, Darren? Sit. Fuckin. *Down*, lad. Are yeh deaf?

Darren sinks on to the dusty floor. Shuffles back so that he leans against the same wall as Sully and so cannot be struck from behind by him or indeed anyone else. Sully regards him amused and side-on as he would a small entertaining animal. Puppy with a plaything, say.

Tommy wheels himself on his chair towards Darren. Castors squeak and he leans, looms like a wave of flesh.

—Two little cunts name of Robbo an Freddy, Darren. Ring any bells?

Very bright, stark light above. Humming fluorescents cast no shadow, expose and illuminate everything.

Darren shakes his head. —None, Tommy.

—Yeh sure?

—Aye, yeh.

—So them fuckin stitches in yer ed an that shiner an that fuckin smack in the nose there, got them fallin down the fuckin stairs, did yeh? Or were yiz fuckin bushwhacked behind Lime Street Station by two lil no-marks names of Robbo and Freddy?

Darren says nothing. Tommy wheels himself back away to a desk topped with a computer terminal with a *South Park* screensaver and opens a drawer and takes out a gun and lays it flat on the mousemat and spins it, spins it. It catches the harsh yellow light on its barrel as it revolves. Tommy's favourite nine-mil, this. Darren has seen it before. Heard it shout, even, and seen what it can do.

—These two lil scallies callin themselves Robbo an Freddy come to see me. Wanner buy a coupla grand's worth of beak, step on it, set themselves up in biz. That's what thee tell me thee wanner do.

Jez Sully laughs. Just one abrupt humourless bark.

—An am thinkin to meself: now where did a pairer blerts like these get ahold of that kinda swag? Jez is thinkin the same, aren't yeh, Jez?

—Yeh. An am also wondrin what's happened to the fuckin *car* youse were given day before yesterdee.

Darren speaks: —I *called* yeh, Tommy. Left yiz a voicemail. Didn't yeh gerrit?

—Not fuckin interested in no fuckin voicemail, lar. Tommy flaps a fat hand. —What I wanner know is where these two little fuckin toerag neds get ahold of *that* kinda dough. Two fuckin grand. Terns out, dunnit, that thee jacked some fuckin pissed-up shite-fer-brains outside Ma Egerton's alehouse cos, an here's the fuckin funny bit, his *mate* told em to. Some dopey twat in a baseball hat, thee said. Know anyone fits that description, Darren?

Flame begins in Darren's stomach. Grinding in his teeth. —Alastair . . .

—That's the one, aye. Dozy cunt in a baseball hat. Accordin to this Robbo lad, or Freddy, whoever the fuck it was, this Alastair one came up to him in the Lime Street Station bar, said he could earn some wedge like, if he jacked the pissed an brain-dead cunt with the fuckin rucksack full of it. Which was *you*, by the way. Said he'd split it with em, like. *Then* it terns out that some postie in North Wales has been screwed an people saw a Morris fuckin Minor at the scene like, an two dick'eds with Liverpool accents an surprise surprise where was fuckin *you* an yer dozy fuckin no-mark *mate* yesterdee? An what fuckin kinda *car* were yiz drivin?

—Yeh, Sully says. —An where's that friggin motor *now*, eh? Fuckin *liked* that car, I did. Classic, like. Pure fuckin quality.

The kitchen door opens. Lenny's there, leaning left shoulder against the jamb, eating a fried-egg sandwich and holding a saucer underneath his chin to catch the drips of brown sauce and runny orange yolk.

—So what I wanner know now, Darren, is this. Tommy scoots on the wheeled chair with shocking speed like a white van pouncing and his big face is suddenly in Darren's the dark eyes wide bright light on dry skin: —WHAT THE FUCK IS GOIN ON HERE, TWAT? WHAT THE FUCK ARE YOUSE UP TO?

Darren's face heated by bad breath and he would recoil but the wall is there against his back and he can see a gun close to him it gulped in Tommy's huge ringed hand but for the barrel a gun a gun: —Fuckin Alastair, Tommy! Tellin you, lar! Nowt to fuckin do with me, man, it's that fuckin Alastair! Believe!

He shows his hands to Tommy, palms out, fingers spread: —Honest to God, Tom! Look! No fuckin fingers crossed, lar! It's that fuckin Alastair!

—Oh, an that Alastair screwed the postie, did he? On his own, like? Yer tellin me that that dozy get –

Squires yells: —Smack him, Tommy! He's windin yer up, lad!

Darren spits words at that voice: —Fuck off you yeh gozzy cunt! Al fuckin –

Choke. Tommy's huge hand, the gunless one around Darren's neck squeezing SQUEEZING the room is abruptly red.

193

—Ey, Tommy . . . c'mon now, mun . . . got to let him speak, first, mun . . .

Lenny's hand on Tommy's arm. The hand opens and Darren gasps and splutters and Jesus Christ some bastard will pay for this shit. Pay for it all, man, no lie.

—Speak, Darren. Quick now, boy, while yew've got the chance.

—Yeh, go on, twat, Tommy sneers. —I'm fuckin *dyin* to hear it, like.

—Alastair, man, Darren wheezes. Breath through his throat like a blade. —That fuckin Alastair . . . I know what happened now . . . that bleedin betrayin *cunt* . . .

Gozzy's voice again: —Whack the divvy, Tommy. Always said he was a fuckin wrong'un, didn't I? Doan need gobshites like that, lar, better off without em. Tellin yeh. Avn't I always said?

Lenny gestures at Squires to shut up. All four faces gather round Darren, leaning leering looming faces without mercy three of them one softer slightly all reflecting the severe yellow light above and washed now in a redness receding.

—Speak, Darren.

—Tell us, lad. Pure cannot *wait* to fuckin know, like.

—It's that fuckin Alastair, man . . . it's *his* doin . . . honest to God . . .

The faces withdraw. Tommy scoots backwards on his chair. —Oh ere we fuckin go. Blah after blah after fuckin blah.

—No, lar, it's true! Tellin yiz! We *both* screwed that postie aye but I was gunner *tell* yiz! Honest! Fuckin *knew* he was up to somethin that snidey get . . .

—Yiz screwed that post office?

Darren nods. One hand encircling, caressing his own neck.

—Both of youse?

—Yeh.

—Without okayin it with me ferst?

—Spur-of-the-moment thing, Tommy. Wasn't friggin planned or anythin, I mean we couldn't find that one-armed bastard, likes, an we were drivin home an saw this postie like, an y'know . . . wasted fuckin trip otherwise, wasn't it?

Tommy grunts. Sully and Squires snort in unison.

—Was gunner tell yeh, Tommy, honest. Honest to fuckin God. *Gorrer* believe me. Jeez, don't yeh always go on at us about fuckin, whatjercallit, fuckin initiative? That's all I was doin, lar. Showin some friggin initiative, man. That's all.

Tommy grunts again. Darren babblecroaks more words, scatters more placating words into the softening air he senses around Tommy. Some minutes later and after a long silence Tommy stands and takes Lenny and Sully into the kitchen and leaves Squires to guard Darren with the nine-millimetre. Voices discussing, mumbling behind that closed door and the gun trained on Darren and Gozzy's smirking face. Darren still on the floor.

—Lovin this, Goz, aren't yeh? Gettin off on this, aren't yeh, you pathetic little terd. Only way to get yer thrills, you. Me unarmed an there's you with the fuckin piece. Wanker.

Squires laughs. —*I'm* the one with the gun, lar. *You're* the one sittin on the deck wither stitched-up ed an onions up yer fuckin nose.

Darren laughs too. —Oh you're gettin it, lad. Yer friggin claimed, Gozzy.

—Just one wee twitch of the finger . . .

—You haven't got thee arse, twat.

—Try me, Darren. Go on, make a fuckin break for the door. I'd pure fuckin *love* yeh to.

Sitting there facing each other just some pistolled air between them and how that air crackles and spits with the weapon in it. Seems to hum. Whether it hums louder and zings tighter for him with the gun or he who is targeted is one mystery which neither could answer. Nor could the miner who drew the metal nor the smithy who shaped it nor he who designed it nor he who built the factory that produced it nor indeed the Bosnian who sold it to the Ulsterman who then sold it on to Tommy's elder brother Joseph and nor Joseph himself even familiar as he is with what guns can do, the breeches in the world and the rifts wrought by them. The horrible consequences of their efficiency.

—Sammy Gallagher, Darren. Remember him? Same thing's gunner happen to you, lar. Saaaaame thing. Whatjer think about that?

Darren does not respond, remembering as he is Sammy Gallagher in silence. Remembering how that man was ironed. Reflecting on how that man can still be spotted in some of the more obscure pubs at the docks or outskirts, sipping Guinness solitary in the pink gleaming patchwork of skin he must live within and dare to bare. Sammy Gallagher and how he screamed and the smell off him of melting fat. *Hiiiiissssssssss.*

Tommy is back in the room. Always disturbed

BOOK THREE

Darkened swirls in his failing vision far above him through and above the burning money falling, softly falling, the little crackle of their flames the only sound except that of the high circling swirls some faint mewling. Birds perhaps or the slashes of life leaving or mere biological imperfections visible now as his bad blood pumps and pools and life leaves but winged they are so birds they are, circling and squealing high overhead or maybe angels come to claim his deserting soul in the taloned and gnashing wise he warrants. Just a few more seconds and he would welcome them. Count to six and embrace them he would, smile maybe as they swoop on to his displayed heart still beating but now slowing, slowing so quickly, time enough please let there be time enough for the winged things from the sky to plummet and remove him from this, the standing staring man with the gun and the small shop behind him and the mountain behind that and this soft seesawing rain of burning money some flakes of which land in the rent cavity of his chest and are doused with a hiss in the blood-puddles there and the still as yet thumping heart, slowing, slowing, those soaring calling winged things above oh please let there be time. Enough.

As if it was meant to be, really, as if some god or other force benevolent to Alastair alone was directing these events. Was looking out for only him. He'd just about given up on searching and was heading back to his nan's house for a smoke and a lie-down and thought he'd go the Upper Duke Street way in case some sexy women came out of the modelling agency there opposite the gates of the Anglican cathedral and indeed one did and he followed her arse over the road to the bus stop and *fuck* if it wasn't one of them little bastard scallies sitting there on the bench in a brand-new Diesel anorak all buttoned up to his spotty chin, that frigging Freddy one. Sitting there like Lord Shite with some kind of frigging smirk on his dial like King of the fucking Kids. He saw Alastair and he was up and running instantly but too late, Ally grabbed him and dragged him into the cathedral grounds and the women at the bus stop both old and young, sexy and unsexy were shouting to leave him alone he's only a kid and Freddy was screaming for help cos he was being mugged, he was being molested and Ally smacked him one on the chin to shut him up and wrestled him through the gates and down the steps and swung him around four times by the hood of his new anorak choking him with the collar and then let go and he bounced off the cathedral wall like an ant against a whale and slipped on the wet moss and Alastair booted him twice and stamped on his thigh to deaden his leg and now here he is crying, holding his leg in both hands, snot from his nose and cack all over his good new duds and Ally's leaning over him like a scavenging bird a rigid finger like a beak in Freddy's damply crumpled face.

—WHERE THE FUCK IS IT, YOU, YER THIEVIN LITTLE GET?! WHERE'S THE FUCKIN MONEY?! TELL ME, KNOB'ED!

—I don't know . . . aw please man it was Robbo he's fuckin hid it somewhere it was his idea anyway he –

Boot. Not a particularly hard one but under the chin so that the teeth clack and the skull thunks back against the cathedral stone.

Clack. THUNK. Ah shite.

Freddy wails.

—I'm sorry, lad, but al friggin do it again you don't tell me where that friggin swag is. I *mean* it. Don't like doing it like but al carry on fuckin doin it until you tell me where you an that fuckin shit'ed no-mark mate o' yours have stashed that fuckin wedge. Unnerstand me?

Wail, wail. Some blood on his lips and blackly grouting Freddy's teeth now and Alastair puts his own face in his own hands then crouches so that their eyes are level. He raps the boy's knee with a knuckle.

—Ey, lad, look at me. Open yer eyes.

Freddy does. Them red and drowned eyes.

—See this? Alastair points at his own face. The markings on it. —See what you an yer mate did to me?

For some reason this makes Freddy wail again and louder. Alastair sighs and stands upright.

—Aw just tell me where the friggin money is, lad, ey? Tell me where it is an al leave yer alone and yer'll never see me again. Simple as. An if yer *don't* tell me where yer've stashed it am just gunner keep on wellyin yer until yer do, alright? It's *that* simple. So what's it gunner be, lar? *Your* choice.

Wail, sob. Bit of pleading, etc.

A voice behind Alastair: —Ey, lad. Birrouta fuckin order, innit eh?

Alastair turns.

—He's only a kid, lar. Leave im alone.

Junkie drawl from the stick-man figure in the shadows underneath a tree not dark enough to obscure his baghead pallor like a sick moon there beneath the hanging branches or jaundiced bauble appended. Alastair bends and picks up a stone and flings it at that shape.

—Fuck off, smack'ed scum! Nonna your friggin business, yeh junkie twat!

The shape dissolves, becomes shadow itself. Ally turns back to the cringing figure at his feet.

—So what's it gunner be, Freddy lad? Yer gunner tell me whereabouts *my* fuckin dough is or am I gunner give yiz a few more digs?

And this played out at the foot of this colossal edifice beginning now to blare with light as dusk comes. Vast shape of stone laid over decades into one pattern of human reaching a world's air contained within and witnessed by the high gargoyles and angel faces carved that only the birds see and can it be said that this trans-action, this withheld pain for money exchange does not belong here or that it somehow constitutes a proximal wrong? That the deep dissatisfaction which oils its motion is somehow inimical to the massive mystery embodied in the enormous surging of stone and glass above it? Or even that those driven by the chemical need in their cells to drift like phantoms through these trees and shrubs and tombstones should in any way be banished by the structure they scurry insectile about? That their arcane rituals and hard longings could ever find a better backdrop than this. There are birds here, gulls and pigeons and sparrows and crows, arising from these darkening gardens to roost for the coming night in unreachable cornice and architrave in the stars beyond danger like nothing but the souls of those who so move seemingly motiveless around at this cathedral's foot and if meaning of the sought-for sort is to be found here then perhaps it is in the being of these creatures to which the sky is skin.

—Right. That's it.

Alastair raises a foot to stamp on Freddy's knee and Freddy screams and jerks his legs up to his chest. Points at a grave some yards away, a crumbling flat sarcophagus on a low plinth.

—What? Wharrer yeh pointin at?

—The fuckin money. It's in there. Doan hit me.

—Where? That grave?

Nod.

—Yer fuckin kiddin me, aren't yeh? It's here? In that grave?

—Yeh.

—I don't fuckin believe yiz. Too good to be true, this, lar. *Show* me.

He yanks Freddy to his feet and leads him over to the grave. A slab has cracked and come away from its partner on the sarcophagus and Freddy moves this to one side and reaches in and extracts a rucksack which he hands to Alastair.

—There. That's all there is left.

Alastair opens the bag. An angled spotlight from the cathedral high, high above drops enough illumination for him to see that there is money inside the bag. Much money.

—Yer happy now? Am fuckin goin.

—Hang on, will yeh.

Alastair grabs the hood of Freddy's new coat.

—Ow much av yiz spent?

—Few hundred quid. Robbo bought a fuckin –

—That's all?

—Aye, yeh. We *was* gunner buy a loader friggin charlie an set arselves up. That was thee idea, like. All fucked now, tho. Thanks to *you*.

Alastair laughs. —Oh, thanks to *me*, is it? *My* fault, yeh? Owjer werk that one out, then? Cheeky friggin . . .

He shakes his head, not without some kind of amused admiration. Putting the blame on him like that. A Tommy in the making, this little scal. A Joey, even. A Willy frigging Hunter. See this sobbing wee get in twenty years' time lording it round the city in a Shogun or whatever the Big Men will be driving by then. Floating around between the buildings in plush Anti-Grav units or their own private monorail trams or whatever the fuck it'll be.

Without letting go of Freddy's hood Alastair drops

the bag and wedges it tight between his feet. Digs in his pocket with his free hand and takes out his mobile phone.

—I'm gunner call someone up an you're gunner tell them that Darren Taylor has ripped them off. Got that? Darren Taylor. What name?

—Darren Taylor.

—Good lad. You're gunner say that Darren Taylor has skanked *all* the money an is gunner buy a shit-load of cocaine an set imself up in biz an he's been calling Tommy Maguire all kinds of dick'ed around the city. Been sayin that he's a big fat poof an everythin. Alright?

Nod. —Then can I go?

—Aye, yeh, then yer can fuck off. If this person asks yeh questions or anythin just ignore em an gerron with sayin what I've just told yeh to. Alright?

Nod.

—Don't worry, I'll be here to help yeh, like, if yeh need it. Ready?

Alastair keys in a number, puts the phone to his ear. It rings. It's answered.

—Yeh?

—Tommy? It's Alastair.

—*Alastair* . . . where *are* yiz, mate?

Oh that sweet voice Tommy. 'Where are ye, mate?' all curious and inquisitive and friendly. Sweet as a viper. Sweet as a stoat.

—Noner your fuckin business where I am, lad. Got someone here wants a werd with yiz.

He puts the phone to Freddy's ear.

—Hello?

—Who's this?

—Me name's Freddy. There's –

—Freddy? Same fuckin ignorant lil get came to see me this mornin? *That* Freddy?

—Someone called Darren Taylor has got the money. He's ripped yeh off big style.

—Yerwha? Are you fuckin –

—He's bought imself a loader charlie an is settin up his own business. He's been goin round the town n all tellin everyone that yerra dick'ed, all washed up. An that yerra big fat fuckin hom. An that yerra big blob of fuckin lard with no knob who takes it up thee arse.

Alastair laughs. Tommy's voice:

—*Listen* to me yer fuckin little prick. You're dead, lar. Fuckin dead. I'm gunner –

Alastair takes the phone away from Freddy's ear and puts it to his own.

—Hear that, Tommy lad? Yer've been fucked over, lar. Terned over, taken for a twat by Darren fuckin Taylor. *Darren* fuckin *Taylor*, man. Softarse. He's laughin at yeh, Tommy. Pure fuckin *laughin*. Takin yeh for all the stupid cunts under the sun. Wharra yeh gunner *do* about it, man?

—Alastair, listen to me. Stay there. Tell me where yer are an al be over soon *as* an we can avver chat about this. This needs fuckin *sortin*, mate, dunnit? This is all gunner –

—Pure friggin *laughin* at yeh, Tommy. 'Tommy Maguire the fat dick'ed,' he's sayin. Wharra yeh gunner *do,* man? Wharra yeh gunner *do?* Whole bleedin *city's* laughin at yeh.

Ally turns the phone off and drops it on the ground and stamps it beneath his foot until it shatters. Still clutching Freddy's collar he squats and takes Freddy down with him and extracts the SIM card from the split handset and pockets it then stands upright again taking Freddy with him once more their movements mirrored as if in some dance of courtship. Or as if linked by some means invisible apart from Alastair's extended clutching hand not in itself strong enough to affect this concrete conjoining.

—Let me fuckin go, now, lar. Yeh said I could fuckin go.

Alastair lets go. Freddy shrugs his coat back on to his shoulders properly and walks away. Back straight, head high, just walks away. No scurrying. Ally stoops and extracts a bundle of money from the sack, a small brick held together with a thick elastic band.

—Ey, lad.

Freddy turns. —What now?

—Eeyar. Catch.

That bundle tumbling through the darkening air. Freddy catches it, examines it, pockets it. Does not say anything but leaves the gardens at a sudden sprint and then when he has climbed the stairs and is back out on the road above he presses his face against the railings and yells:

—Al see you again, knob'ed! Gunner *find* you, I am! Take an ammer to yer fuckin knees, lad! Gorra brother an he's gunner fuckin *do* yiz! You're *dead*, knob'ed!

Alastair looks up at the yelling figure and sees him in silhouette above and against the street lights clinging to the railings like a shadow imprisoned. The figure shouts some more abuse and threats then flees and Alastair bends and rezips the rucksack and hoists it over his shoulder as he stands. Turns to regard the cathedral at his back which he may never see again and maybe some beneficence falls from it at this moment. Maybe it's all true, what they say. In the fortuity of finding Freddy and taking him to the very place where the money was stashed maybe there's some sympathy, maybe there's some

yeh but Freddy was evidently sitting on that bench to be close to the dough to guard it, wasn't he? So it's no surprise cos – aye but if that modelling agency had've been on another street – if it had've been set up elsewhere – if Freddy had been sitting on any other bench – if the slab on that grave hadn't've been cracked – if they'd hidden the rucksack somewhere else – if they if he if if if if if if if if if if if if if if if if if if if –

Alastair leaves the gardens. It's a fucking *big* cathedral. Junkies reappear to float ghostly through the trees and gravestones like desultory, departed souls. One from inside the oval shadow of his hoisted hood and with candleflame eyes watches the skinny figure with the rucksack and baseball hat ascend the stone stairs.

Oo the bag is nicely heavy. As he grins Alastair feels scabs crack on his face and thinks that before he boards the train he'll wash his face in some public toilet somewhere, make himself look a bit more respectable for what he's got to do. There's a toilet in Central Station, a nice cleanish one with soap and towels and everything. He's heading there anyway.

Station.

★   ★   ★

Darren's mobile trills in his pocket like a baby bird chirruping 'You'll Never Walk Alone'. He takes it out, regards the display screen which shows Tommy's number, turns it off and puts it back in his pocket. Fucking Tommy. No need to speak to that fat bastard or any of his toady minions like Sully or Squires or Lenny fucking Reece. Jesus, that Lenny – just caught him unawares, that's all. And then the hot shock of that burger in his face all stingy in his eyes and he couldn't see for a bit, was blinded, couldn't do fuck all about being frogmarched into the cab or anything cos he couldn't frigging see and the *shock*, man . . . Plus he's one *strong* bastard, that Lenny is. Big strong Welsh bastard. Not so big that he won't bleed, tho. Soft skin, every human being has got this soft, rippable skin that parts easily under sharpened steel or splits under heavy blunt objects. And the *amount* of blood . . . Darren saw someone get shot once – T with his nine-mil – shot in the leg, through the artery, like. The *blood* . . . spurted four feet in the air. Could've had a frigging *bath* in it, no lie. Or like the old lady in the post office and the way her scalp unzipped aye but bigger, younger, maler people as well Christ only cowards only focus on leathering old ladies and how *else* would she have opened the safe, by asking her nicely? By saying 'pretty fucking please'? Ruthless, man, that's how you've got to be. Merciless, like. Get hold of a Walther from somewhere and line them all up, all of them, Alastair Sully Gozzy Lenny Robbo Freddy and Tommy himself, one shot each back of the head walk down the line pull the trigger take this youse *cunts* –

Bang. Bang. Bang. Bang. Bang. Bang. Bang.

And seven bleeding sacks of shite on the deck who'll never treat *any*one like a divvy ever, *ever* again. *See* ya.

Darren sits on a bench in Williamson Square and lights a cigarette. Pigeons strut muckily around him and burble until they realise he has no food to offer them at which point they drift away again, through and around and scattered flapping by the legs of people out early for the night, blotchy white feet in strappy heels, polished shoes and trainers and boots. Darren blows smoke and thinks anger at them all, pigeons included because they can fly. He turns his mobile on and rings Alastair again for about the seventeenth time in the past two hours or so and this time he receives a strange, lifeless tone as if he's called Mars. He turns his phone off again, replaces it again in his jacket pocket. Dribbles smoke at the floor, the sooty paving slabs dull-sequinned with colourless coins of flattened gum.

Where oh where will Alastair be? Where will he go to spend that money? Too stupid to leave town where will he go? Too brain-dead even to hide for a while, lay low for a while he will *not* go to his granny's house for shelter or maybe he will because he is *that* thick. Or:

Pub. Or:

Knocking shop. Or:

Where else where else where will his appetites take him . . . With the ready cash to assuage his hungers where will he drift to where will he go, around this city Darren can see him wandering in his skinny inadequacy in that antwacky shelly and that perpetual frigging baseball cap and that gob hanging open never-shut, drool on his pimply chin and the stained white socks tucked into his antwacky trainees and the way he walks all drippy and feeble and ineffectual just bumbles through the world brain-dead get that he is, breakable little arsewipe with a body susceptible to so much pain and pain it will suffer oh how it will split and bleed that face flattening under Darren's fist and feet Jesus the rage in him the fury in his head pushing at the bone, pounding at the bone such a sharp throbbing in his head against the inside of the skull pound pound pound the bone which is going to surely –

Crack.

That's it.

That's that bastard's luxury. *That's* that bastard's Spanish villa.

Darren crushes the end of his cigarette and leaves the square and walks to the gyratory and boards the next bus that will take him to Liverpool 8, bound as it is for the Dingle and St Michael's and areas beyond. He buys a ticket and finds a seat upstairs among the bright people going out and their chatter and invisible perfume clouds and he peers through the window at the passing city, the night's illumination beginning to burn. He disembarks on Upper Parliament Street and cuts through the estate behind the Coronation Buildings, the corporation houses all identical and the music behind their windows either techno or reggae, always techno or reggae. Beyond this estate lies some old terracing cross-hatched around patches of waste ground that once held buildings either obliterated by *Luftwaffe* bombs or razed in the riots and never built on again, left fallow for dandelion and nettle or as dumping grounds for unwanted household appliances or old mattresses or on occasion burnt-out cars sinking into mud and bracken like mastodons. Darren enters one of these terraced streets and halts at a house whose lower windows and door have been covered with sheet metal, three big sheets riveted to frame and jamb. From an upper window a faint light pulses. The number 18 is painted in red on the steel.

Darren presses the intercom button at the side of the door. On certain streets like this one in appearance in other areas the net curtains would be twitching up and down the street on each side like some prolix secret signal, some abstruse and coded conversation conducted via flap and jerk of cloth. In some areas, along some streets net curtains *do* twitch. Eyes *do* pry. But not here, not unless they check for police. Only ever police.

The intercom crackles. A voice all drawly answers:

—Yeeeeee-aaaaahhh? Oo dissssss?

—Darren, lad.

—Hoooo?

—Darren. Darren *Taylor*.

—Know none Dah-*ron* Tee-looorrrrr. Bye-bye.

—Darren fuckin *Taylor*, yeh fuckin fool. I'm *known* ere, lar. Ask Herbie, if he's there. An then just fuckin lerruz in.

Faint voices through the intercom system kind of robotic, mechanical. Like sentient machines concocting a plot. Then:

—Hoooo-*kay* Mistah Tee-looorrr. You go round *back*.

213

Darren does, down the urinous ginnel between ashpiles of burnt clothing and through a gate into a garden where three pit bulls tied to metal stakes driven into the bare-soil lawn burst into instant violent insanity at the sight of him until a black guy in a deckchair smoking a cigar the size of a rolling pin waves a rolling pin at them and tells them to shut the fuck up.

—Y'alright, Darren? What's happenin, kidder?

—Y'alright, Jegsy? Guard duty tonight is it yeh?

—Someone's gorrer do it, lar, avn't thee?

—Is right. Catch yiz later.

—Nice one.

Darren pushes the back door open and enters the kitchen empty of every appliance except the electric cooker on which all four rings burn fiercely to heat up the saucepan on each in which water boils around small glass jars. One man, tall and skinny with a woolly hat and goatee beard, attends at once to them all, raising each jar to check and gently shake, his hands describing fast jerks and circles over the hot hob like some kind of legerdemain. Some magician this and indeed something of the alchemical to this scene and the very process itself carries or is surrounded by such an aura. The honed focus on this man and his deep desire to intensify and improve. Purify, depollute. Unclear he is as to which salts separate and why and which new ones are formed or why but knowing only that they will if his quick hands and assessing eyes are inspired. Knowing only that they *will*.

One small, cracking sound behind the burbling bubbles. The man raises a jar and regards it and smiles at the small chalky rock decocted from liquid and hisses 'yesssssss'. Darren goes into the gloom of the adjoining room and scans the wall-bound faces as his eyes adjust to the lack of light and sees no Alastair. No Alastair, only ten or so people like him both male and female assessing Darren in turn with a gaze communal and focused strange. Faces both white and brown and shades in between lining this room like variegated flowers lit hydroponically by the huge throbbing TV screen showing *The Matrix*.

Another man in a woolly hat rises smiling and approaches Darren. They clasp hands and punch fists knuckle to knuckle.

—Darren, man.

—Herbie. Seen Alastair?

—Alastair? Herbie rolls the word around in his mouth as if tasting it. —Don't know that name, my friend.

—Aye, Herbie, yeh do. Dozy get always wears a basey? He's been here with me before. Few times, like.

Herbie nods. —Oh yeh. Haven't seen him, no. Not for weeks. Last time was . . . He drifts off, thinking, then slips into some kind of trance in which his dark eyes become as glass for a few seconds and which is broken abruptly by a gold-toothed grin. —Anyway. Have a smoke with me, lar. Seein as yer here, like, yeh?

—Aye, alright.

They move to a corner and sit and Darren takes his place among these people with their eyes boring at the TV screen like awls and small glass pipes being put to lips and billows of smoke lightly rising. Little conversation except that on the television unless tongues and burning rocks could be said to converse which maybe they can in a language comprised of bubbling and of breath. Seated figures in gloom as if placed to await in some ante-room admission or rejection from a different world or anticipating some judgement, as if this is the Day when the souls have risen and these here arranged about have no allotted place. As if whatever power has called them forth does not know what to do with them unplaceable as they are and malleable to no proscribed system extant of punishment and reward. And in their withdrawal and stance isolate and willed can be seen the horror of a glimpsed nothingness and a splinter of knowledge empirically earned of what it might be like to live for ever in darkness and alone.

Herbie produces a makeshift pipe from somewhere, built out of a Buxton water bottle and a Biro tube and some tinfoil. Like something a child might make. Like some plaything featured on *Blue Peter* or at school. He loads it with a stone and smokes it then loads it again and hands it to Darren who smokes too, Herbie regarding him with the odd glassine focus of the crack-high as Darren's own eyes achieve that sheen and focus also. The smoke in the bottle trapped in plastic like a little captured cloud. Some miasma gone maverick and of necessity snared. Darren returns the pipe.

—Nice one, Herb. Ta, lar.

—Norra problem, Dar.

—Herb . . . fuckin top name for you, that, innit? *Herb*. Appropriate, like.

Herbie grins. —Is right. An yer not gunner believe the name of the musher I bought the bugle off.

Interrogative eyebrows on Darren.

—Doctor Rock.

—Go 'way. Yeh kiddin.

—Nah, straight up. Doctor fuckin Rock. He's a proper doctor an evrythin, gorra practice in Huyton.

—What, an he deals gack on the side?

—Aye, yeh. Dead easy for him to get hold of, innit?

—How's that, well?

—Every fuckin ozzy's gorra supply of charlie, Dar. Skag n all. Best fuckin painkillers goin, lar.

—Yeh?

—Oh aye yeh. Y'know on charlie, when yeh snort it like an yer face goes all numb? That's the anaesthetic kickin in, man. That's the –

—I *know* that, Herbie. I'm not fuckin stupid, lad.

—Never said yeh were, mate, never said yeh were. Just explainin to yiz, like, why there's always a good supply of beak in thee ozzy.

Even in this gloom and through the chemical obfuscation Herbie can discern the faint yet fierce flickering in Darren's sharpened eyes. Can see the blaring TV screen reflected wee in each pupil and the tiny figures wearing shades and long leather coats fighting there as of Darren's eternal inner fury given form, as if it has assumed this shape of fighting figures whirling, flying, gravity-defying as if the force and extent of his always-anger can be seen only as such impossible acrobatics, as movements that the human body can never really make.

Yes. *Plus* Darren's been known to slash people's faces with knives. Herbie's seen him do it. There is *that* as well.

—Don't talk to me as if am a bleedin knobend well.

217

—I *wasn't*, mate, I was just sayin —

A stocky cross-legged man sitting close to the television screen turns his head, swivels it on his bulky shoulders.

—Ey, can't youse two keep it down? Tryna watch *this*. Good fuckin movie, lar.

Herbie sees Darren's face begin to swell as he glares at the cross-legged man and soon the high will flop and deflate and it must be cherished before it does not spoiled no not spoiled which is a thing about to happen. Bad words are amassing in Darren's throat like an army. Herbie nudges him gently.

—Ey. See them fuckin towers come down, lar?

Darren grunts. Eyes blazing into the back of the cross-legged man's head.

—Yeh, couldn't fuckin believe it, man, Herbie goes on. —Like a friggin movie or summin, did yeh see it? I was in a boozer in Chester with Dean, barman puts the box on like an —

—Dean?

—Aye, yeh.

—*Wrexham* Dean?

Darren staring at Herbie. His head like a building ablaze and the eyes like windows about to shatter.

—Aye, Deano, lives in Wrexham. You know him.

—Dean wasn't in Chester, man. He was in fuckin New York when the towers came down. He watched the planes fly in. He *told* me.

—Nah, man, he was in a pub in Chester, I was with him. Barman flicks the telly on like and —

—Fuck off, Herbie. Dean was in New York. Don't lie to me, lad.

Something wrong here. The lean on Darren and the gritting of his teeth his breath leaving his nostrils like a horse's and the purple bruises black in the half-light and Herbie recalls Dean's rapt face as he watched the televised towers topple and the replayed planes and the flames and the tiny people falling through such vast space kicking their tiny arms and legs and the explosions and Dean's softly muttered 'Jesus *Christ*' several times over as if robbed of all speech except that name that plea but Darren's leaning here and his teeth are bared and his breathing is quickening change the subject Herbie change it quick:

—So, this erm, this Alastair one. Why yeh lookin for *him?*

Darren's breath slows to nearly normal. His expression softens: —Wha?

—Before like. Yeh asked me if I'd seen Alastair.

—Did I?

—Aye, yeh, yeh did. Soon as yeh came in. Don't seem like yeh wanner give him some good news either, if yeh don't mind me sayin. Got summin to do with them bruises, has it?

Herbie nods at Darren's face. Darren stares down at his knees. —That mudderfucker Alastair. That *bastard*. Oh Jesus. —Is he?

—*Fuck* yeh.

—Why? What's he done?

And what story follows told by Darren so it follows that betrayal is the theme. Of a one-armed absconder somewhere in Wales and of a fruitless quest to find him undermined by Alastair's innate stupidity and then of a post office cased by Darren for weeks and the stubborn old lady proprietor who had to be given a belt before she'd open the safe and all that fucking money and then Deano's party in Wrexham cos he'd just come back from New fuckin York Herbie not friggin Chester and then the Lime Street Station bar and being jumped from behind by two little scally bastards who skanked all the money and then Lenny, ambushed again, and Tommy and their names are Robbo and Freddy know them? And it turns out that that Alastair cunt is behind it, believe that shite, that betraying fuckin bastard can't believe he's done this thought he was a bleedin mate can't trust *no* bastard these days man and how they're gunner fuckin bleed when –

—Fer fuck's *sake*. Cross-legged man's head rotates again. —Fuckin gob on *you,* lad. Can't yeh just fuckin button it? Important friggin film, this, not that you'd know fuck all about *that.* Youse wanner gab all fuckin night, take it out to the friggin yard or summin an lerruz watch the fuckin film in peace. Honest to God.

He turns back to face the telly. Darren says:

—Ey, lad.

And Herbie gulps heat.

Swivelhead again. —Wha?

—Want yer fuckin face ripped, cunt?

The man sneers. —By *you*?

—By *me*, yeh.

—Wanner friggin try it? Come ed, then, prick.

He stands. He is big. Floor-bound faces crane up at him then at Darren as he stands too, shrugging off Herbie's entreating hand as he does so and the big man steps forward and Darren's right hand strikes like

220

a snake. No blade flashes or catches the light from the TV screen, nothing like that, just Darren's hand darts in the half-dark and seems to slap the other man's cheek yet there is no retort, no sound of crack or clapping just that one swiftly swiping arm.

One or two gasps. Herbie groans low: —Aw fuckin hell man . . .

The big man stops dead, raises one hand to his face. He takes that hand away to examine it for blood and as he does so and against the pale blue light of the TV that side of his face yawns away. Little blood as yet except that splashed across the television screen in a dotted line across Laurence Fishburne's head, just that slow splitting in two of his face as one cheek sags to show teeth where teeth should never be seen.

Darren leaves to screams. A big black guy stands in his way, gold teeth and necklace gleaming, blocking the door. Boxing gloves in the colours of the Jamaican flag on a thick chain around his neck.

—You want some n all, lad? Darren says. Looks him sneering up and down. —Youse Yardies and yer fuckin bling. Nowt down for yeh.

Dull blade. Hooded eyes regarding Darren as the black guy steps aside and Darren leaves the uproar behind him.

Insane dogs again in the garden. The brandished rolling pin.

—See yeh, Jegsy.

—What's goin on in there, Darren? What's all the fuckin fuss about?

—Fuck knows, mate. Don't ask *me*. Think some

little blert's OD'd or summin. Am out of here before the bizzies tern up. Fuckin amateurs, lar, eh?

Jegsy from his deckchair watches Darren leave the garden and barks at the dogs to shut up but this time they don't, panicked as they are by the sounds of chaos from the house, the screaming and the shouting. Jegsy sighs and rubs his face. Never easy, this shit. Nothing ever is. All is chaos. Ash is everywhere.

Darren, small in the street, running down towards the lit city. Across waste ground of weed and wreckage where a tree of flame once stood, a tree of fire with a lifespan measurable merely in minutes yet an aeon in its echoing.

The concourse at Central Station is heaving and long lines stretch from the ticket offices, watched over by a pair of transport police like buzzards; black-dressed, hands clasped behind their backs with their elbows spread like wings. Alastair joins one queue of rush-hour length and waits patiently, the rucksack held to his chest at all times and when at last he reaches the window he buys a one-way ticket to Wrexham. He shows his ticket to the police at the barrier and they nod him through and he goes straight to the manky public toilet at the top of the escalators and enters one of the cubicles there and drops the toilet lid and sits on it, the sack of money at his feet on the pissy tiles. He holds his face in his hands. He examines his fingernails, badly bitten. He notices a glory-hole in the left-hand wall of the cubicle and takes out his keys and scores in the paint around it these words:

Then he takes up the rucksack and leaves the toilet
and descends the escalators to the underground and
boards the next West Kirby train and alights at Bidston
where he waits twenty minutes for the Wrexham train,
he alone on the empty platform in the dusk dropping
on to the marshland surrounding and the zipping lights
and perpetual muffled roar of the motorway and
beyond that the high lights of the tower blocks beginning to snap on in the marooning sky. A New Brighton
train passes and he regards the passengers on it, their
featureless faces blank and purulent under the fluo-
rescent bulbs like yellow water. Like a train of the
drowned. The Wet Hell Express. He smokes three cigarettes in succession as he waits for his train shivering
in the cold and when it arrives he gets on and finds
a window seat but soon he can see nothing except
his own reflection, soft doppelgänger in the streaky
glass, and the illuminated names of the stations the
train calls at, those on the Wirral southbound like
Neston and Parkgate and then abruptly those in a
different tongue as he enters North Wales like Pen-y-
ffordd and Gwersyllt and Caergwrle, where on the
opposite platform northbound the signs point now in
the direction of Lerpwl. Not far from here, she was
born. Nearby, his grandmother was born he thinks but
what vast barriers she had to cross both physical and
in the form of the Eryri range and others. Others
which he can comprehend but never really articulate,

kin to the Cymric signs that flash past the reflecting window; on the inside, he can pronounce these words.

Wrexham; Dean's do. Two nights ago? *Last* night was it? Jesus, how eager time seems to die. To escape the burden of its appointed role and office. Life itself in its headlong rush like this train. One hurtle through a drizzly darkness.

He gets off at Wrexham General and climbs the stairs alongside the racecourse ground where he went once to see Tranmere play just for the chaos in it and he legged it when the locals began to pelt the group he was in with bottles and he hid beneath a bush on the platform until the train came. He crosses this bridge over the railway track and carries his sack which seems very heavy now into the edges of the town to the bus station where the many bays and waiting buses bewilder him, as do the wall-mounted timetables with their confusing place names and times like some arcane treatise on the movements and reactions of ferrous metals. The booking office is closed but he can see a uniformed man in there behind the counter so he raps on the window with a knuckle. The man ignores him so he raps harder and then the man looks up.

—We're closed.

—Aye, I know, but I need to get to Cilcain.

—Where?

—Cil. Cain.

The man approaches the door so he need not raise his voice.

—Where'd yew say?

—*Cilcain.*

—Next bus quarter to seven.

—In the morning?

—Yes. The man nods and gives Alastair a look. —Or yew could always get a taxi.

Alastair leaves, approaches the cab rank and asks the lead driver the fare to Cilcain. The quoted price seems absurdly high so he traverses the bus station, weaving between waiting travellers and over and around the swaying or prostrate jakeys these places seem for some reason to attract and enters the big grey bunker of a pub propped up against the row of shut shops.

Noisy bar. Some footy on the big screen. Ally asks one of the bar staff the price of one night's single room and the price is reasonable, is at least a lot lower than that quoted by the cabbie so he accepts it and is shown upstairs to a small and stuffy but clean-seeming room, bed table portable telly shower and hospitality tray, with an unrestricted view across the bus station. Alastair showers quickly then takes some money out of the sack and hides the sack beneath the bed and goes down to the bar and finds a seat in a corner and drinks until he is drunk and says not one word to anyone or even himself and when the bell rings and the lights flash to signify last orders he throws whisky into himself and ascends the stairs to his room like a pinball, bouncing from corridor wall to corridor wall and finds the door to his rented room and enters it after several bungled attempts to get the key in the lock and collapses clothed on the bed. He gurgles as he snores. On top of much money.

Peter's up at the bar. Peter the Beak. Must be swelter-ing in that long black leather coat but he *never* takes it off. Told Darren once that it was like Samson's hair, that he'd lose all his special powers if he ever took it off. *What* frigging 'special powers'? Divvy.

Darren taps him on the shoulder and he turns and grins and they punch fists.

—What y'up to, Dar?

—Tryna find Alastair. You seen him?

—Alastair?

—Aye, yeh know, dopey twat, always wears a base-ball hat.

—Oh, *him*.

—Aye, yeh. Seen im, well?

—Tonight?

—Yeh.

Peter shakes his head. —Not for days, man. Weeks, even. Last time I saw him he was with you.

—Aye, well, he's not tonight. Need to find the cunt, tho. If yeh see him make suren give me a bell, yeh? I'll av me moby on.

—Alright. What happened to the face?

Darren taps his nose. —Keep *this* out. He turns to go but suddenly remembers something. —Ey, guess who *I* saw thee other day?

Peter shrugs.

—That berd you were seein. That cracked slapper who strangled her boyfriend, what's her name now?

—Kelly? Peter is abruptly upright, back straight, taller than Darren. —Where djer see *her*?

—Chester. Adder kid with her n all. Lil baby, like.

—Chester?

—Yeh. Just crossin the road, norra bother on her. Merdrin fuckin whoo-er if yeh ask me, like.

Peter's face unreadable as he thinks. Darren taps the side of his nose and makes a sniffing sound. —Info like that's werth a wee bump, Peter, innit?

—Not carryin tonight, Dar. Night off. But I'll make sure yeh get boxed off soon as, yeh?

—Aye, well. See that yeh do.

Bighead longcoat arsewipe and Darren leaves the bar and once outside his mobile gets a signal and immediately it screams at him to indicate incoming text. It's from Tommy. He reads it:

DAZ

ALLS SOUND

MONEY BACK

NO PRBLMS

GIZ CALL M8

He reads it twice, deletes it then presses the hash key and puts the phone to his ear. Tommy answers on the third ring.

—Darren. Where *are* yeh, lad?

—Just got yer text, Tommy.

—Aye. Yeh haven't been answerin yer friggin phone, av yeh?

—Tryna find that fuckin Alastair, that's why. Been all over the fuckin city an –

—Fergerrit, lad. No need any more. We've got the money back, every fuckin penny. Get yer arse round ere an yeh can take yer share an we can avver toot an a bevvy, alright? To celebrate, like. Sound with that?

—This straight up, Tommy?

—Wha?

227

—Straight up, all this? Money back an all that, God's honest truth?

—God's honest truth, lar. Al tell yeh all about it when yeh get ere. Am choppin the beak up now an Lenny's pourin the Baileys. Want someone to come an fetch yeh?

—Nah, yer alright. I'm only round the corner.

—Alright well.

—See yiz in ten.

—See yiz in ten.

Darren ends the call. Tommy's voice was calm. He even sounded happy. Trust here in this world is as faint as the breath of a moth's wing but without it there is only an abyssal plunge. Only friction burns on your face from the speed of the passing air because *that's* how fast you fall.

Darren walks down into the city centre, hands in pockets, fingers caressing the metal of the Stanley knife. Has a life of its own, it's thirsty for blood. It's like a tiger. No, *he's* the tiger, Darren is, terrible beast of prey stalking the night-time city, ravening, of immense and terrible power. Huge he is and hungry. He'll be in ozzy now, that rude bastard round at Herbie's. Getting his kite stitched up. Deserved it, tho, the gobshite. No fuckin manners. Tryna make Darren look small, well who's the dickhead *now*, eh? Bastard. Deserved it. Asked for it. They always, *always* do.

The beams from the Tower restaurant have been turned off now but some pollution palling the city still casts a reddish sheen on the moon's face. Darren looks up at it, it lights his way, it leers into Alastair's cheap rented room scores of miles away. Blood-red visage of a wrathful god regarding them all, all who mix and move and sleep and walk and all the buildings and vehicles they exist within. *Everything* they have built.

OTHERS

CABBIE

Aw Jeez it's norron. Tellin yeh, this is *well* out of friggin order. Pays good an all that like, but *this* is what yeh get, these battered balloon'eds bleedin all over yer back seat and Lenny just tellin yeh to drive. Oh aye thee pay well these friggin so-called gangsters like, but sooner or later one of them no-marks is gunner take revenge on thee easy target an who's that gunner be? Fuckin Muggins here. *Me.*

—Aw Lenny lad, wharrer yeh tryna do to me? Get me into fuckin trouble, you will.

Big feller, that Lenny. Big Welsh feller like. Must av some strength in them arms cos he's only using the one to hold thee other lad down like no bother. He's thrashin around, tryna escape but Lenny's got one hand on the lad's neck an is forcin his ed down between his knees. Some strength in that arm, tellin yeh. An a loader friggin dough in his other hand, like, which he passes through to me.

—Aw stop yewer skriking, Shirl, he says in that funny voice. Dead relaxin, that accent is. Feel like noddin off just lissnin to it like. —Buy yewer missus something nice on-a way home, see?

—Yeh burrit's out of order this, lar.

Big wedge this is, tho. Glance down at it as I edge

230

out into the traffic. Few tenners, few flims an all. *Nice* one that, man. —Where djer wanner go, anyway? Tommy's gaff is it?

Course it's Tommy's gaff. Where the fuck *else* would it be? That lad Lenny's holdin down, he's done somethin naughty an I don't envy the poor get. Can't tell who it is, not with his ed bein held down like that, but it could be Maggie fuckin Thatcher an I still wouldn't envy the poor get when Tommy gets ahold of em. Bad piecer werk, that Tommy one. Somethin friggin pure *wrong* about that lad, no messin round. Got them *eyes* like . . . bad, bad man. One bad, *bad* man.

Still, if it's *his* friggin money I'm not complainin. Big wedge in me shirt pocket like, feels fuckin *boss* in there, it does. Fuckin *top*. Lenny wants me to hurry up, put me foot down like, but in *this* traffic? And *this* bleedin rain?

—Jokin, aren't yeh, Len?

Big feller doan answer. Just gazes out the window like. Wipers need to go on now cos the rain's comin down in buckets.

Can smell onions. Onions n tomato sauce an meat. One of em must've adder burger before thee got in. Or used it for friggin aftershave cos that's wharrit smells like. Pure friggin *honks*, lad. One of the weekend whiffs, that burger smell – do a weekend shift an that's all yeh smell all night, greasy burgers like. Chips as well. An chicken wings. An also sick and piss an even shite on a few occasions, some dirty bastard who's cacked his kex wantin a lift home. Thee drink *too* much, that's the problem. Aye we all enjoy a bevy like, but some of these young uns . . . can hardly friggin *stand*, some of em. No lie. Young girls lyin there in the gutters like, showin everythin . . . not right, lad. Just not fuckin right.

So, yeh, we all need perks, don't we? Bein a fuckin mobster's cabbie has its perks, like, an this big friggin wedge in me pocket is one of em. Buy Charlene somethin nice, me first granddaughter, like. *Ice Age*, she *loves* that film. *Loves* it, she does. Al nip into that Toys R Us place on the way home an buy her the DVD. Pure *loves* that film, ar Charlene. Bit partial to it meself, must admit. Makes me laugh. Big kid I am oh aye, the missus —

Shoutin from the back. Lenny's ignorin it, still holdin the lad down, still just gazin out the winda. Funny feller, that Lenny. Big, gentle feller like, speaks all soft, would never in a million friggin *years* guess that he worked for Tommy Maguire. Or Joey, rather; I mean, Joey's the brains, the bossman like, Tommy's just the cold psycho who puts the fear of shite into people. Friggin loves doin it, n all. Bad, bad man, that, tellin yiz. Friggin *hate* it whenever I've got him in the back, like — just this yowge friggin menace behind me. Like drivin around with an open friggin *fridge* in me cab, knowmean?

One mad friggin job, this, tellin yeh. *Mad* friggin job. Been at it over thirty years an it gets no easier, in fact it gets *werse* — all the nutters in this city now. Only last year I gave a lift to a girl terned out to be a fuckin merdra. Merdered her friggin boyfriend, like. Strangled the poor sod. Gave her a lift home from the pub like, on the dock road, shouldna done cos I'd been drinkin, but, y'know, pretty young gerl seemed upset about somethin carn have her walkin the city onner own at three in the friggin mornin, so I gives her a lift like an at the lights down Catherine Street she jumps out the cab an legs it into the church. Terned out that she later went home an tied her boyfriend to the friggin bed an choked the poor get to death. Friggin pervert, like. Shockin. Just goes to show yeh, dunnit? I mean who'd a thought it, eh? Pretty young gerl like tha . . .

Shook me up a bit, that did. No messin round. Fair got me goin a bit, that did, when I read about it in thee *Echo* . . . I mean, what's happenin ere? What's happenin to people?

This friggin traffic, lad. Gunner take owers to get to Tommy's gaff at this bleedin rate. An me belly's rumblin n all; the smell from the back is makin me hungry for a berger. Big berger with double fries an a Coke. Can't, tho; doctor's sworn me off. Dicky ticker. Gorrer stick to salads an boiled fish – salads an boiled fish! Fuck *that*, lad. Gunner gerra big bagger chips an some gravy, I mean they're only friggin *spuds.* Carn go wrong with friggin *spuds*, can yeh?

Group a scallies blockin the road. Pissed up by the looks. It's like that film: 'Some day a *real* rain will come an wash all the scum off the streets.' You *know* it, lad. Fuckin *love* that film, me. No messin. Might treat *meself* to a DVD n all, there's enough cash in me pocket to buy moren one. *Ice Age* n *Taxi Driver*, sound. Wither big bagger chips. Or a pizza, even; there's *vegetables* on a pizza. Healthy, like, innit?

FRANKIE MAGUIRE

Best thing I ever did, lar. Best thing I ever did bar *none*. Wake up every mornin in the sunshine with the parrots squawkin on me seven acres an I think: You've fuckin well *made* it, Frankie lad. You've fuckin *made* it, son. No more drizzle, no more bizzies on me case, this is the fuckin life. It's made. *You're* made. This is pure happiness. Oh fuck yeh.

No regrets. Not one. Doan even miss me brudders, an thee probly don't miss me, either; the postcards I send em probly get binned unread. But I couldn't give two fucks, man; the parrots squawk somewhere on me seven acres an the sun always shines an I am Top fuckin Man. No regrets. Not one.

JOEY MAGUIRE

When Joseph Ferdia Maguire was eight years old he saw an angel. He was feverish and bed-bound after being pushed in the canal and swallowing water three days earlier by a bigger boy who laughed and threw stones at him as he floundered and yelled and who then ran away, and among his sweat-soaked sheets and the stink of vomit from the bedside bowl Joey had also seen gigantic spiders on the ceiling and zebras hiding in the curtains, but when he was eight years old and seriously ill Joseph Ferdia Maguire also saw an angel at the side of his bed. It was white and tall with a thin face. It cloaked him all cool with its wings and put a cool hand on his forehead and Joseph felt the sickness being sucked out of him into that hand.

He was special, the angel said in a voice that sounded only in Joey's head, clear among the clagginess and the buzzing, a deep voice of no determinate gender. Special, and he was being saved for great things.

The fever lifted early the following morning and Joey ate Ricicles and toast and jam for his breakfast. By mid-afternoon he was playing football in the garden with his father Shem and his uncle Dusty. Doctor Muttu came round and declared himself amazed, said Joey must be especially strong to come so quickly out of such a sickness but that he must not exert himself for a week or so just in case. And that he must drink plenty of liquids. And to eat only soup.

That night, before he went to bed, Joey went in to check on his little baby brother, Thomas. He was lying on his back in the cot like a big blancmange and Joey peered at him through the bars and knew instinctively that something was wrong, that a baby's face should not be purple like that, and he also knew (but *how* was a mystery) to reach gently into the soft and toothless mouth and tweak the tongue and pull it up and away from the back of the throat and this he did. The whoosh of breath then into that tiny mouth was very loud, very deep. He watched through the bars as his baby brother's face faded from the colour of plums to the colour of strawberry ice cream and then vanilla ice cream and then he went to bed and slept soundly and dreamed that a kindly thin-faced man with wings held him and flew him over the estate, down into people's gardens, across their moon-blued roofs. It was a reward, the thin-faced man said. A prize for being good. Transvection, although that was a word which Joey did not know.

Joey forgot that dream the next day, as the business of tracking down the boy who pushed him into the canal and making that boy eat dog poo as punishment occupied his thoughts. The angelic visitation, if that is what it was, simply became one blurred moment of his fever and he quickly forgot the incident as he also quickly forgot the delirious episode itself. Now, he does not recall ever being seriously ill as a boy, and indeed all he knows of his childhood is that he had one and that it was unique, that something happened in it to make it unique. There was no thin-faced gentleman, no life-saving gesture, no ecstatic soaring. But it was unique. It was unlike all others. And he *did* find the boy; and he *did* make him eat dogshit. Down on his skinned knees on the park grass, sobbing, vomiting as he lapped.

ALASTAIR

Don't like this, lar, no way . . . not really for me this but *fuck* knows av gorra do it . . . we've *all* gorra do it sometimes, like . . . in this werld . . . y'know . . . just gorra be done sometimes, man, no two ways about it . . . just gorra be done . . .

Now I must be violent.

Cos I mean if I don't then it'll friggin happen to *me*, like . . . fuckin Darren or Tommy or one of *them* . . . cos if I don't, if I *don't* then —

No. Cos they're not fuckin gunner *catch* me, are thee? Am not gunner be here. An gunner be *where* am a gunner be

in *that* place.

That post office in that village what was it called the name of it what was it

erm

Cilcain.

That's where am gunner be.

Cilcain.

But am never gunner get there am I not unless I get friggin violent . . . pure *gorra* get that dough back, man . . . an if I avter get fuckin violent to gerrit back then so be fuckin *it* . . . just gorra be done . . .

But not *too* . . . erm . . . not *too* . . .

. . . erm

don't wanner waste him like or anythin Jeez no . . . he's just a friggin kid . . . just little fuckin babyscals, the two of em . . . just wanner scare em really . . . just make em, y'know . . . what's the werd . . . the werd is

Jesus . . . fuck . . . sometimes I get so confused . . . always have been since that time in the Copperas Hill sty when the fuckin bizzies . . . so many times thee booted me, like . . . never been the same since . . . can't . . . things I can't fuckin do like in me *ed* it goes all cloudy this way . . .

But yeh – violence. *That's* what's gorra happen now. Some kind of violence, like.

Just to scare them. Just to get that money back.

First tho av gorra get some kip . . . pure fuckin knackered me, like . . . no lie . . . get back to me nan's an avver smoke an a birruver kip . . . maybe gerra birra scran as well . . . pick up a bagger chips or summin . . . or somethin . . . yeh, somethin . . .

Lights comin on. Moon comin out. When I was a

kid me nan bought me oner them things, them things that dangle above yer cot like, that hang from the ceiling . . . forgotten what they're called . . . a model of the sky, like, all the stars an the moon . . . I used to always be tryna catch that moon . . . it had a face drawn on it . . . a smiley face . . . like a smiley god or somethin it was hangin there above me an I was always reachin up for that smiley moon . . . that model moon . . . I thought it was God . . . burrit was just a

   that modellin agency, oh aye yeh . . . they'll all be leavin there at this time, all them sexy berds like, *that's* the way I'll go home . . . back to me nan's, like . . . see them all comin out at this time them dead sexy women . . . see them . . . on Duke Street, like . . . that modellin place . . . opposite thee Anglican . . . looks nice at night-time all lit up, thee Anglican does . . . aye but them models . . . thee all come out at this timer night . . . there's

   there's *one* . . . friggin arse on her, lar . . . just perfect like . . . God in them tight kex . . . there's

   there's

   im

   there's oner them fuckers

   can't believe it man little fuckin thievin gobshite sittin there on that bench

   bastard he made these marks on me face an I need that money I *need* that fuckin

   now I must be VIOLENT

FREDDY

Oh yeh fuckin buy *you*, gerl. Fuckin buy *you* now oh

aye you'll fuckin *cream* when yeh see the brewsters *I've* got stashed, oh aye you an a thousand friggin others includin that Madeleine O'Shea, oh yeh yer all gunner *cream* when yiz see what Freddy lad's got stashed away can buy yiz fuckin anythin can buy *you*

Look at me I'm wearin Diesel
Wearin fuckin *Diesel* I am oh aye
yer all gunner
all gunner
fuck it's *im*
It's *im*
ARGH GERROFF ME GERROFF ME I WANT ME MAM I'VE DONE FUCK ALL GERROFF ME LAD AL GET ME BRUDDER FUCK OFF FUCK OFF GERROFF I'VE
MAM MAM MAM MAM MAAAAAMM
HELP ME SOMEONE HELP ME

DARREN'S VICTIMS: NUMBER 23 (COUNTING ALASTAIR AS ONE)

All I wanted to do was watch the fuckin film. No fuckin *need* for that, man, no fuckin *need* . . . all's I wanted to do was toot a little rock an watch me favourite friggin movie like, an now look now look I

—Mmmm. It's too deep for glue. Sometimes we can simply glue these clean cuts together but not if they're as deep as this. Has to be suture, I'm afraid.

Me mouth works. *Tries* to: —Wiw . . . wiw urr ve . . .

—Don't talk, you'll make it worse. It's very deep.

His fingers are in my cheek. Jesus Christ I can feel his fingers going *through* my face my face through my fuckin *face* shouldn't be able to do that his fingers in me my face my face what's HAPPENED TO MY FUCKING FACE

Some blackness as this I'm falling falling into. Painkillers, wharrever they've jacked me up with kicking in strong. I can hear another voice, *two* other voices. Two doctors. I hear the words 'plastic surgery'.

Plastic surgery on my face. My face needs plastic surgery.

Oh Christ that bastard. Totally fuckin uncalled for. This is my life now changed for ever nothing will ever be the fuckin same again ever ever ever EVER

That talk we all had last night about *The Matrix* when we were all stoned on that oil an Michelle she said that them brothers who made the film had taken the blue pill and are in the know an thee made that film to warn us all it's more of a documentary than just a movie an we all went wow an we an we an an an an an

an fuck that how *pathetic* it was, me

Me, how fuckin *pathetic* I am goin on about *The Matrix* my fault this is all my fault I must be shite for him to wanner do this to me for him to hate me so fuckin much I must be shite this is all my fault this wound this pain no life ever the same again

all my fuckin fault

my face needs plastic surgery it is *that* bad

That's how *bad* my face is cut up is damaged thee need to reconstruct it

The Matrix oh aye we live in The Matrix reality is

240

This is reality

This is fucking reality

Me, lying on my side an I can feel one half of my face slipping over thee other half an I can taste my own tears as they trickle through the hole in my cheek into my mouth mixing with the gushing blood an that should never be allowed to happen cos

cos

In reality my face is whole

In *reality* it should not be

PLASTIC FUCKING SURGERY WHAT SCARS WHAT SCARRING PAIN BLOOD AND MY FUCKING LIFE WRECKED THIS IS REALITY THIS IS REALITY THIS THIS THIS THIS THIS THIS THIS THIS THIS FUCKING

FERDIA MAGUIRE AND FAMILY (WHAT'S LEFT OF IT): 1849

The fog bank is a whitewashed wall a mere stone's throw from the shore rising sheer from the grey sea like something more solid than fog. Little waves emanate from it to lap the sand and shrieking gulls drift through the milky vapour like wraiths or souls unmoored, recently released but if that is the case then the entire sky would be black with them and the sound of their screeching would burst ears. Ferdia stands and waits for those little waves to swell, to tell of an approaching boat somewhere in that fog and bound for the shingle shore on which he stands.

Shelagh is a shape close to him, a dim figure asquat on the sand–and–stone beach and attended by three smaller shapes like familiars. She has been weeping for days, it seems, weeks. One of the smaller shapes bends double and coughs and retches. Aoife again. Any more of this and she'll be spewing up her own lights.

—That Aoife once more? Ferdia's voice is gulped by the fog, as is Shelagh's affirmative murmur. —She still bringing up the blood?

More murmuring, more retching. This could be the loss of child number 3 in as many weeks but what is a man to do with a child so hungry and wasted that its lights and liver can be discerned as dark patches beneath the stretched skin like the transparency of a sprat? Feed it more grass the likes of which only bring on the dysentery? Or visit the Hollow of the Blood again where the vein of a calf can be slit open and famished mouths can be pressed slurping to that awful spigot? Chances must be taken. Death must be defied glutted as it is here, now with cairn-topped mass graves carbuncling the fields, uncountable new ones every day.

The retching stops. Aoife cries loud.

—She well?

—She's not. She's ill and will die and her soul is claimed like yours and mine and all. They're only childer, Ferdia Maguire, and damned them you have.

—Ach, would ye ever shut that hole? Ferdia spits then reflects that to swallow that mucus may have provided some nourishment. —Sure and don't we need money? You know of a man alive who'll take us off this island without a coin, do you?

Shelagh shakes her head and reaches and gathers her children to her, three where there was recently five, three where there will soon be two. —Not alive, no. All charity in this place is sunk in the earth. Those who live and breathe belong to Lucifer and there is nowhere to go from here. We exchange one Hell for another and nothing more there is to it.

Ferdia sucks on a shell. For the salt, for the salt. The pain in his stomach is vile and howling and there is a wailing in his head too as there has been for months since this began, since the dark cloud passed over the country and infected the people with an evil just as the prátaí were infected with the blight. But then the occupiers were of an evil anyway with the evictions and the burnings and the potatoes on the other hand hid their rot beneath their unblemished skins and they came up from the ground as they always do tumbling like pebbles and only revealed their black hearts when cleft. All goodness gnawed at, eaten away. Tiny cankered animalcule and the apocalypse they can sow. A mere blink of time to scrape people down to the bone, to suck muscle and flesh into the horrible hollow air which alone can sustain no life.

—One Hell we exchange for another and no way out of it there isn't, Shelagh mutters again and then sinks her head into her bundle of children and begins to mutter a prayer in the old tongue. Soft sibilants and rolling plosives beneath and akin to the small crash of the waves.

And truly it has been a Hell, a deathscape designed by demons in finery. After the crops failed and the grain was removed to feed others away over a sea and the clergymen called wrath down on the heads of those who sought to seize the corn and Trevelyan withdrew whatever meagre aid there was all Mhaigh Eo it seemed walked the storm from Doo Lough to Louisburgh. All Mhaigh Eo, with the rain and the lightning and the never-ending hunger taking children and the old and the cairn-crowned graves appearing along the trail in bog and sudden pasture and running roadside and in uneven lea where the great forests once stood now tree-stripped to make the navy of a malign alien race to ferry away that very commodity which could lend respite to this vast ravage. And then in Louisburgh these marchers drenched and dripping and semi-naked skeletal were poked and inspected by the Poor Law Guardians who instead of declaring them official paupers and allotting them three pounds of meal per family unit instructed them all to be at Delphi Lodge, the private fishing lodge of the Marquis of Sligo and ten miles distant at 0700 hours. Without stint the rain fell and under a tree denuded of leaves the youngest Maguire died and rage would have grown then had not pain and exhaustion swamped it although some among the wanderers there were who spoke of redress and revenge yet such words in the mouths of such scarecrows wet and emaciate provoked only sobs from hollow stomachs. And then the march to Delphi Lodge which exposure took more of the very young and very old, some left sitting upright at roadsides like milestones calibrating the distance to Hades and when this legion battered, bedraggled arrived they found the Guardians at breakfast and would not be disturbed. And so a wait followed. A long wait. And unwilling to be interrupted at table the Guardians sent the ragged horde on their way home. Home to a barren farm and empty shell of a house from which soon they were to be dragged for non-payment of rent.

And tumbrils laden with grain and other crops and livestock too under armed escort traversed the empty land to the docksides where great ships laden with such produce took it elsewhere. From those who would die without it to those who didn't need it.

So fury *did* grow, as it must; those who starve amid substance can in their gurgling guts find rage. Can as they consume themselves from within find that they have strength enough still to make a fist or fling a rock which is precisely what Ferdia Maguire did on his way to Westport harbour; providence offered him one of Boycott's Ulstermen broken-legged at the roadside, having been tossed by his horse, and it was easy to brain the beseeching bastard with a rock and steal the effects from his pockets which comprised but a clay pipe and a pistol with no shot and some money. At the first blow of the rock Shelagh began to bewail the fate of their immortal souls and she continued in this vein without cessation all the way across to Westport sands, through deserted village and past burning barn and fields of wooden stumps and fallow pastures reeking with the dead and patrolled by the black birds who eat such moribund flesh. Wept she did in ditch and under hedgerow as they concealed themselves from government patrol and from weapon-wielding indigents, animate skeletons crazed and with furnace eyes. And when the second child died and his grave was just a scrape in the earth and down into the Hollow of the Blood they went where a man accepted money to open a calf's vein and in turn they knelt to suck and she stood blood-faced and weeping in that hollow beyond the gaze of Redcoat or Guardian indeed like her they all stood, thick blood clotting on chins and cheeks and most of them weeping and the calf lowing too. And secretive down into Westport harbour with the youngest child carried and vomiting blood not her own not even of her species over her weeping mother's back and as a family of famine they entered the harbour, a clan of want among the jetties and pilings. Ferdia bought four small fish from a man in a coracle and these were eaten raw and quickly, ungutted and unboned. A man approached and said that for a fee he could carry the entire family safely over to the great port of Liverpool where so many countrymen have fled that they say it outrates even Dublin for sons of Erin and that any man can find paid work on the docks there. Ferdia asked the man the fee. The man asked how much money Ferdia had. Ferdia told him and well then that's the fee the man said.

So Ferdia and family Maguire wait hungry on the white sand and shingle surrounded by the white fog. Shelagh bawls still into her remaining children held and huddled to her but Ferdia, Ferdia . . . there is an energy alive in him from somewhere. From the gulped blood or the raw fish or even from the shell-salt he is swallowing, there is an energy from somewhere within his weakly beating chest. Maybe from the Boycott Ulsterman rotting now and skull-split at the roadside like so many before him and them undeserving and he most assuredly not. Maybe it is that man's stolen spiritus now that throbs in Ferdia and distils here on this fog-cloaked empty littoral into rage. A rage in this blood and seed and in whatever other blood and seed they might produce and down further through the bloodline to the many childer he will generate and nurture and to their issue also and for ever on so far that Ferdia cannot see it. Can see only a heaving metropolis somewhere over the sea where those of his blood will possess proud power and never suffer in this way again or want for anything other than perhaps what the blight and breaking of this world can never give.

—Not coming, Shelagh says, a grey shape in grey vapour. —Stranded here we are. All die on this beach we will and –

—Hush it, woman, Ferdia snaps. —I'll be dead from your screeching if nothing else kills me. Sure isn't there enough suffering to fight without you making it worse?

She prays again. Buries her head in her children and prays again in Erse and does not see the waves swell nor the small boat drift out of the fog towards them nor hear the slap and drag of oars on water.

Ferdia sees it. Ferdia hears it. And sees also the rope cast out towards him and sees the city over the sea where there is a life to be lived and money to be made and food to be eaten and sees in that city the yet-to-be of his blood and the might in them he will cultivate like he once cultivated potatoes and he will tell them and instruct them to tell their childer too and so on and so on into the next century and beyond that it is not by hoe or spade or rake that a man survives but by a rock. And by his willingness to use it.

CRACKHOUSE

Built as part of a terrace out of Shropshire brick and Blaenau slate shortly after the First World War and largely by veterans of that conflict, the first tenants of number 18 were the Jones family, stonemason patriarch employed on the construction of the Anglican cathedral, with wife and small child and two further children born under that roof. In 1929 Mr Jones fell eighty feet to his death from scaffolding and Mrs Jones took her three now fatherless children deeper into Cheshire, to be closer to her parents. The house lay empty for three months and was then occupied by a single old lady whose son had made much money in the armaments industry and had purchased the house specifically for her to age and die in which she duly did, shortly before another global horror sent flame and steel shrieking from the sky to obliterate surrounding houses, seeking to destroy the ack-ack guns which had been stationed in the streets roundabout, one of whose crew lived in the house for much of the war and, like the house itself, survived it with only minor damage; an eye here, a window there. After hostilities ended the local council bought up many of the houses in the locality and number 18 was rented out to a convalescent nurse from North Wales who had entered the city initially to be in service but was now employed as a carer for soldiers mutilated in both body and mind. Kate was her name, and her heavy drinking led to a neglect of her civic duties and she was soon forced to vacate number 18 after long periods of rent-avoidance and she was replaced by a Jamaican family who had been shipped to the port on a sister-ship of the *Windrush* at the invitation of the Attlee government with the promise of paid work in the restructuring of bomb-damaged British cities. The head of the family was employed as a labourer on the reconstruction of the docks centred on the site of the *Malarkand* explosion and his wife worked in service for a family on Faulkner Street whose forefathers had made their giant fortune through using people of her skin colour as a mere barterable commodity. Relentless hard work allowed this couple to save enough money to move out to a more desirable property on the northern outskirts of the city and they were replaced by another Jamaican family whose stay in the house was brief, swiftly driven out as they were by the small but viciously vocal group of locals who were offended by their melanin. From 1970 to 1972 a Chinese family occupied the house, newly come from Shanghai, but they drifted down dockwards where for several centuries their compatriots have gathered and still do. Three Irishmen then moved in, two of them employed on the underground rail system then being extended and the third remaining in or close to the house to attend to the various outlaw Republicans who had been invited to use it as sanctuary; he kept them company, offered support, maintained a watchful eye at the window. These men moved out when the exigencies of their secret calling demanded that they should, to break any possible trail, and were replaced by a docker recently made redundant who lived alone and who, in 1981, watched in terror and awe from the overgrown back garden as Toxteth burned, the flames so high that they spat above the roofs of the Coronation Buildings below the only just completed cathedral. Disappointment and depression and a form of freefloating fear led this man to a reclusive existence in number 18 and in the late eighties he became the second person to die in the house in a static storm of horded and rotting items of a thousand sorts. He lay undiscovered for three weeks. The clean-up operation took days and after it the house was thought unlettable so it lay empty apart from the various junkies and drifters who used it for shelter until the doors and windows were replaced by thick boards and it was bought for a quarter of its original worth by a man called Herbert who had accrued much money from dealing in illegal drugs and owned several such places scattered around the city and its environs and he is there still and is at this moment attempting to subdue the rage and hysteria that has followed an horrific facial wounding in the house's main living area. Shurrup, he is shouting. You'll attract the fucking bizzies. The wounded man has been driven to the hospital and his attacker has long fled into the city and there is bloodspray on the walls and TV screen and it will remain on the walls turning blacker then greyer for two years until Herbie will be shot dead in an altercation along Granby Street and the ownership of the property will revert to the council, Herbie of course dying intestate, and the council will sell it and others like it to a multimillionaire from Ireland who will renovate them all extensively and impressively and will make more millions selling them to those who will relocate or return to the city in 2008, drawn there by the City of Culture celebrations and the global attention they will receive. A family will be made in number 18, *two* families in fact, the second of which will be forced to flee during the Peace Riots of 2011 when the house and its immediate neighbours will be firebombed and will be so damaged as to warrant demolition and they will be flattened and will be no more.

FATHER DONAGHY

Lord give me the strength. Give me the power to find the words to make solace for these lost souls. Lord You have chosen me as a mouthpiece for You down here on earth in this desolate city and fallen so far we. Help me, grant me the strength and the wisdom to calm these terrified souls and allay their fears and give them in turn the strength the resilience to to to. To cope. To survive down here among all this. To find some peaceful place which I *know* is attainable tho chain of loss and canyon of grief this is and always has been.

What can I do? Feeble and fallen, tell me what can I do?

Lord grant me the. Give me the. Bestow upon or let me find —

Mrs Taylor again. She came to confession this morning and to what did she confess? To nothing but fear and sadness and concern for her children and no sins they.

Only maybe in the doubt but which of us is pure enough is strong enough to never feel such doubt, to never hear or heed that persuasive voice? Faith, that's all I can tell her; keep faith in your heart. His ways perplex us poor as we are in our faculties to approach an understanding of His plan and it may seem like every waking day is a trial of our faith but accept that trial we must. Faith itself is irrational and strange and seemingly foolish too and that adds to the difficulty of its sustenance. But keep it we must for it is all we may have.

But He shreds innocence, she told me. Innocence apparently offends Him for He shatters it at every turn and why is He so eager to augment that which we turn to Him in desperation to oppose? These were not her words but were her meaning. Why is His guidance not so immediate, so tangible, why are His ways discrete from us so that life's struggle itself becomes further, driven as we are to fight to find any suggestion of strength to offer a possible way to face up to each daily obstacle? These were not her words but were her meaning, and whenever she addressed me as 'Father' her accent rendered it as 'farther', and it is apt, that, suggestive as it is of the ways in which these people hereabouts push things, the world, their lives, push themselves away from firm ground to the lip of a chasm incessantly. And this is a plan we must trust, I told her. To question is healthy spiritually but to expect an immediate answer is hubristic and the core of it all is faith and trust. Then she told me that she cannot trust in a scheme that apparently seeks to destroy innocence and all it brings her is more suffering. And I could not answer her except again to repeat the word 'faith' even though that word could barely leave my lips such platitude it had become.

What can I do, here? What do You expect me to do? What do You *think* I can do? Why choose a man to represent You here on the soil who lacks entirely the skills to do so? Send me guidance. The reward of understanding for this endurance is surely not too much to ask.

And she spoke about her son again, she always does, the bad one or rather the *baddest* one; Darren. I remember him when he was a boy, at the masses. On several occasions I had need to speak to him alone and I could see it in him even then, how he was coming apart even then. The mischief in him and oh sure there is mischief in all healthy children but in him I could see the potential of it to curdle and sour and it has. It has. It has become malign in him. The yearning in his heart has broken a hinge and offered ingress to something that should have been resisted and sure where should he have gone? Where could he have sought instruction in how to resist? Alone here we are. I am approached for guidance by these souls adrift and I just don't know what to say or what to do I am rudderless myself I am lost too.

And now to visit St Mary's primary school, where last week the chapel was desecrated. Foul words painted on the walls and the floors urinated on and I must calm the children and the teachers too and attempt to explain to them why such a thing happened. It's been cleaned up now, but I saw the devastation and felt the shock of recognition of a prayer so pure, so articulate, so full of longing. The expression of a roaring soul dissatisfied and disappointed and set aimless on this world and of course our hearts will remain restless until they rest in You. And a broken and contrite heart, O Lord, You will not despise. There will be forty children looking to me to make some sense of the destruction and what shall I tell them? I need Your strength, here. This burden is great. Mrs Taylor is right now for all I know at the edge of Victoria Dock contemplating the dark and oily waters in which so many of Your children have died cold and alone and terrified. She needs strength. *I* need strength. Until it arrives from You I will find it in whiskey. Just a glass or two before I visit the school because I am too weak without it, too weak in the basic which is true of Your creation entirely. Your favoured creation. Us screaming billions. And suddenly as the whiskey burns me within I realise that You too have Your Hell and it is Your love for us. And suddenly I feel strong.

O God, I am sorry for having offended You. I detest all my sins because I dread the loss of Heaven and the pain of Hell. But most of all because I have offended You, O God, who are all good and deserving of all my love. I resolve with the help of Thy grace to confess my sins, do penance and amend my life. Amen.

And now: outside. A collar Your armour. Outside, to explain to children the darkness of Your plan and what can children know of this? What can *any* of us know?

JAMIE 'GOZZY' SQUIRES

HA HA HA HA HA HA HA HA HA HA HA HA HA HA HA HA HA!

Tommy, you prick. Darren, you little fuckin gobshite tied to a chair in a puddle of yer own piss an yer dim fuckin dial uglier than it normally is an that's sayin somethin. An Joey, you, Joseph fuckin Ferdia Maguire; you soft fuckin no-mark shite-for-brains fuckin has-been. This is thee end of *youse*, oh aye, this is thee end of *youse*. Don't wanner punch fists with me, Joey, no? Well *fuck* yiz then. All's I was tryna do was say tara. *Fuck* yiz.

Go off an meet them Irish lads, he says. Two Coggies name of Stevie an Ray. They're waitin for me in a Transit van down the Pier Head an in the backer the van should be four AKs in good nick, two Brocock ME 38s (shite if yer ask me; them airgun conversions always are), an a Mach 10. Okey-doke says I, an off I friggin goes. To meet a coupla Irish mushers, oh aye, but the ones *I'm* gunner be meetin ain't gunner av no shamrock tats on the backs of ther hands, oh fuck no.

I take out me moby an tap in a number. Ulster accent answers:

—Aye, Jamie. How about ye?

—All ready an waitin, Willie. Do yer stuff, lar.

—Ther on the dock?

—Yeh.

—Sound, so. See ye down thur.

I close me phone. Can't help laughin. This is me, Jamie Squires, about to set imself up in biz an I've got evrythin I fuckin well need; pieces enough to arm a small fuckin army an a pair of loyal wacko Billyboys to fuckin shoot em. Fuckin sound *as*. This time next year it'll be: The Maguires? Remember them?

Wharrever happened to *them* two fuckin arsewipes? An Willy Hunter n all an that soft get Stega an *all* the fuckin others, *all* of em.

I nip into Ma Boyle's for a Guinness, give Willie an his twin Wally time to do the job. Am calm enough even to pick at a pinter prawns with me stout, an halfway through it me moby goes off. It's Willie an all's he says is:

—Ye all set thur, Jamie? Glug-glug time.

Sound. I neck me ale, leave the pub. I can see the Transit just over the road, two fellers wearing Rangers shirts in the cab. An there'll be two blerts wearin Celtic shirts tied up in the back an tonight them same green-an-white hoops are gunner be feedin the fuckin fishes in the slime at the bottom of Vicky Dock.

Oh yeh.

The van beeps. Willie or it could be Wally waves over at me an I wave back an cross the road. Cross the road to a better fuckin life, aye, a better fuckin world. No more Tommy, no more Joey, just Jamie Squires without the 'Gozzy'. An Willie n Wally as well, of course.

So first stop: Victoria Dock.

Second stop: To see Fat Tommy. His fuckin number's *up* an that's that.

Money. Guns. Power. The world is fuckin *mine*, lar.

Could yeh go a sausage supper, Bobby Sands?
Could yeh go a sausage supper, Bobby Sands?
Could yeh go a sausage supper, yeh filthy Fenian
   fucker,
Could yeh go a sausage supper, Bobby Sands?

YES! OH FUCKIN *YES!!!*

Helicopter. Dead low helicopter. Germans! But dead fuckin *low.*

A voice in a megaphone. A big loud voice. What the fuck is

DARREN: HIS STANLEY KNIFE

noun: Brit. trademark: a utility knife with a short, strong replaceable blade (Concise OED).

The basic model, designed and developed in the late nineteenth century by the Stanley Rule and Level Company in New Britain, Connecticut, and widely cloned since then, is fifteen centimetres long with a ridged slider on the top by whose operation a triangular section of blade can be made to protrude from one end and lock in place. This blade is extremely sharp and double-ended, trapezoid in shape and reversible. The handle contains storage space for spare blades and consists of two die-cast sections of steel (or, increasingly, plastic) screwed together. The blade can be locked in both stored and deployed positions. The artefact displays a considerable finesse of design; it possesses perfect weight and comfortable grip. Nor is there need of a screwdriver to open the handle; a small coin, or a sturdy fingernail, will suffice.

Darren uses the Stanley 10-079 5-3/8" Retractable Utility Knife (catalogue description). He stole it from the carpenter for whom he mated when he left school and undertook one of his very rare occasions of socially acceptable work; on the third day the carpenter called him a lazy twat so Darren stole his knife and walked off the job. It is grey of colour, once gloss, now matt, and it is sleek like a shark or a missile. The attractiveness and efficacy of its design is not lost on him. Darren first brandished it as a threat in the late 1980s when he had just turned twenty and he accompanied Joey on a debt-collecting job over the Mersey in Birkenhead. Darren showed the indebtor, a Don Johnson fancier with the sleeves rolled up on his suit jacket and an orange tan and blond highlights in his hair, the knife while Joey showed him photographs of what such a knife could do; the freshly ribboned face of a man held up by a grinning Tommy and Sully. Did you kill him? the man asked. Joey replied: Bits of him I did, yeh. The man paid up. And the knife first tasted blood shortly after that event during a fracas in Leeds city centre after a Liverpool–Leeds United game. Darren does not recall many of the details only that, as his victim lay on the road holding his cheek together, it was not Darren but the knife itself that seemed to say: You don't know how to deal with this, do yeh? I've scarred you for life. What the *fuck* are yeh gunner do *now*?

And then the brief moment of fame on 11 September 2001. Box-cutters, the hijackers used. People in Britain asked: What is a box-cutter? Deployed on that day for cutting anything but boxes it is the transatlantic name for Darren's companion used as if in strange denial of its origins, as if in deliberate neglect of the man who gave it its name. And maybe that is as it should be concomitant as it is with the adopting culture that loves to fight and wound but which baulks generally at murder. That, like the knife itself in the apposite hands, parades the ability to cause horrific injuries and hideous scarring with little or no possibility of death.

So Darren and his blade flee from number 18, from another opened face. How easy it is to cause chaos; how little physical expenditure it takes to become the most important person in a crowd. Darren used to tally his victims with a notch cut into the handle of his knife, but he has long since grown out of that affectation. Although, when he watches *Gangs of New York* for the second time (on video, fast-forwarding through all the boring bits), it is a practice he will think of taking up again.

Darren and his knife, they hum through the city.

YARDIE GUY

Me *knew* im gunna be baaaaad news d'moment im come through do'. No, *befo'*; d'moment me hurd im voice on intercom, seen. D'moment im carl me neerms. Only man carl me dem neerms be either fuller barls or loathin for im life an eager t'lose it, mon. Knahmean?

But dat bad bwoy no way gunna mash my mellowness, mon. D'ganj be doin im good, good work seen an me be atinkin about ow well a nice lil rock go down right now at diss mo-*ment* but fo' de time heer bein me happy jessa sit right heer, mon, see all de boys an girls awatchin theer fillum, that maaaaad fillum wid all-a dem flyin people tink dey be so cooool in theer shades, mon. Jessa *fillum,* my brothas, my sistas. Jessa fillum. Not be real life, mon, seen.

Dat man, dat baaaad bwoy, im dat my bwoy Herbie carl 'Darren'; now, *im* is de real life, oho mon, yes. *Dis* be d'real world, wid *dat* man in it. Im an is bleerd, me meanin, an ow quick im be to *use* dat ting, mon. Bwoy jess ax im be *quiet* so's ee can enjoy is fillum dat's *arl* im do an nex ting im on *flo'*. Straight, nex ting im arl *bleedin* on de flo' an badbwoy Darren doin is run. Me mellowness done *fucked* heer mon, knahmean? Done be pure *fucked*, seen. No room fo' dat bleedin in me mellowness.

An dis Darren, im her in me feerce starin at me gold. Im gotta look on im kite dat might be carld a *sneer*, knowomsayin? Baaaad teeth on d'boy. Baaaaaaaad breath out of im.

—You want some n all? im say. Threat'nin *me*, can anyone b'lieve. —Youse fuckin Yardies an yer fuckin bling. Nowt down for yeh.

Can only be carld a *sneer*, seen. Only carld a *sneer* an it be directed at me, b'lieve? Directed pure at *me*, mon.

Me watch im go. Theer's all dis hollerin around me now, arl dis shoutin an ascreamin an feer bitta *bleedin* goin on additional. But me tinkin bout dat baaaad bwoy, dat Darren; me tinkin im *awight*. Mean, im got *barls*, mon, im got barls. Theer's a feelin in me dat it not gunna be long wait befo' me an dat Darren mon be meetin up ageern. An me don't know whetha it be t'plug-a man's knees or offer im graft, knahmean? Cos a man like dat, I gots t'do *sumtin* widdim - gots t'*deal* widdim sumway. Ceernot leave im out in de world alone, mon. Gots t'*deal* widda bwoy like dat through war or peace mon, de one or de otha. War or peace, mon, seen? Unnerstan me? Knowomsayin? Peace, mon, or waaaaaaarrrrr.

SAMMY GALLAGHER

Like I'm wearing Marigold gloves all the time, them pink shiny ones with the pads on. That's what me hands look like now. Dunno about me face cos I don't look in mirrors any more if I can help it, an I close me eyes when I'm in the shower or the bath but I can't help thee occasional glimpse, like. An wharrit fuckin looks like . . . what *I* fuckin look like. No wonder Marie buggered off. No wonder she took the kids. Tried to grow a beard to hide it like but the hairs only grow on the unburnt bits. Just these patches of long black hairs comin out of the pink raw stuff, horrible. I am horrible.

It was out of order. It was all my fault. Too big for me fuckin boots I thought I could –

It was well out of fuckin order.

It was all my fault.

That's all that goes through me ed now, them two phrases, unless I'm bevvied. Which I always friggin am. Only way to deal with it, see, only way to drown the memory of me own stupidity. What was I thinkin of? How could I av been so fuckin soft?

Every day yeh think it'll get berrer, that yeh won't wake up with them two phrases goin round n round in yer ed: It was out of order it was all my fault. It was out of order it was all my fault. Burrit's *always* the same. *Always* the fuckin same. An then yeh think: is this me, now, for ever? For the rest of me life is this all I've got, just the booze an them two phrases? No family, no friends, an oo's gunner employ a freak show like me? Can ardly leave the house, unless it's to the offie or the Railway at thee end of the road where thee let me sit in the corner by the bogs an get hammered. Victim Support was no bleedin good either. What could thee do? I am beyond their help. I am friggin ruined. Pure fuckin ruined. I am not the man I once was, them an their fuckin iron changed me for ever. Their *iron*. Fuckin evil bastards. But it was all my own fault.

If only thee had've used a knife. Or a gun. If only thee had've killed me cos I wish now I was dead. Thirty-fuckin-five years old an me life is over, fucked, ruined.

ALASTAIR

Since he was a boy and he went fishing at Bala Lake and startled a basking viper beneath a weeping willow Alastair has been dreaming not *of* that serpent but that he *is* it. That he is all one muscle; that he is convincingly camouflaged, able to hide from the world; that he packs poison; that the universe has shrunk to just one hunger, easily assuaged. These have been wonderful dreams yet he wakes from them invariably with a skin-prickling sadness when he slips into water and the dreamed shock of that catapults him out of sleep which it does now, here in this cheap room at the edge of a town called Wrexham at the inland edge of Wales.

He does not know where he is. Half drunk still he sits up on the edge of the bed with the blackness rushing to buzz and flicker against his face like flies in swarm. He flaps at it with loose hands then holds his face in those hands then gropes and staggers to the toilet and shower room, a converted cupboard by the door. He fumbles for the light switch and flicks it, squints his eyes against the rude glare. Swills his face at the tiny sink then examines that face in the mirror; sees the cuts and bruises, the swellings subsiding. Sees the skin sallow and puffy with too much alcohol and not enough sleep. He urinates an ochre syrup into the toilet bowl then turns the light off and crosses the room in the darkness to the window where he parts the thin curtains and gazes out over the bus-station concourse, the empty apron and the deserted bays lit up weak yellow by the surrounding sodium. Chip wrappers and placcy bags like lungs roll like tumble-weeds across the blank tarmac and on the roof of the public toilets a lone gull screams, convulsing its entire body as if vomiting sound although behind the glass Alastair cannot hear it. He watches this bird for some moments, this creature lost among concrete and calling into the darkness forever unanswered. He sees it spread its wings then sees it taken up by a sudden gust wheeling through the lamplight and higher, beyond that watery glow into the upper night above.

It is cold in here. A warp in the window frame is letting in a draught and Alastair can feel this like an icy digit stroking his cheek as if the outside world is trying to entice him even freezing as it is. Somewhere in it and outwith the town's illumined rim is a place or an event or both that Alastair can hear calling and has been harking to for days. Since before Dean's party.

Since the futile trip to Aberystwyth to find and hurt further a one-armed absconding man. He envisages it as two footprints in blooded mud the contours of which will fit no feet but his.

It is very cold in here. He lights a cigarette but the first pull makes him gag so he stubs it out and climbs back into the bed, curls up under the starchy duvet that smells unfamiliar, that has a texture of unwelcome. Outside, the wind continues to wail across the abandoned tarmac escarpment and down into the dark and deserted streets of the town, and he is coaxed by this sound into reseeking his hiss, his secret scaling, but the brief sleep that follows is as hollow and bereft as the outlying town itself, the howling blackness tearing down the alleyways and passages as if in hunt of any survivors of some kind of apocalypse and finding not one.

This Alastair, he has *been* a viper. He has known in some way a strength of some sort. But his succeeding sleep is empty and he will wake early with no memories of that, agog as he is for what he is about to do. For the only thing left here for him to do.

LENNY REECE

Oh no no no mun this is not good. Some kinda beatin aye no worries bout that see but this –

THIS –

Tommy's got the nine-mil to Darren's head. Both of em screamin, they are. Darren's tied to-a chair an Gozzy's holdin his head still an Tommy's got-a gun pressed against-a top of his skull, *in* his curly hair all

264

matted with-a blood from-a beatin he've just received. Squires is grinning. *Lovin* this he is, see. An Tommy's screamin an yellin an he's gunna pull-a trigger, mun, I can see it comin I can see it about to happen it's –

Not good not good. Like that time some years ago when Joey gave some scally a load-a money to go off to Amsterdam an pick up some drugs an none of us ever saw the boy or the money again an Tommy convinced isself that a lad called Noel was in on it an took me round to his bedsit an after a big argument with this Noel one stood an put a cushion across his face an I thought he was gunna suffocate him but then he pulled out a gun an put three fuckin bullets into that cushion. Made me sick, it did. Totally fuckin unnecessary, it was, see. He's not right, Tommy. Not right in-a head, mun. In his early twenties Noel was that's all an now he've got no life just cos Tommy needed to save face an he's gunner do-a same thing again, here, he's gunner put a bullet into Darren's brain an weaselly little scally that he is this is not right, mun, not fuckin right. Somethin fuckin wrong here, mun, aye.

This has to be stopped. This has to be prevented.

—Where the fuck djer think *you're* goin?

—Toilet, Tommy. Need a slash, see.

—Alright well. Be quick.

An then he resumes his screamin at Darren an Darren resumes his screamin back but he's beggin, now, Darren is, he knows what's about to happen like an he's beggin, pleadin. I can smell his piss. See it on the floor, underneath-a chair.

Tommy's gunna shoot him. Tommy's gunna *kill* him. An this isn't-a way of-a world, mun, no, not this. It's brutal aye an it's dog-eat-dog but it don't need-a go this far. No fuckin way, mun. It's only a few grand. No one deserves-a die for that amount-a money, mun. Tommy will go on about the principle of-a thing an that mushers avta be taught that he can't ever be taken for a cunt an respect an all that shite but bollax to *that*, mun, no one deserves-a die over a few thousand quid not when Tommy isself drives a thirty-grand Shogun an owns three properties including one in fuckin Marbella an four grand-odd to im is pocket fuckin change. Fuck *that*, mun. What's about to happen yur is nothin but pure fuckin murder an if I can prevent it from happenin then I will.

I go through-a kitchen where Shea Neary's in a frenzy, snarlin, frothin at-a gob, whipped up by all-a commotion like. The whole place is goin mad. I lock meself in-a bog, take out me mobile phone. Scroll down through-a list-a names like until I reach Joey then press YES.

JOEY MAGUIRE

What do I hate most in thee entire friggin world, lar? What do I hate most? Not Bluenoses or bizzies or even Mancs, it's the fuckin number 350. *That's* what I can't fuckin stand, them three fuckin digits. That number's like a fuckin *wall* or somethin, a fuckin mountain; I just can't fuckin get over it. It's just pure too fuckin much.

—There yeh go, Joe. Dezzy slaps more weight on the bar above me, a disc on each end, like. —Yer topped out. Yer on 340.

But fuckin hell I'm not spunkin a fuckin fortune each month on 'roids only to be stuck on fuckin 340.

Not stickin that shite in me veins only to be stuck on 340 fuckin pounds, no fuckin way, lar. Pure *is* not gunner happen. That is *not* the Joey way.

—Whack another ten on, Dez.

—Ten?

—Each end, aye.

—Yer goin another *score*?

—You herd me. Bump it up to 360, lad.

Dezzy does. Then he tightens the collars. The fuckin bar's bendin in the middle like it's gunner snap. Them weights look pure fuckin *yowge*. Like a fuckin *gorilla* couldn't lift this, lar. It's too much. Too much.

Not for Joey friggin Ferdia Maguire, tho. Fucks no, not for me. Strength is the thing, lar, no messin. That's all I've ever been taught throughout me life like, that yer've gorer push yerself and *keep on* pushin yerself an when yeh think yeh can't push yerself any more yeh just fuckin *push* yerself again. Me dad, me grandad, an probly his grandad before him; just fuckin *push* yerself, son. That's what thee've always said. Be fuckin *strong*. Even when yer starvin, be fuckin *strong*. Some thin-faced feller from me childhood probly one of me uncles like, he told me about the strength inside yeh. About how it's *always* fuckin there.

Be strong. And trust *no* cunt.

Me arms reach up. Thee grab the barbell at either end, just behind the weights, like. Me back sticks to the bench with sweat. Dezzy steadies the bar with a loose grip on the middle and –

Me fuckin phone rings. Me moby in me coat pocket, I can hear the friggin thing ringin.

—Aw fer fuck's sakes.

—Leave it, Joey. Do the lift, lar.

—Can't, Dez. Waitin for a bell off me daughter, like.

Fuck's sakes. I gerrup off the bench an fetch me phone. Lenny's number shows up on the wee screen burram up now so might as well answer the fuckin thing. Sometimes it's important.

—Len. What's happenin, kidder?

An he tells me. That fuckin brudder of mine. I'm back in the country five fuckin minutes an the off-is-fuckin-chunk knob'ed's only gunner do some more slaughterin, inny? Don't that friggin cack-for-brains ever learn? Am tempted just to let the divvy gerron with it like, an waste wharrever fuckin no-mark mule he's gunner waste but if I do it'll bother me for fuckin *months*, lar. Some friggin burden, this, tellin yeh, bein the fuckin conscience of the family, likes. Some fuckin burden. Specially with a fuckin brudder like *that*.

I tell him I'll be round in ten. Just round the corner. He tells me to give it toes like before it all kicks off big time an I doan even get changed, just fuck off round there in me sweats. That fuckin brudder, tellin yeh. Saved the cunt's life when he was a babby likes an I've been savin the dick'ed from himself ever fuckin since. Shoulda just let the bastard choke.

Honest to fuckin God. Avin a conscience, lar . . . some friggin burden, tellin yeh, no lie. Some big friggin burden to carry, this.

TOMMY MAGUIRE

IT'S HAPPENIN AGAIN IT'S ALL FUCKIN HAPPENIN TO ME AGAIN BETRAYAL

BETRAYAL BETRAYAL YER BEIN FUCKIN LAUGHED AT TOMMY LAD

Like me Uncle Dusty bein shot before me very fuckin eyes an I was only thirteen fuckin years old some Billyboy cunt from over the water comes over an waits for him in the pub

BOOM

and Jesus Christ the blood

BETRAYAL

KILL THIS FUCKER

SHOOT THIS FUCKER

Pure fuckin *laughin* at yeh, lar

WASTE SMOKE SLAUGHTER

Like Noel that time after that cunt Colm fuckin Downey ripped me off an NO CUNT RIPS OFF TOMMY MAGUIRE should never av trusted that jippo bastard no way an he's got blood on his hands now that bastard. BLOOD on his hands cos it was *his* fuckin fault that that Noel lad got bumped pure fuckin innocent musher like but that fuckin Colm

BETRAYED

His fuckin fault that I hadter waste that Noel an I hope he's fuckin miserable that Colm cunt wherever the fuck he is now his life fallin to shite around him, hope he's got SARS AIDS cancer an me with me Shogun an me three fuckin gaffs an moren that RESPECT an fear aye FEAR no fuckin money can buy this friggin gun in me hand know that with one wee twitch of this fuckin finger

That Colm cunt comes back to this city an his fuckin knees're gone elbows n ankles n all six-pack the bastard

THAT'S WHAT YER GET FOR LAUGHIN AT
ME

But BETRAYAL

Make im a cripple

Fuck im right up like Sammy fuckin Gallagher

Like DARREN FUCKIN TAYLOR'S gunner be
pure *is* gunner happen

Like a hundred fuckin others cos no cunt rips me
off or treats me like a knob'ed fuckin NO ONE does
I am DEATH to the toerags I am DEATH to these
no-marks fuckin scum I am DEATH to them who
think ther better than me think thee can make *me*
look a twat I AM

There's a knockin on the door. Darren fuckin Taylor
that'll be.

I nod at Gozzy to goan answer it. Ee nods back an
does.

This cunt's gunner *die*.

BUS DRIVER

Can't say that I noticed him, really, to be honest.
Boy just got on, paid his fare, went and sat at the
back. Noticed that he kept his rucksack held all tight
to his chest like and when he got on that early in
the morning I thought to meself: Aye-aye. Here's
trouble. I mean you *would*, wouldn't you? Scouse
lad with his face all bruised and cut and the baseball hat
and that, that shellsuit? Mean, a boy like that gets
on the bus and you're automatically on your guard,
aren't you? I'd heard of the Cilcain robbery, like, but
I didn't make the connection and anyway as I say,

all's he did was get on, pay his fare and go and sit at the back. Why should I have noticed him? Perfect passenger, he was. And *them* you don't notice. *Them*'re the best kind.

And it's still a job I love, to be honest. I've been doing the Wrexham–Mold circular for years and I never get bored. Up early, open roads, day all new and fresh, badgers and foxes and all the other animals you see at that time. It's brilliant, I love it, to be honest. The early run, like, the roads're all empty and I go through all the little villages on the way, across the Vale of Clwyd, beautiful it is, see. Breathtaking. I'm too busy looking out at the scenery and concentrating on me driving to notice one particular passenger although as I say I *did* notice this feller when he got on but after that . . . well, he just kept himself to himself, like. Didn't even notice when he got off at Cilcain although he was probably the only person to do so at that time of the morning, to be honest. I mean, I was just enjoying meself, as I always do. It was a beautiful morning. But I *do* recall stopping at Cilcain because I remember watching some big hawks circling over the post office, the one that was robbed, big buzzards, they were. But that's all I remember, really . . . as I say, you tend not to notice the good passengers, them who cause no problems, just pay their fare and sit quiet. You tend not to notice them, and they're the best kind, to be honest.

ALASTAIR, HIS GRANDMOTHER
KATE: HER LEAVING

Pwy sy'yna?

Alastair	my boy	is that you?
Alastair	and	oh
		all my lost children
		yma
		aaaaaaahhhhhhh

herdd
perffaith
herdd

MUGGED

Come to Wales, Simon says. Stay in my parents' holiday
cottage, he says, do some climbing, canoeing, get drunk
in the pubs, have a great time of it. Shag women called
Rhiannon, show the boyos how to drink. Have a *great*
time, he says. What he *doesn't* say is: Come to North
Wales and get rolled by some scar-faced Scouser for
ya mobile fuckin phone . . .

Capel Garmon: that's where Si's cottage is. So I got
the London–Chester train and took a bus out into the
hills and did a bit of walking on my own and spent
the night under canvas on my own by some river. Few
spliffs, few tinnies, did a bit of writing . . . didn't sleep
very well tho cos of all the noises. God, the *noises.*

Snufflings and scrapings and screechings all night outside the tent, felt like I was camping in Africa or somewhere. So I woke up knackered, like, and packed up the tent and took a walk to the nearest village for a bite to eat and a cuppa and to catch the bus out to Si's place at Capel Garmon, and just as I turn the corner I see the bus pulling away. Missed it. And standing there as if he's just that moment got off it is some scally in a baseball hat holding a rucksack to his chest and he calls me over and what does he do? Only takes my fuckin mobile, doesn't he? Only mugs me for my fuckin mobile . . . Honest, he's like some Harry Enfield Scouser, he is: Ceeeerrm down! Ey, lar, ey! Ceeeerrm down!

Oh yes, come to wonderful Wales and get mugged by some Scouse bastard in a shellsuit with cuts and bruises on his face. Oh nice one, Si, nice one, my bravvah. And all those noises in the night as well . . . tellin ya, this is the Wild West, my friend. Too fucking right. This is the Wild West.

And he goes off with my mobile, round the corner somewhere, and I'm just about to chase him and knock him on the back of his head and take the fucking thing *back* when he reappears, like, and just hands it over. That's all he does, just hands it straight over back to me. Says sammink to me in that awful nasal accent and then waves and walks away. Waves! Politest mugger *I've* ever encountered, not that I've met many, like . . . in fact, to be honest, he was the first. And it could've been much, much worse . . . but he was still a fucking Scouser, tho, wasn't he? All the fucking same, man, them bastards, all the fucking same. Lucky I didn't get me face Stanley'd.

I checked my phone, made sure it hadn't been spat on or anything, and then I checked the timetable at the bus stop, so I didn't notice where Terry or Barry or whatever his Scouse name was went. Didn't see. The timetable told me that I couldn't catch a bus to Capel Garmon from there anyway so I just carried on walking, thought I'd get to the next village then call Si, tell him to come out and pick me up in his new 4x4 he got for his birthday. So yes, I had a bit more on my mind than what some brain-dead Scouse scally was up to. I did hear a gunshot, yes, when I was walking down the lane to the next village; I heard the crack, but I just thought it was someone shooting pheasants or grouse or whatever. Didn't see anything, just heard the gunshot. Thought to myself: there's some yokel's breakfast sorted out, innit? Wasn't until I watched the local news that night at Si's place that I realised what had happened. But what can ya do? And what can ya expect? Some scally mugger trying to get into your shop . . . Jeez, *I'd* shoot the bastard too. I stayed at Si's for a week – canoed on Bala Lake, climbed one of those mountains with the mad Welsh names. I did the Adam and Eve jump but Si wouldn't do it, too chicken-shit. So he's getting slated for weeks about that one. So yes, apart from that fucking Scouse mugger, my time in Wales was quality, or *most* of it was . . . I mean, I didn't do the jump either, to be honest. But I wasn't as scared as Si was. But Jeez I was pleased to get back on the train again, get back to some fuckin civili-sation. It's the Wild West out there, my bravvah. And it follows ya; I mean, two days back at home and me mobile rings; some fucking Scouser tellin me that he knows I'm in on it all cos the call came from my phone. Threatened to rip my arms off, said he was blind in one eye now cos of me, and that he was going to murder me and someone called Alastair together. I told him that I didn't know what he was talking about, that I don't know anyone called Alastair, and switched me phone off. Wrong number, must've been. But I'm monitoring all me calls from now on. But ya see what I mean, how it follows ya? Just can't get away from it, man. It *follows* ya.

EMRYS

Buzzards. He hears them squealing. They must be soaring low over the shop and the adjoining fields, scanning for newborn lambs in the pastures, for unprotected new lives to rend and destroy and if the events of the past few days have taught him anything then it is the necessity of protection; the moral imperative to guard the innocent, to shield the vulnerable from harm and hurt. Which is what Frank's gun is for.

Still in the hospital, she is. She may never leave it alive.

Buzzards. Big, brutal birds. Wheeling and screeching above the shop. The way they kill rabbits: not strong enough to kill them outright or carry them aloft they will swoop and strike, swoop and strike until the rabbit is dragging itself broken across the field still seeking sanctuary trailing its guts behind and the raptor will then eat. Whilst the rabbit still lives. It will eviscerate and eat the eyes of the still-living thing.

Protect the innocent. Shield the susceptible, the unsafe.

Frank's shotgun in his arms feels perfect. The shape of it, its heft. Like some sword of justice. He carries it outside into the bright morning and shields his eyes as he scans the sky and sees no birds in the glare but hears them and there is a figure, a shadow crossing the road towards him. Shellsuit and baseball hat and battered face and holding a rucksack tight to his chest this figure stepping out of the sunlight and approaching him and Emrys knows what this is it is the evil returned the badness come back as it will and will again.

She may never leave the hospital alive. When he saw her on that horse. Forty years. Stillborn baby and the tears and the infant badger found in the barn and that time they came and shot the sheep. Take this off me I cannot bear it.

The figure stops. Holds out the rucksack in its arms towards him. The split and swollen mouth opens to speak beneath the eyes blank in the shade of the cap's peak and Emrys levels the gun and twitches his finger. The index finger of his right hand, it twitches once and quickly. To protect the innocent. From harm to safeguard them.

DARREN

If there will be one event that, for the rest of his life, he will regret ever happening it will be, here and now, the pissing of his pants. *Not* a good way to confront death. Although it will *not* be it will feel, until he eventually *does* die, half blind in Melbourne, Australia, in a motorbike accident at the age of sixty-three, like the final indignity. Like *the* ultimate indignity although of course in the days to come there will be many, *many* more.

ANOTHER NURSE: WENDY MURRAY

Sometimes they get to you; sometimes there's one among the hundreds of others that gets to you, that stabs your heart. That makes you realise the futility of it all and the pointlessness of existing for so many years just to die alone and adrift in the corner of some terminal ward with a view of the gridlocked traffic from the window, had you the strength to just sit up and peer out through the glass . . . and all the other illnesses around you . . . and within you, everything failing, shutting down . . .

Kate died today. The ancient lady in Ward H who in her rare moments of clarity had the mental energy of someone half her age, she died today, shortly after her grandson or was it her great-grandson, rough-looking lad with the beaten-up face, came in to visit her. Over a century old, she was. She went as Wendy was washing her; as she lifted up the left arm to clean the oxter, sun-parched powdery shell, the old lady gave out one last rattling breath and all the life left her, all the more-than-a-hundred-years of it. Wendy was asking her if she'd received a telegram from the Queen when she turned a hundred. Suspected that her words made no sense to Katie if indeed they could even be heard but enjoyed chatting to her anyway, enjoyed it especially when the ancient lady would respond in Welsh, how songlike that language came from her withered lips. Did she send you a telegram, sweetheart? and that was when Katie died. Just rattled and went limp. And Wendy thought that the last word Katie heard in her life was an endearment, was someone calling her 'sweetheart'. And she felt a cold skewering sensation inside her chest, beneath the starchy uniform, within her thin skin.

She called for the duty doctor who arrived and noted the time of death. No point in even attempting to revive such an ancient human being; her ribs and lungs would be shattered by the defibrillator and the unacknowledged yet widespread triage system in operation throughout Merseyside hospitals forbade it anyway. So that's all he did, the doctor, just noted the time of death and looked into Wendy's face and told her to go and take a break, have a few minutes' rest.

On her way to the nurses' station she stopped at a vending machine and bought two bags of crisps, ready-salted flavour, a can of Coke and a Snickers. She'd been watching her weight recently but there's solace in salt and sugar and E-numbers. There's a kind of energy. Some comfort. As she ate and drank alone she watched the local evening news which told her of an incident earlier that day at Liverpool docks, a shooting incident; evidently, armed police had been trailing men suspected of gun-smuggling from Northern Ireland and had followed their Transit van to the docks where a firefight had ensued. A grim-faced reporter with the Cunard building as a backdrop spoke of a 'hail of bullets' in which four men died, one a local under-world figure police named as James Squires. In the back of the van was found a 'substantial' amount of firearms and also two men trussed up in rope with heavy weights tied to their bodies; one of these died in the shootout, the other remained in hospital in a critical condition. Sergeant O'Malley appeared on the TV screen and spoke of his fears of a coming gangland war for control of the city's lucrative drugs trade. Then back to the studio where the newsreader informed Wendy that no police officers were hurt in the incident and on to the next report of another fatal shooting this time just outside Wrexham, a burglar shot dead by the owner of a post office whose wife was in hospital following an earlier break-in. Police were investigating.

Wendy thought: 'Seriously injured.' She thought: 'Critical condition.' And she thought of other gunshot wounds that she'd treated, of the appalling damage guns will inflict. Of the way bullets blast and blunder through miraculous delicacy, through processes of fine-tuning measured over millennia. And her heart sank when Sister Thomas entered the room and told her she was needed now to help treat such a wound; some young thug complaining that he'd been shot in the eye and that he was going to kill the people who'd done it, only he wasn't using the word 'people'. Hysterical, Sister Thomas said he was. Highly agitated. Very probably about to get violent.

Shot. In the eye. But the patient had calmed somewhat when Wendy arrived at the scene; still and supine he was, with a nurse on each of his arms and a leaning doctor closely examining the damaged eye, shining a light into it, squinting. The patient was typically dressed; trainers, shellsuit trousers tucked into white sports socks, fingers chunkily agleam with sovereign rings. One of the nurses explained to Wendy how this man had been shot in the eye at extreme point-blank range with an air rifle; it hadn't been loaded, but it was fired at such close quarters that the blast of compressed air had popped the eye from the socket and damaged the eyeball so severely that it would almost definitely have to be removed. He'd been given a sedative to calm him; he'd arrived at the hospital in a fury. Wendy smelled urine and studied the patient's face and remarked to herself how one eye might be irrevocably ruined but that the remaining one was working enough for two; surrounded by the blue bruising of some older wound it was darting madly from face to leaning face, flitting across features with the lips below it grinning and nostrils flared with the sedative-high. It took everything in, this one eye; gulped all before and above it with a hunger great and rapacious. And when it swooped on to Wendy's face it locked instantly on to the hirsute wart on her upper lip and the subconscious zeal with which it searched for and the skill with which it found her weak spot made her flinch, made her unsteady on her feet. Made her feel sick, this simple glimpse into a soul so attenuated and weakened that its gusto for cruelty propelled the motion of one eye even as its twin was dying. Even as it was being removed. That there could exist a need for power so great that it narrows ocular function down to one sole perverse purpose even in sedation, even in pain.

The unknowable darkness in that one eye. Wendy dropped her gaze from it, down towards the scabbed mouth. It was sneering at her.

A stretchered overdose case crashed then through the nearby double doors with calls for assistance and, thankful, Wendy moved away from the eye to help. And on her way home that night upset and exhausted she decided to leave her job. Eating curry and chips alone in her flat above a bookmaker's she decided that she'd had enough; enough of death, enough of injury, enough of the knowledge of the human heart's hopelessness and the suspicion of its terminal unperfectability. Enough of slashed faces, like the one brought in yesterday; enough of a world in which as a punishment a man is ironed, about two years ago, brought into Accident and Emergency with his face, his hands dripping yellow with melted skin and fat. So she handed in her notice the following day, and two months from now she will find work in the gift shop of the Catholic cathedral and in a year's time she will commence a platonic affair with a priest a full decade older than her and this affair will become physical when, unable any longer to resist temptation, this gentle and kind and caring man will leave the priesthood and they will marry and then as Wendy Murray-Donaghy she will bear three children to him. He will for ever carry with him a deep sense of disappointment and sadness at the failure of his calling and he will die first and seven years later at the age of seventy-nine Wendy will pass away at her home on the Wirral overlooking the Dee estuary and beyond that Wales and the huge bridge that will be linking the two by then, she will expire attended by one of her grandsons who had just popped in to see if she needed any shopping and his concerned stare into her face will be the last thing she'll ever see, his eyes, his pair of beautiful, bright blue eyes.

ALASTAIR

NO NO THIS SHOULDN'T BE HOW IT WORKS
NO I'M SORRY THIS IS FOR YOU LOOK
HERE'S MY HERE'S YOUR NO NO IT
SHOULDN'T HAPPEN LIKE THIS MY VOICE I
NEED TO SPEAK HEAR MY WORDS PLEASE
LISTEN NO DON'T

I'M SORRY DON'T

shoot

To wake in pain. Or *not* to wake in pain, that's the aim, that's what he craves, to wake safe in his own bed without a vicious booming in his head and with the surety that the stalking pain of the world has found someone else, has locked on to another target, someone somewhere not him. He hasn't caused enough pain himself recently, that's what it is; he hasn't tipped the quotient of suffering in his favour. If he can cause enough people to hurt so that he exhausts the city's supply of anguish then he'll be able to come conscious again without this ache, without this breaking. Without a throbbing in his skull so sharp that it clangs and jangles in his back teeth.

He hears voices, in this unique darkness of his; Squires' voice, followed by Tommy's:

—An Snake Tong Tony's in on this caper, is he?

—Aye, yeh. Euro Objective One, lar, them cunts're fuckin brewstered. Tony Tong's settin up this import business, some fuckin spices from China or somethin. Piecer piss, Goz. Sully's round there now, likes, patchin things up with Tony, learnin the ropes, altho it's gunner take him fuckin years, soft get tharry is.

—An so yer apply for these funds . . .

—Yer apply for these funds to, to *diversify* into legit businesses. Simple as. Investment in domestic and commercial properties an opening trade negotiations with other countries, that's what theer lookin for, lar. Tellin yeh; easy fuckin graft, this. Stega's been at it for ages.

—Who, Stephenson? One snidey get that Stega, lar. Stay well away.

—Aye, Goz, but Joey's been at it n all. Tony Tong, same thing. Not seen Tony's new bar? Used to be the Shangri-La club? *You've* been there, Len, aven't yeh?

Darren can't move. His arms, his legs, they are concrete. And the voices are like chainsaws in his head, he blacks out to block them out but when he reawakes they're still there, still rattling and snarling in the razor dark:

—Tellin yiz, lads, that fuckin brudder of mine, his fuckin conscience'll kill him. He's all for goin completely fuckin legit, believe that shite?

A snort. —More or less already *is* straight, lar.

—That's what I've told him. Joey, a said, a said buyin debts for half theer price then sendin a coupla mushers round to collect em in full, that's exactly what big fuckin businesses do. Only difference, *they* buy em off banks n stuff and *we* buy em off dealers an twats like tha. That's thee *only* fuckin difference.

—Aye, an *them* cunts're friggin legal. Bailiffs an stuff. That's another diff.

—Aye yeh. But –

Roar. Blackness. Black*out* again. And reawake still to Tommy's voice:

—An another fuckin thing, what's this fuckin Leo Sayer revival all about? Never could stand that fucker, me.

—Not aware that there *is* one, Tom.

—Aye, Len, there is. Seen the twat on the telly, aven't we, Goz? Member when he used to dress up as a fuckin clown? In the seventies? Clown is *right*, lar. *Shoot* that knob'ed, tellin yeh. Fuckin shoot him. Ever heard that joke about the bus in Belfast, and —

A groan escapes. Too eager to express some mountainous pain it flees his broken mouth before it can be gulped back.

—Aye-aye. Gobshite's awake.

Something cracks his face, snaps his head to the side. Old scabs inside his mouth reopen and he tastes the copper of blood.

—Wakey-fuckin-wakey, dick'ed.

—Slap im again, Tom.

—Wakey-wakey. You've got a fuckin story to tell us, Darren.

His eyes open to stare into a black hole brightly circled that is the entire cityscape. He can see down into that hole, can see the spiralling set into the metal that will cause the bullet to spin as it exits thereby maximising impact damage. He can smell cordite. Then he can smell urine, his own. He doesn't want to die.

Too excited for breakfast Alastair pays for the room and leaves the pub, squinting into the sunlight that bounces off the windows and flanks of the buses arranged in grumbling queues. He crosses the tarmac apron of the bus station and consults the timetables on the wall and notes the number of the bus he requires. He has seven minutes to wait. Despite the arrayed vehicles there is no one but him waiting here at the stand and small hidden birds are singing from litter-strewn tree and bush and the grey skies and drizzle of the last few days have gone and there is a strong sun in the pale blueness above and no cloud at all. Soon his conveyance will come, soon.

—WANNA FUCKIN BULLET IN THE BRAIN CUNT WANNA FUCKIN –

—JESUS TOMMY I NEVER

—I'M GONNA FUCKIN DO IT LAD YERRAH FUCKIN DEAD MAN NO CUNT LAUGHS AT ME TIME TO DIE YEH FUCKIN – . . . Ey, Lenny; where the fuck djer think *you're* goin, lar?

—Need a slash, T. Him pissin isself; smade me wanner go as well, see.

—Alright well. Be quick. TIME TO FUCKIN DIE DARREN YERRA FUCKIN CORPSE LAD THIS IS WHAT YEH GET YEH FUCKIN

The bus arrives. Alastair gets on, pays his fare, takes his rucksack to the back seat and sits down. Gazes out the window at the bright and waking town as he leaves it. He sees a milkman and a stray ginger cat; he sees many papers.

—NO TOMMY PLEASE I NO TOMMY I

—HERE IT FUCKIN COMES LAD TIME TO FUCKIN DIE DARREN YEH FUCKIN

—Do it, Tom, do it! Pull that fuckin trigger, lar! *Waste* that no-mark get! *Laughing* at yeh, Tommy! Pure fuckin *laughin* at yeh, lad!

—DON'T LISTEN TO IM TOMMY THAT

GOZZY CUNT I NEVER I NEVER NO PLEASE DON'T FUCKIN

Wrexham spreads and scatters into low brown council estates and these soon too dissolve, absorbed by the surrounding green. As if that word 'green' could sufficiently encapsulate the thousand tones and shades of that colour lying and rising roundabout. How much greener green was when as children we'd yet to learn the word 'green'. How immeasurably more wonderful grass was as we crawled like quadrupeds through it whether in meadow or on hillside or even in the scrappy squares of dogshat and littered vegetation that separated then and still do the big beige blocks of corporation housing. Green the grass and green the leaves. Green the lichen, green the weeds.

Alastair holds the sackful of money tight to his beating chest and gazes out the window at the land beginning to swell, into the hills he moves through and towards the blue glassy mountains now visible in the near distance. He recalls this landscape as a recent acquaintance, familiar as he is with it from the unsuccessful trip to find and hurt for his sins the one-armed absconder. Three days ago, was that? Four? Seems like an entire childhood since between then and now was that THUNK and the falling old lady. The awful way she crumpled and in a coma in Wrexham General may not survive heavy blows to the head with blunt instrument probably badly brain-damaged doctors say if she should pull through. Trauma trauma and

THUNK. Darren, that psycho evil bastard. Yeh but

the fucker'll be tampin now, won't he, runnin round the city tryna find this fuckin money . . . tryna escape Tommy . . . that bastard that evil fuckin . . .

THUNK with the hammer disgusting crime on a defenceless old lady. Catch the thugs who did this says the policeman on telly and bring them to justice, shocking wicked cowardly. This

Aye but she might be out of hospital. She might now be at home, back at her shop or her husband may be there but what if it's empty? What then? Post it all back through the letter box note by blood-soaked bastard note all of it every last red penny. Because there must be more than this. Just get rid of the fuckin stuff just return it, give it all back because because there must be more please God let there be more cos otherwise this is this is all unfuckin –

The bus slows to a crawl to squeeze past another bus along a narrow lane, high hemming hedges on each side. Just two, three inches between the two vehicles, that's all. Length of a thumb. Alastair regards the other bus, close as it is, notes its destination (RHYL) and that the driver of it is a woman and that she carries no passengers and that someone has finger-tipped the words 'CLEAN ME' into the dried muck on the rear window. And that that muck is made up of a million brown pointillistic particles each one seen in close focus cracked and scaled like the surface of a salt lake. Each one and there are millions.

A torrent to him, the world is now. Each of the leaves that brush against the glass by his face, he sees their spines, their veins, the tiny frilled holes where grubs have fed. And the twigs from which they depend, knuckled like fingers, gnarled like the twisted fingers of arthritis like

Kate. Or those hands that handed to him his fudge and dropped his change. Curled atop starched white sheets in a hospital like –

The bus speeds up. Through a village still sleeping apart from a postman in a yellow rainproof although the drizzle of the last few days has now gone and the air hums blue, yet still cold. Alastair wonders what made that drizzle, how it was formed. Why it fell on him as he lay beaten to blackout in the gutter outside Ma Egerton's pub. And why nobody stopped to help him unless of course down that quiet back street nobody passed in the mere minute or two that he spent unconscious.

Rhyl. It was going to Rhyl, that other bus. He recollects visiting the funfair there as a child. Several times, he went, often with Kate. And he wonders, here on this bus among the swelling hills, whether Darren, whether Tommy, whether Joey did the same, and whether like him they stood spun like candyfloss and awed by the mad machines that whirled people through space and scattered the screams of their lovely terror out over the throbbing lights and through the spokes of the Ferrises like the gearings of giant clocks. Wonders whether they stood dazed like he did in that gorgeous gaudy kingdom, the sweet smells and oniony smells and barks and blarings and saw something in those strobes of a vista open only to a child's grace, pre-caries pre-sex pre-knowledge of a certain sort but known certainly to the lost and the lonely that tend for some reason to orbit those loud crowds as they do bus stations yet do not commingle since to do so would insist that what they search for is not only un-attainable to them but is even in any form demark-able wholly unknown, and that that unknowing is part of the knowledge unwanted, never yearned for. And part of Alastair long interred but still writhing asks whether something of that wonder is ever able still to survive. Or whether it ever dies entirely. And thinks probably that at a certain age in such places among exhaust and bodies moving aimlessly that it does.

The bus enters another village and Alastair sees a sign, half hidden in a hedgerow as if it too is organic, a peculiar privet. It reads: CILCAIN. Alastair thumbs the bell-button and moves towards the front of the bus, towards the doors. The bus decelerates as it approaches the shelter. Considering what he's already done he will risk injury or worse should he return to his home city but after what he's about to do if indeed he does it he will never be able to go back to Liverpool ever again. These small villages hereabouts with their barns and bus stops and small pubs and post-office-cum-grocery-stores and their crumbling stone shells adja-cent to the huge dwellings built recently to house the rich and also the hills and mountains above and the rivers and woods too, these places must now and for ever be his portion in the world, his cold and only home, if he gets off the bus, if he actually does what he's planning to do. They will be from now on what he lives within adrift for ever until he dies.

The bus stops and hisses. Alastair disembarks, with his rucksack. The bus pulls away and leaves him there.

*   *   *

—NAH TOMMY DON'T FUCKIN DO IT MATE
PLEASE TOMMY LISTEN

   —Someone at the door, Tom.

   —FUCKIN IGNORE IT WELL! THIS CUNT'S
GUNNER –

   —It's Joey, T.

   —Who?

   —Joey. An he ain't lookin too fuckin chuffed.

   —Aw shite.

   —What should I do, lar?

   Sigh. —Answer it, well. Lerrim in.

The post office; it's just a small, whitewashed building
beneath a tree. That's all it is. High above it three big
birds soar, circling on thermals, making high squealing
sounds as they search for prey. Hawks of some kind,
Alastair thinks. Like vultures in a Western. Don't see
such things in town, no hawks, no, but plenty of fuckin
vultures, oh aye yeh; millions of *them*. Without wings,
like.

   There is a telephone call to be made. *Two* telephone
calls to be made. He has only fourteen pence in change
but there is a hiker, boots and a knapsack, walking
towards him.

   —Gorra moby, lar?

   —Pardon?

   —I said av yeh gorra mobile phone, lad?

   —Yes, I have.

   —Giz it well. Need to use it.

   —It's, it's got no credit. I've –

   —Give me yer fuckin mobile phone!

Alastair's hand held out. The hiker delves into the

pocket of his Gore-tex and takes out an Ericsson and places it on the waiting palm.

—Can I have it back when you're finished with it? I need it round here, don't I?

Ally ignores him, walks over to the lay-by beneath the tree where he and Darren parked the Morris Minor what seems like an age ago. The Morris Minor; beneath running water now. Newts and frogs for passengers, a stickleback for a driver. He regards the phone, notes with a smile the Orange display in the LCD and taps in 453 and listens to a robotic female voice inform him that his remaining balance is twenty-two pounds and seventy-three pence, goodbye. No credit, the hiker said; lying fuckin knob'ed. Gobshite. Alastair taps in another number from his memory, General Enquiries at the Royal Liverpool Infirmary. A voice answers. He gives it a name. The voice asks him if he is related and he says 'grandson' and is told that sadly that person is no longer with us. She passed away during the night. He terminates the call then taps in another number from memory, hears it ring and knows that it will be playing 'You'll Never Walk Alone' in Darren's pocket somewhere. He waits for it to be answered but after several rings it is transferred to voicemail. He leaves a message:

—Darren. It's me. Djer know where I am? I'm at that postie in North Wales, lar. I've got the swag with me an djer know wharram gunner do? I'm gunner give it *back*, lar. Every fuckin penny. I'm gunner give it back. Djer know why? Cos yerra fuckin wacko. Yer fuckin soft in thee ed, lar. An yeh know somethin else? I told Tommy that you've skanked the money. So if he's not friggin wellyin yeh now then he soon fuckin will be. Like that, Darren? Like all this shite, do yeh? You are *fucked*. Pure *fucked*. Av a nice life, yeh evil fuckin psycho sacker shite. *See* ya. *Fuck* off.

He turns the phone off, goes back over to the hiker who's still standing in the same place and gives it back. Just hands it over. The hiker looks down at it in his hand and beams:

—Ah thank you very much, my bravvah. Quality, man, quality.

Alastair grunts and waves his hand and moves away. Soft southern blert.

He moves. His feet take him over the road. The rucksack held again to his chest feels like it is full of sodden sand so heavy has it become yet light inside he is as if all burden has been sucked from him, drawn into the sack and with the money it holds within. Something new awaits him in that small white shop, shadowed by tree, under the hungry circling birds.

Lenny comes back in. Joey's right behind him, steroid-swelled deltoids bulging from his sleeveless sweat top. He stands and surveys; there's Darren tied to a chair, his face a mask of blood, there's Tommy standing by him with a guilty gun at his side. Gozzy there with a clenched fist held out towards Joey at chest-height which Joey looks down at incredulous.

—The fuck's that, Goz? I ain't punchin fists with *you*, lar. Ain't a fuckin social visit, this. Thought you ad some people to meet today, anyway?

—Aye, yeh, I do. Just thought I'd –

—Yeh thought fuckin notten, lar. Just gorra call from

Raymond on me way round here, he's waitin on yeh down the dock. Like we arranged, remember?

Gozzy just stands there staring. Strange glint in his misaligned grey eyes.

—The fucker yeh waitin for? Fuck off down the docks! NOW!

Gozzy does. He just leaves.

—An *you*. Joey points at his brother then that pointing hand turns over and uncurls into a flat palm. —Giz that fuckin gun.

—Nah, Joey, listen, lad. This lil fuckin get's just –

—I don't care, Tom.

—He's fuckin ripped us all off, Joe! He's screwed us over! He's fuckin –

—Tommy, I couldn't give two fucks what he's done. I'm not avin you bringin the fuckin glare down on us again cos yeh can't control yer fuckin soldiers. Giz that fuckin gun.

No movement. Joey roars:

—GIZ!

Tommy flinches and hands the gun over and Joey takes it and stuffs it down the elasticated waistband of his kex and pulls his top down over it. A sniggering is heard. It's Darren. Pink bubbles pop at his split lips as he laughs.

—The fucker *you* laughin at, knob'ed?

—You. Distorted Darren's words are, coming as they do from such a damaged mouth. —Yer just a little kid, aren't yeh? Scared of yer big brudder. Like a shitein little fuckin –

Tommy punches Darren again with a fist the size of a melon. Droplets of red spatter across the computer screen.

—Oi!

—But he's fuckin laughin at me, Joe! Yeh *heard* him, didn't yeh? He's takin me for all the cunts under the sun, lad!

—No one's gettin wasted here, Tom. Don't care what he's fuckin done, no one's gettin smoked. Len; need a word.

The two men go off into the kitchen. The dog barks four times then calms as it recognises the incomers. Tommy stares down at Darren. Darren all smashed grins back up at him, sees Tommy's stupid jowly face up there by the ceiling, above his bellies. Sees over that flabby shoulder some postcards from Australia stuck to the wall, remembers that the eldest Maguire brother, Frankie, lives in New South Wales and has done for several years. Land of opportunity. Small cities. Plenty of immigrants opening restaurants and bars and eager for them not to be burned down. Step One.

Money for the airfare. Easy. Bit of dealing through Peter. Then

Cos he can't stay here. Not after this. Unless he gets in with the Steg or Willy Hunter and gets some payback off this fat fucker cos he's gorra get it, this bastard. Oh aye yeh and that friggin Alastair who

Darren feels his phone vibrate in his pocket, hears it playing its tune. Tommy shakes his head but Darren has no intention of answering it anyway even if he could, even if his arms weren't roped to the chairback. After a few bars it stops and moves on to voicemail. Darren'll answer it later cos he knows he's going to survive this now. Knows he's going to get out of this alive cos did yeh see the way Tommy shat it when

Joey came in? Pure shiters. Is right; fuckin bully, Tommy. Hasn't got thee arse to –

Joey comes back in with Lenny and a rifle which he hands over to his brother.

—The fuck's this, Joe?

—That's all yer gettin, Tom.

—It's a fuckin *air* rifle, lar.

—Aye, I know.

—Aven't even got any pellets for it, lar.

—Hard fuckin lines, well. But that's all yer gonna get. Can't trust yeh with a proper shooter, likes, so that's yer lot. Fuckin kid's gun. An I *mean* this, Tom; I hear that *this* knob'ed here or anyone else has been fuckin slaughtered then that's you an me fuckin finito. Unnerstand me? Fuckin end *of*. No friggin brudder of mine. Unnerstand? Come ed, Lenny.

Joey leaves with Lenny who glances and shrugs at Tommy. Doors slam. Tommy regards the rifle. Darren laughs.

—Ooo big fuckin man with his airgun, eh? Fuckin big man! Gunna shoot a few pigeons are yeh, big bad gangster man! Fuckin *airgun*, lar! Not even friggin loaded! Big bad fuckin gangster man with his –

One of Tommy's huge hands engulfs Darren's blood-bristled skull. The thumb and forefinger stretch the lids of one eye apart and that eye blood-laced and terrified spins and darts in its socket. The barrel of the rifle is jabbed into that eye, actually *against* it, screwing into the tear duct.

—Think am fuckin funny, yeh?

Darren gurgles laughter. He can smell his own piss and his eye screams with pain but still he gurgles laughter. This won't kill him. It will hurt a great deal but he will come out of this much more alive and bigger and stronger and badder. So he gurgles laughter, of a sort.

—Well laugh *now*, dick'ed.

So much ahead of him. Oceans and deserts and revenge. There is so much to live for.

—Mudderfucker no-mark thinkin am fuckin funny, let's see yeh laugh *now.*

The world is his and it shines brighter than he ever thought possible. Tommy pulls the trigger.

Them big birds. The blue sky and the distant mountain and how light the money feels against his chest like a kitten like a lamb, a bushel of wheat like something hollow, barely there. And his chest too with this sensation as if he's been emptied out removed from the bloodied sludge of existence. Become something else.

There it is, the post office. There is a man. There is a shotgun raised.

As if weightless enough to soar with those big birds, over that mountain. As if transformed enough to adopt their effortless grace, high as they are, remote as they are. Something of their grace some way shared.

And oh what clarity; what intense resolution of sight. The webbing of the man's hand that grips the stock of the shotgun, the soft flap between thumb and forefinger; Alastair sees that it bears two tiny blisters. Peppercorn-sized. He wonders how they got there. Wonders what burnt the man.

The sunlight bounces off the man's spectacles,

making him light-eyed. Words amass and jostle in Alastair's throat, words like SORRY and FORGIVE and PLEASE and NO and LISTEN but he cannot utter them, suddenly supine as he is with his chest torn open and the money falling around in tatters set aflame by the storm of white-hot shot, the storm that lasted a second. Some of those flaming shreds seesaw down to land inside Alastair's rent chest and sizzle in the puddles there and in their falling stands a man and behind him is a shop and behind that is a mountain and behind that is a sky in the wide blue of which soar and circle three winged things, so high, so high. Their spread wings to catch him. A breeze blows across him and soothes his exposed slowing heart and so high they are, those winged things, high enough to see the whole of Wales up there. Liverpool as well, even. The island entire.